Finding Kris Kringle

By

Joan Byrd

Deep Indigo Books
Published by Indigo Sea Press
Winston-Salem

Deep Indigo Books
Indigo Sea Press
302 Ricks Drive
Winston-Salem, NC 27103

For information regarding bulk purchases of this book, digital purchase and special discounts, please contact the publisher at indigoseapress@gmail.com

Cover Design by Joan Byrd
Manufactured in the United States of America
ISBN 978-1-63066-579-1

I dedicate this magical classic to children of all ages, whose faith is believing is seeing, and where the portals of childhood still remain because it never left their heart.

Do I believe Santa Claus exists? He exists as much as snowflakes, silently falling on a snow-covered ground—as much as an evergreen forest sparkling with frosty ice crystals under a winter moon—as much as angelic voices singing Silent Night—as much as the sound of sleigh bells and sleigh rides through the snow—and the magical wonder of Christmas through the eyes of a child.

Praise God, He lives, in the hearts of all who believe in Christmas miracles!

—Love, Joan

CHAPTER 1

A perfect silence fell across the high snowy peaks as a gentle snow drifted down upon an already snow-covered ground. There were no sounds of birds singing in the tall evergreens that surrounded the hidden village that set nestled between two great mountains. There were never any visitors coming to the small remote enchanting village and with good reason. The festive holiday village, always alive with twinkling lights of red, green, blue and white, that shined throughout the small community year-round, was protected by an invisible heavenly presence. The Lord had place the angelic guards around both the village and surrounding countryside to ward off anyone adventurous enough to climb to the top of the world, the North Pole.

Hidden away inside the small village lived one-hundred small people only growing to three to four feet tall and the happy group worked under the watchful eye of the man in charge of Kringle Village, Nicholas Kristopher Kringle and his wife Martha were loved and respected by each resident and the cheerful group called them Father and Mother Christmas.

Nicholas had become a very important symbol of the Christmas season, especially for children, whose letters magically made their way up to the North Pole in plenty of time for the elves, as Father Christmas happily named them when they asked him for their own identity, to complete all the toys that were asked for. Nicholas had a deep love for little children and making them happy on Christmas morning was the main reason he was so pleased with the elves great ability to make whatever a girl or boy asked for.

Many years prior, Nicholas and Martha tried to make all the toys themselves, but seeing the number of children asking for a special gift increase, the humble man prayed that God would send him some helpers, talented with making toys for children. Then the village magically grew as did the number of toymakers when God sent down one-hundred gifted Cherubs who transformed into Santa's elves.

Nicholas had been called many things throughout his 2,000-

1

years reign beginning with A Giver of Toys. Because there were so many versions of her husband's name, Martha sewed a handstitched canvas with all his given names, Father Christmas, St. Nicholas, Kris Kringle, Santa Claus, Ole St. Nick, Jingle Kringle, and Giver of Toys. She framed it and hung the beautiful tapestry in their big den for Nickolas to enjoy his many names.

Martha had purchased all the stories, songs, and videos pertaining to her devoted loving husband but his favorite was always TWAS THE NIGHT BEFORE CHRISTMAS. So as Nickolas sat back enjoying his morning coffee and sugar cake, Martha had pulled up a chair to once again read his favorite out loud. As he happily listened to his wife's dramatic reading, the happy man settled down in his big green velvet chair, preparing for his favorite part. When Martha got to the place where it described him, he sat up, a big smile on his lips.

"With a little ole driver so lively and quick, I knew right away, it must be St. Nick!" Then Martha looked over at him and gave her version. "His blue eyes how they twinkled! His nose like a cherry! His cheeks were so merry! The beard of his chin was as white as the snow and his small-little mouth was drawn up like a bow. The pipe that he held tight in his teeth made the smoke circle his head like a wreath. The jolly ole elf had a round little belly that shook when he laughed like a bowl full of jelly!" Martha joined her husband in laughter. "Nickolas darling, that makes me laugh every time I read it!" Martha got up to take the empty plate and smiled down at her handsome thirty-three-year-old husband. "I am certain all the artist and Santa helpers who have you looking fat in that red suit would never recognized the real Santa Claus. My adorable 6'4", black hair sporting a neatly trimmed dark beard and mustache, is the perfect male figure who keeps my heart a flutter throughout these many years!"

"And my very beautiful-young wife has made our many years together completely enjoyable." Nickolas got up and walked to the fireplace to place on another log before catching a glimpse of himself in the mirror hanging over the mantle. "You are right darling. Should I decide to wonder down below the Pole and be among those living in the many towns, they would never think the stranger among them was the jolly ole fat man." He laughed recalling the many past Christmas's when he magically changed into Santa Claus. "Tis a real treat to be transformed every Christmas Eve into my jolly ole fat self." Nickolas gave a wink into the mirror, then took Martha's hands. "It is time to make my rounds and check on the elves progress. Barnabas said they have already started working on this year's toys."

"Why so soon?" Martha walked over to put the worn book up on the shelf. "I'm aware there are many children who asked for the same kind of toys as many have asked for in past Christmas's. Things like dolls, balls, and bikes never go out of style for kids, but darling Christmas is still six-months away. It's only the 24th of June. Isn't this supposed to be the elves free-time off until September?"

"Martha dearest, these anxious toy makers grow restless trying to find projects to keep them busy for eight months. They are happier when they are making toys." Nickolas gave his wife a kiss before reaching for his coat. "Starting early just means the toys will be even better. Now, the elves can slow down and take their time."

"Our lovely group of elves certainly enjoy their labors of love." Martha had walked over by the window to watch the parade of happy little people making their way down Candy Cane Lane to the Toy Factory." Martha smiled down as she watched the elves in the back pick up snow balls and give them a playful toss to the elves in front of them. "The happy-group should be there when you arrive Nickolas." Martha turned to see her husband putting on his heavy overcoat before tying on a wool scarf. "Nickolas, are you walking down this morning instead of taking your warmer inside tunnel?"

"I thought I would clear my head if I breathed in some nice cold-fresh-air!" Nickolas gathered his gloves and wool hat, gave Martha a gentle hug and walked out the door as his caring wife walked back to the window to watch her husband make his way down Candy Cane Lane.

"Clear your head? From what, dear husband?" Martha had been totally confused over Nickolas's unusual words.

CHAPTER 2

In The Toy Factory

"Good morning Father Christmas!" Barnabas, the head elf, greeted Nickolas with a cheerful attitude as the bright-faces of the happy workers chimed in with their own joyful greetings. "As you can see, the workers are at their stations waiting for your instructions before they commence to making toys!" Barnabas pointed out the patterns for the latest bike styles. "As you see Santa, the workers at Bikes and Trikes Station are ready to get started on the latest styles preferred by kids in this modern world."

Nickolas smiled down at the anxious workers before glancing over the new design then turned his attention on the many colors of paint and noticed a few new shades near the end of the bucket line. "Barnabas, I recognize most of the colors but several of the new shades are quite different." Nickolas reached for two of the new shades and raised his eyebrow, a sign of his disapproval. "I approve all the colors except #6 and #7. Demon's Delight and the Dark Angel will never be delivered by Santa, nor anything else relating to evil. See that they are removed from these heavenly grounds Barnabas."

"As you wish Santa! You are the head man Kris!" Barnaba snapped his fingers and the two unexcepted cans of paints magically vanished. "Station B&T, you may begin your day's work and keep all those smart looking wheels looking safe enough for the good little boys and girls!" Barnabas gave his boss a friendly wink and escorted him to the next station, Dolls, Figure Hero's, and Stuffed Animals.

"Barnabas, if you do not object, may I address my workers?" Knowing his head elf enjoyed his high position over his fellow elves, and felt the need to take charge while in the toy factory, Nickolas glanced over smiling at the head elf's flushed face as snickers could be heard throughout the factory. Barnabas cleared his throat before regaining his upbeat personality, then took a sweeping bow in front of his boss.

"By all means Kris, speak away! You are the big cheese around the Pole!"

"Thank you for recalling that fact Barnabas!" Nickolas tuned his attention to the toy makers. "My beloved workers, I have no doubt that every doll, every stuffed animal, or figure hero's will be made to perfection by your gifted hands! Remember our number one rule: CHILDREN'S TOYS SHOULD ALWAYS REFLECT GOODNESS AND LOVE AND MATCH WHATEVER THE CHILD ASKED FOR!"

A rosy-cheek girl with golden hair stepped up smiling and tilted her head out of respect. "Father Christmas, you can count on the workers in D, SA & FH. Our love for small children match your own and it is our delight and joy to please you and Mother Christmas. We love and cherish both of you!"

"You are a sweet-delightful angel Breanna as are all of my beautiful angelic elves." Nickolas passed around his perfect smile. "Mother Martha and I could not love you all better if you were our very own children. We love and cherish each and every one of you. You may begin doing that which you love and remember to slow down since my happy little group can enjoy making toys for almost six months."

Barnabas clapped his hands as he spoke up "You heard our leader, start working and do not dillydally!" the brass young leader waved Nickolas to follow him to the next station. Station #3: Toy Cars, Trucks, Trains & Tracks! Then down to Station #4: Games, Playing Cards, Cubes, Puzzles, Books, Crayons and Coloring Books! Then to Station #5: This & That and Everything in Between!

After checking over all the stations, Nickolas and Barnabas made their way back down the long rows between the huge stations, observing the large group of eighty workers busy at their jobs and listening to the happy chatter. The noise was so loud, Barnabas had to speak up. "I can say one thing Kris our workers never complain about having too much work and too little pay." He chuckled.

"I do believe my toy makers are even more excited this year!" Nickolas squeezed his eyes shut from the constant noise. "Their happy merriment has raised the noise level at least ten decimals!"

The constant chattering noise grew as the clatter of toymaking tools starting banging, zipping, twisting, rolling, blasting, and sewing machines humming throughout the giant toy factory! Then the chatter turned to joyful singing, festive and filled with Christmas spirit! Now the head elf practically shouted over the loud noise.

"Kris, your toymakers are certainly filled with the Christmas spirit!"

"A little too much holiday spirit for me Barnabas!" Nickolas had clasped his hands over his ears to muffle out the loud sound. "Please ask the elves to lower their merriment until I leave the factory!"

Taken back by Father Christmas's unusual request, Barnabas stared over at their leader, the one always filled with the love of Christmas and the first to join in with the merriment and carols. "I shall get on it right now Kris." Barnabas, now no more obnoxious over his position, the head elf only had concern for the man they all loved and looked up to. Having the power to speak to his fellow elves in a quite-calm voice wherever he was, Barnabas addressed the happy-busy workers. "May I have your attention!" With the head elf's sudden announcement, the entire factory grew to a deafening silence as all eighty loyal workers stopped what they were doing to hear Barnabas's unusual interruption. "My fellow workers, if you can refrain from your obvious Christmas merriment until Father Christmas leaves the toy factory, he would appreciate it."

Instantly there were eighty-upset elves staring up at the usually jolly man, now strangely removing his hands from his sensitive ears and blowing out a relieved breath. What had changed that cause Father Christmas to become upset over the happy clatter and chatter, the joyful singing of the Christmas season? Did not this very same loving man declare A TRUE CHRISTIAN LIVES WITH CHRISTMAS IN THEIR HEART YEAR-ROUND! But they would wait patiently until Santa exited the building then resume their joyful merriment. As soon as Nickolas stepped out, leaving the toymakers staring at their elf leader, Barnabas put on a cheerful face.

"Now, do not go around worrying about Father Christmas! He will be back to his old self before you know it. My expert guess is our dear father may have a slight headache brought on by the sudden change in cranking up the old toy factory in the summer instead of the fall, so loud noises would affect it. Being angels, we are never affected with human frailty's like our beloved Father and Mother Christmas, but we can be compassionate to all their request." Barnabas felt, from their relaxed appearance, the workers had excepted his statement. The dramatic leader waved his hand gracefully. "You may go back to making your toys with all the joy and song you like!"

So once again, the sounds of Chattering, Clattering, Bings and Bongs, Rings-Dings-Dongs and Christmas Songs could be heard throughout the big toy land!

CHAPTER 3

Martha Kringle had dressed warmly to go for her own fresh air walk. Her mind was fixed on her husband's strange statement and was totally oblivious of the handsome young elf making his way to her side. Hearing the head elf call out her name, Martha stopped and gave him a beautiful smile as he happily returned one to the beautiful woman. With a sweep of his hand a red rose appeared and giving a gallant bow, he held it out for her.

"A sweet smelling rose, for a delightful lady!"

"Barnabas, you do my heart proud." Martha lifted the rose to her nose and it indeed smelt as sweet as any summer rose she recalled from her long-past. "Thank you, dear friend." Taking another sniff, Martha could not get over how perfect the angelic rose was. "Tis quite lovely and most unusual to see such a perfect rose in this cold land we call home."

"Anything to help warm your tender heart madam." Barnabas noticed her red cheeks and nose. "Dear lady, you look quite frozen! How long have you been out and about in this frigid air?"

"I know my limits when it comes to this Artic temperature Barnabas and the length of my stay is always longer in the summer months up here." Martha pulled her heavy wool coat around her tighter before leading her new walking companion down Peppermint Avenue to take in the cute little cottages where the elves lived as she continued her reason for being out in the cold. "After Nickolas left for the factory and I watched him enjoying the first new flakes of morning snow, I decided I felt like taking my own fresh air walk since being cooped up inside since the last big snowstorm hit the mountain." Martha stopped briefly to gaze down at the shorter walker. "Barnabas, I just now recall how you never leave your post inside the toy factory when our family of elves are busy at work, did something happen to bring you out here to see me?"

"Tis true I am usually busy inside with my hard workers, but I had to come out to look for you over a grave matter." The usual relaxed fellow grew serious.

"Did something happen in the toy factory Barnabas?" Martha suddenly felt this abrupt meeting had something to do with her husband.

An angel's ability to read the thoughts of others alerted the head elf that Martha was aware that something had happened that concerned not only himself but every angelic worker in the factory. Feeling protective of Mother Christmas, Barnabas reached for her hand as he wondered if she too had noticed a difference in her husband. As Martha waited for the head elf to speak, she knew from his caring actions he had read her thoughts.

"Martha, something did happen, most unusual for Father Christmas. He is usually as upbeat and joyful as the toymakers but there seem to be no Christmas joy within the dear man this morning. Things started out like all the other seasonal starts to getting the workers going. Santa and I made our rounds to all five stations for our loving leaders final instructions before starting the toymakers to sanding and hammering, zinging and zanging, twisting and twirling, curling and waving, sewing and sawing and all the other glittering and flittering! After we gave the go-ahead, the happy group of elves started making toys of all kinds! Big ones, small ones, round ones, square ones, short ones, tall ones, thin ones, fat ones! Those toys that are bouncy, the ones that are flouncy, the ones that are cute, the trains that go toot, the ones that are brave and fight dragons in caves, stuff animals from bears to lamas and sweet baby dolls that say mama! Like always, the chattering began from all the excitement of making toys for the good girls and boys and within minutes the singing rung out with one Christmas Carol after another! So, with the noise of the many different sounds, the big toy factory was filled to the rafters with loud joyful sound!" Barnabas had been chatting instead of sight-seeing since he had been down Peppermint Avenue many times walking to and throw from his cottage to other places in Kringle Village and hadn't noticed they had walked back to the Kringle's big three-story house. He gazed up at the largest middle window and knew Father Christmas was somewhere inside his large den. "I could tell Kris was getting tense from the loud sound ringing in our ears but I did not get concern until he covered his ears and stated loudly: 'BARNABAS, PLEASE ASK THE ELVES TO LOWER THEIR MERRIMENT UNTIL I LEAVE!'!"

"Dear Lord! I too heard my Nickolas speak words before

leaving for the factory that did not match my patient husband's loving demeanor. Nickolas's said, he thought if he went for a walk he could clear his head if he breathed in some cold-fresh-air! Clear his head from what Barnabas?"

"I assure you dear Martha, I cannot begin to imagine what Kris Kringle needs to clear his head from." The head elf looked thoughtful for a minute. "To ease the large group of workers minds from worry over Santa's unusual behavior, I simply told them Santa might have gotten a rare headache due to our starting back six-months earlier and at the time I told them it sounded possible, but now I'm not so sure." Barnabas looked bewildered as he gazed up at the empty window. "What can we do Mother Christmas? We have no access to doctors up here. Up until now, there hasn't been a need for one."

"My good friend, I do not think Nickolas's problem requires a medical doctor." Martha blew on her cold hands and motioned toward her home. "Barnabas, this job calls for a higher being. The good physician."

"You speak of our heavenly creator and God! Jesus our Lord!" Barnabas stopped to open the front door for Martha. "I shall have all the elves to pray for Father Christmas dear Martha. The good Lord knows best and is sure to already know Kris's problem." The caring elf helped her up the frozen steps. "Keep me informed. I'm just happy we got a six-months to find the cure Kris needs so he'll be ready to become Santa again!"

The Kringle's Large Den

Martha found her husband sitting quietly in his overstuffed favorite lounge chair, his eyes closed while his hand kept thumping the wide armrest, keeping the beat to the old classic, I'm Getting Nothing for Christmas. She slipped quietly from her overcoat, wool hat and gloves before stepping behind Nickolas and laying her ice-cold hands over his cheeks causing him to sit up.

"Martha, you are as frozen as an icicle!" Nickolas took her cold hands and pulled her around on his lap, then started rubbing her cold fingers briskly. The devoted husband gazed into Martha's beautiful blue eyes as he teased her. "Dearest Martha, didn't we have enough snow-people built down in town square without you volunteering to become one?"

"I suppose I lost track of the time while making my brisk

morning walk when I was greeted in the courtyard by a perfectly charming elf who came bearing this perfect red rose!" Martha pulled it gently from her pocket and lifted it up under her husband's nose to smell. "Smells as lovely as it is beautiful, wouldn't you agree darling?"

"Yes Martha, it was a lovely gift and since roses do not grow anywhere near the North Pole, this perfect flower had to come from angelic magic. My guess could only be one ambitious head elf, so why was Barnabas out walking instead of seeing over the workers?" Nickolas knew the angelic elf wasn't flirting with Martha, he was most-likely confiding in her, sharing his private thoughts over some important matter, most likely his own strange behavior in the toy factory. "Did this little visit have anything to do with what happened in the toy factory right before I left?"

"Yes Nickolas, Barnabas and the toy makers were all upset and were left speechless when you yelled out." Martha touched his face gently. "My dearest Nickolas, I too grew concern when you stated you would be walking to 'clear your head'! Nickolas, I knew something was wrong with you when you chose to go to the factory by walking outside instead of taking the underground tunnel in your sleigh! Martha took his hand. "Darling, what is going on? There is something that's bothering you so please tell me. You must know I am always here for you Nickolas."

"It's the children Martha, the big change in their behavior. I have watched the naughty list growing day-by-day. Today's children are without discipline from both parents and teachers and the little brats take advantage of the situation! They mock the children who believe in me and worse still, those precious little lambs that follow the teachings of Jesus!" Nickolas lifted his wife up and walked to the big window to gaze out at silent snow falling peacefully. "The letters to Santa keep getting fewer and even some of them are from the arrogant bullies writing me just to make fun of the overweight old man who should have retired from his fantasy world a long time ago, then asking me for ugly things like live well-built strip dances or some X-rated DVD's!"

"I agree adults have made it easy for children to misbehave. These parents are the same little precious children who once believed in the magic of Christmas Nickolas. The modern age has taken away discipline and spanking the disobedient child so they

11

feel they have free liberties to do as they please." Martha joined her unhappy husband by the picture window that made them feel a part of nature and gave a soft sigh. "The little darlings know they have the upper hand and their parents disregard the Lord's holy words to spare the rod, thus spoil the child."

"Indeed, they do their children a misjustice Martha, by allowing them to get away with bad behavior." Nickolas brushed through his thick hair with his fingers. "If things don't change soon the naughty children will outweigh the good ones in the near future and at the rate they're going, pretty soon this old world won't need a Santa Claus!"

"Nickolas, there's really no need to take on so my dear." Martha could finally feel the warmth coming back into her frozen fingers and toes, so she removed her scarf and top sweater and laid them aside to put up later. Nickolas always came first to the devoted wife. "There are still many sweet children in this beautiful world who believe in you Santa. It's true those spoiled brats can be horrible and deserve only coal in their stocking."

Nickolas turned his attention back down on the village square in time to view the four stable elves walking the reindeer around the courtyard. His attention remained on the daily routine below his large window as he spoke. "To me, the worse kind of child is the one that does not believe. They start out small, never believing in Santa Claus and in return, they receive no toy from me! They grow into know-it-all adults and fail to believe in the Lord, our Savior, thus, do not receive Eternal life in heaven!" Nickolas turned to face his wife, tears lacing his piercing blue eyes, an emotion not witnessed by Martha since they lived their eternal life high atop the North Pole. "It's these children that breaks my heart the most Martha and they grow more in number with this new generation!" The loving man focused his attention on his concern wife as she made her way over by his side to gather his hands in her own. "The truth is, I am depressed over the change in our sweet children Martha! I fear there is no turning back! Together, you and I have been making God's children happy for over 2,000 years! This is the first time since I began being The Giver of Gifts to children that I cannot feel the joy in giving and I have the desire to hand this job over to a more modern Father Christmas!"

"But Nickolas, no one could ever replace you!" Martha watched as her devoted husband turned to look once again into the courtyard, now empty except for a new round of fresh snowflakes. She lifted her eyes and said a silent prayer before joining her upset husband. "Dear husband, have you forgotten, this is no ordinary job you have been blessed with, nor is this place we call home. It is not registered on any map because it cannot be seen by human eyes and we along with the angelic elves can survive here comfortably having constant light 24-7. Nickolas, you and I live forever at 33 years old for all eternity here in Kringle Village because you became Nickolas Kristopher Kringle, the Giver of Gifts to Children."

"I know you are right Martha but how can I get back to feeling the true Christmas spirit? The joyful spirit I used to witness on the faces of all the good boys and girls! What am I missing from all the hustle and bustle? From all the shopping and spending?"

"Nickolas, maybe what you need is some time off to go back when you did have that true Christmas spirit. Time to go back to when you did have that incredible love and joy for every child you saw in the old neighborhood streets of Bethlehem playing with make-believe toys made from sticks and rocks. Go back to when your God-given gift for carving lifelike things from wood became a mission to serve needy children by making them that special toy they pretended to have. You begin your unselfish hobby by carving smooth wood into sheep, cattle, donkeys and carts, then hid them at the needy child's door post." Hearing the warm familiar voice of the One who had granted both Nickolas and Martha their Christmas wish, the loving couple turned to look into the incredible caring eyes of Jesus. "Nickolas, my brother, then as you remember how that spark for making one small boy happy, grew into a flaming fire as you and Martha happily created many special toys to fulfill the dreams of many more poor children. Then, as you remember making all those children happy long before what became Christmas, I will help you recall your very first Christmas or should I say, 'The Very First Christmas! The night that lit your heart with more love than you thought possible! You will recall it was not making children happy that placed the real Christmas Spirit in that big heart of yours Nickolas, it was one tiny baby, lying in a manger inside a humble stall. This is what placed that amazing gift of Christmas Spirit inside you and Martha and IT SHALL LAST FOR ALL ETERNITY!"

Nickolas knew, with another heavenly gift from his Savior, he would find his way back to the Giver of Gifts and regain the true Christmas Spirit!

CHAPTER 4

The Judean Hillside Outside Bethlehem

Nathan, the senior shepherd, watched his loyal band of shepherds busy at their post. Nighttime had fallen over the quiet hillside on this cold-crisp starlit night. The millions of twinkling stars danced over head as the devoted men took turns warming up by the blazing fire, built not just to ward off the long night's chill, it also helped keep away unwanted wild dogs, wolves, and large cats, prowling the hills for a lamb supper.

As the sheep settled down the shepherds gathered around the fire to give night watch as they quietly talked, took out their packed supper to enjoy while they kept their eyes and ears pilled for any disturbance out in the large herd of sheep. While Nathan drank down his warm broth he listened to the shepherd talking quietly, as not to disturb the sleeping sheep. The head shepherd knew there was one faithful shepherd who would remain quiet and not be drawn into the local gossip. Nickolas was too busy carving away at the perfect smooth wood clutched in his hand. Nathan smiled when he noticed what the carving was.

"I can see some lucky boy is going to be very surprised and happy to find that handsome donkey at his doorpost Nickolas."

"I saw young Thomas this morning playing with a group of neighbor children who I recognized as living on Wellspring Street, the upper side of the city. Each boy held a costly store-bought donkey except for seven-year-old Thomas who had managed to find a stick with enough stems to break off all but four, and declared he had a fine donkey with mismatched legs." Nickolas smiled to himself, recalling their made-up game. "All six boys got down on the sidewalk and would pretend to gallop their donkeys across the make-believe road, making their donkey kick up its stiff back feet while the happy boys made neighing sounds."

"So, you are saying young Thomas was let in the game even though his donkey was just a stick?" Nathan always got caught up in Nickolas's stories concerning the children of Bethlehem.

"Well, Thomas stood over them watching for a while until the rich boys asked him to join in the game. They had been brought up to be kind to all God's children, rich or poor, so the game was going well until a loud crack could be heard from the stick donkey."

"Do not tell me the stick donkey lost one of his mismatched legs?" Nathan suddenly felt sorry for the poor boy.

"Thomas's happiness suddenly took a disappointing change as the group pretended to gallop across a sandy embankment and his stick donkey struck a rock and popped off both back legs. The five rich boys could not control their laughter over young Thomas's disaster and kept repeating, who ever heard of a two-legged donkey running around on tiptoes?"

"I guess it hit the young fellow hard, seeing his friends making fun of him like that." Nathan held his hands over the fire, rubbing them together. "What happen then?"

"The other five continued to rib Thomas about the stick donkey with words like: That was one sick-stick donkey! You rode his legs right off! Why don't you go ahead a put him out of his misery!"

"I guess it is easy to make fun of someone's bad luck when you have been given a well-built toy." Nathan knew what must have happened next but he always enjoyed hearing this good shepherd tell the happy ending. "Is this when you stepped in to give poor Thomas hope?"

Nickolas laughed, knowing his old friend and boss knew him well. "Yes Nathan! I cannot stand back and watch a small child cry, so I stepped from behind the old Chestnut Tree and after calling out his name I made my way to him and lifted his trembling hands in mind. I could tell his young eyes were studying my face and within seconds the trembling stopped only to be replaced by sad tears. I asked Thomas if he was a good boy for his mother and father and after he tearfully said he was, I told him that the Giver of Gifts has seen him playing with those other boys and everything that had happened. Then I softly told Thomas if he would stop crying and say his prayers before going to bed, in the morning there would be a special gift waiting for him outside his door."

"So, the special gift waiting for young Thomas by his doorpost will be," Nathan's eyes dropped on the perfect object in the gifted man's hand, "this remarkable-real-life donkey!"

"Tis right my trusted friend. I will deliver it straight down to Passion Street where I will meet Martha who will bring me the toy cart made specially to attached to this donkey." Nickolas smiled.

"So then, when Thomas meets his five playmates, he will not only have a fine donkey of his own but a cart to boot if needed to haul a tiny stone!" Nathan held out his hand for the carved donkey. "May I child-test it Nickolas?"

"Certainly!" Nickolas noticed the other shepherds had stopped talking and had stood up and walked over to witness what was going on. "Nathan, you may show my fellow shepherds what it takes to bring joy to a child."

Nathan got down and started moving the life-like donkey in what looked like a slow trot, then neighing softly, the head shepherd put the carved donkey into a kicking motion, while the group of excited men got down on the ground to watch closer as they laughed with childlike joy.

"Wow Nathan, any child would love to get this!" Ruben watched with wide-eyed wonder. "I bet my little Susanne would love to get a cute carved lamb!"

"Or a wooden shepherd holding a staff!" Mark, the youngest among the shepherds, smiled down secretly wishing it would be made for him.

"A carved shepherd would be perfect, but he would need at less one carved sheep with a tiny lamb!" Nathan stood up to hand the perfect gift back to its creator, giving him an approving wink for making so many grown men feel a childlike wander again.

CHAPTER 5

Stepping back behind a low wall to observe the young boy's reaction after finding his promised gift, Nickolas and Martha waited quietly, sure of young Thomas's early arrival through his family's door. As a cock crowed somewhere nearby, the door flung open and an anxious-wide-eyed boy stepped out and looked down at the doorpost to see a packaged, wrapped up in a strip of woolen cloth and tied up with a green vine on which red berries grew.

Seeing her son's unusual early morning interest, Thomas's mother followed him to see what had drawn him out so early. The patient woman waited and watched as Thomas picked up the package and stared down with a smile as big as his young-bright eyes. Hearing his mother give a sigh, Thomas turned to show her his gift.

"Look mother, it must be the gift promised me by the very nice man who had seen my poor stick donkey fall on the rock mountain and break his back legs off!" Thomas quickly sat down to unwrap the present and when he saw what it was he let out a squeal of surprised joy. "Look mother, my very own donkey and a cart, to go on my donkey! None of the other boys have a cart!"

"Son, that is the best-looking donkey I have ever seen! Why, those bought ones don't hold a candle to this fine animal!" Thomas had handed his mother the donkey to check out for herself. She easily attached the cart, picked off a couple red berries and placed inside then set them down for her son to see. As she enjoyed watching her little boy so happy, she paused to look around the empty street, unable to see the loving couple watching the happy moment. "Thomas, did that nice man tell you his name?"

"No ma'am, but he did tell me who would be bringing this wonderful gift to me this morning and where it would be waiting." Thomas stood up and joined his mother in checking out the empty street, hoping to get a glimpse of the mysterious giver. "His title is THE GIVER OF GIFTS!"

Tears flowed down the mother's face as she said a prayer of thanks to God for the Secret Giver who lit up her little son life with total happiness.

Word had spread about this mysterious person who brought beautiful gifts to needy children. Back inside their small dwelling on the edge of the city, Nickolas and Martha looked over the growing list of children. Concern for her devoted husband being overtaxed with making toys and holding down his fulltime job shepherding from six p.m. to six a.m., Martha touched his hand.

"Nickolas, I too would love to continue giving secret gifts to all these children, but continuing to keep it up once a week is not only draining the income you bring home, which is needed to pay our bills and seed for the back garden, but you work twelve-hours in those hills and I have taken on all the house duties as well as the garden. We simply cannot survive on all the joy giving to these children bring us."

"Of course, I am aware this has become a strain on what short time we do have together and the extra expense." Nickolas laid the list down and gathered his wife in his arms. "I never dreamed it would take off like it did. The number of children has increased by tenfold. If we are to continue making children happy, then we must choose one day out of the month." Nickolas walked to the window and looked out. "Winter is coming on soon and my supply of wood ripe for carving will be harder to find."

"Nickolas, I have hope in my heart, knowing that our good Jehovah will supply us with whatever we need so we can continue to make children glad." Martha was studying to decide which day of the month would be the best. "What to you think about the last Friday in the month. We could never choose the Sabbath day, the seventh day of each week, but the sixth day rings in the Sabbath so it just feels right."

"Good as any and it does have a ring to it." Nickolas turned to give her a smile. "Now, we must find a way to let the children know they will start receiving 12 gifts a year, one a month on the last Friday." Nickolas rubbed his beard in thought. "Martha, can you think of any way we can make the gifts even better since we're expecting anxious children to wait?"

"I am glad you asked Nickolas. As a matter of fact, I have been working on that very thing to surprise you." Martha walked over to a closet and took out a cloth-covered item. "This is just one example of how to bring your carving to life." Her eyes glistened as she laid the package in her husband's outstretched hands and watched him open it, letting out a gasp. "Do you like it?"

"Like it? Martha, this is exactly what I have been trying to imagine when I make my carvings!" Nickolas laughed, feeling almost like a child himself "Dearest Martha, you have brought my shepherd to life by giving him a face and color!"

"The happiness on your handsome face is all I need!" Martha felt nothing but love for the good man standing in front of her. "Nickolas, the ideal came to me one day while I was in the market. Why, I did not even know I had the gift of painting until I ran into a complete stranger." She could tell she had her husband's full attention. "The truth is, I cannot recall ever seeing a man that short and bless his dear soul, when the wind gave a big buff and his curly hair blew up, I swear, his ears beneath that thick bush of black hair were pointed on top."

"Pointed ears? No kidding?" Nickolas gave his wife a slight grin. "My beautiful wife wouldn't be pulling my leg now, would she?"

"I would not, dearest husband! Although I tried to act normal after witnessing such an unusual sight, the stranger blushed a bright red and produced an unusual bottle filled with seeds and said they were a gift from Jesu'. He told me to plant them, give them a drink of water, then watch them grow to produce berries of every color on God's promised rainbow." Martha blushed when Nickolas laughed. "The soft-spoken man gave me small brushes and what he called a painting tray, then told me to go make the carved toys come to life and make the children feel gladness in their hearts!" Martha was expecting her husband to laugh again but Nickolas had grown serious.

"Martha, this unusual man you described must have been sent from God. An angel perhaps."

"Then I'm not crazy." Martha closed her eyes feeling relief. "I too felt he had to be a heavenly being, but I never pictured the heavenly angels looking quite like that."

"Did the seeds grow berries of every color in the rainbow?" Nickolas looked back down at the shepherd, painted with an array of colors.

"More like every color of God's promised rainbow that filled the sky over the ark!" Martha assumed the first rainbow seen by man must have been amazing. "So, first I started with these eatable berries, that would be safe for children, then I was guided by an invisible being to other plants, roots flowers and bark, all safe for children. I ended up with twelve brilliant colors that I would paint on the carved items you left stored in the garden shed. Then I would place the items inside a strong cypress box and heat it over flames until it was dried and the carved wood shone like a smooth stone."

Nickolas held it up for the sunrays to reveal its beauty as he admired it. "Never has there been another toy or trinket like this before Martha!" Nickolas gave her a big smile of approval before laying it down and walking over to his workbench to retrieve his own surprise carving for her to check out. "This one is made especially for girls. Tell me what you think?"

"Oh Nickolas, it is a young maiden carrying a water pitcher!" Martha took the carved figure and noticed she had her features. "Older girls will cherish this exquisite gift my dear and once painted a fine trinket to display in their room." Martha could not contain her excitement when she walked over and pulled out yet another surprise to share with her devoted husband. "Nickolas, it looks like you and I saw a need to give little girls their own special present to play with." Martha held up what appeared to be a baby made from rags. "As you probably guessed, I stuffed the arms, head, body and legs with scrapes of leftover material from my sewing and stitched them up into a baby. By dipping pieces of rope into black or yellow dye, once dried I plaited each side and cut fringes in the front for fringe bangs. Then with my small brush I painted on two black eyes with lashes and brows, outlined a nose, painted on red-lips and cheeks and named her: Daughters of Little Ladies! What do you think Nickolas?"

"My dear Martha, I can see every good-little girl in our city wanting one of these life-size rag babies!" Nickolas checked out the cute rag baby and knew if sewed tightly, it would pass the child test. "I can find only one problem with this fabulous gift for girls! The name you chose is a wee-bit long precious. It needs to be easy for a young child to ask for."

Martha nodded her head in agreement as she thought a moment then gave her husband a smile. "I believe I have found the perfect name for this adorable baby! Since it is made from rags similar to the one my mother made for me, the first part will be named Rag! My mother called it daughter of her little girl then I changed the name to daughters of little ladies, but if we take the first letter of each word it spells DOLL. So, we add the rag and call it a RAG DOLL!"

Nickolas chuckled out, obviously pleased over the name. "Rag Doll! Martha, I grant you every little girl in Bethlehem will ask for a Rag Doll from the Giver of Gifts!"

"While every young maiden will cherish having their very own Martha doll." Martha enjoyed watching Nickolas blush, knowing he had carved the young maiden to look just like her. By painting her hair raven black and her eyes royal blue she will be my tiny twin."

"My wife is wise beyond her young years." Nickolas gave her a warm hug.

"Making toys for good girls and boys makes my heart young husband, but in years I would hardly call a fifty-year-old-women young." Martha glanced from their small window to the gently sloping hills that would soon take her shepherd husband away for his night watch. "The sun grows low in the western sky. Soon our time together will be gone for another long night."

"It is not easy to leave you alone my dearest to endure another long night here below the hills but work will keep us going." Nickolas had joined his wife at the window. "There is plenty here to keep you occupied while I am away."

"Tis true there is never a shortage of work my dear, like packing your night supplies and supper." She gave him her sweet smile and walked over to the pantry and pulled out what she needed for packing her husband a good meal and a small jug of homemade wine. "That should ward off the winter chill."

"Just enough to keep me warm and little enough to see that I do not fall asleep." Nickolas took the wrapped package. "Promise me you will keep busy until bedtime as not to miss my delightful company."

"Dear husband, since I can no longer have children, this thing you have started with the village children, has filled that empty place in my heart!" Martha patted his cheek. "I grant you Nickolas, I shall not become desolate nor filled with despair as long as I am making toys for all 'our' children in Bethlehem."

"Then you and I have the same desires! The same dreams for making the wonder of magic come alive in the hearts of children! A special place for children where make believe can become real! A place that is only meant for children who believe!" Nickolas had a faraway look as he spoke the things that had lived within his heart. He felt Martha's soft hand on his causing him to look down and smile. "Martha, the years have slowly crept up on me and I find climbing the Judean hills take me longer to reach the sheep and herders, so this is why I leave a few minutes earlier these evenings."

"I thought as much." Martha reached for his over cape and wrapped it around him securely, pulling the hood over his head gently. Reaching for his staff, she placed it in his outreached hand. "Nickolas, what will happen to all those precious children we have spoiled after we are gone? We cannot leave them searching endlessly for presents that simply are not there." She could not contain her sad tears. "Surely our caring God would not leave the little ones wanting."

"My dearest Martha, my faith in the great Almighty tells me our most high God will intervene and make things work out." Nickolas shivered, suddenly having a sense of being extremely cold. Something from outside the window caught his eye. It was something white falling from the sky and covering the ground. Realizing he might be having a vision since he was wide awake he asked Martha if she saw something falling outside. When she said she did not and reached out to touch his outstretched hand, he heard her gasp.

"Nickolas, your hand is ice cold!" he snapped from the vision and reached up to feel his face and found it cold as well. "Dear husband, do you have a fever?"

"Martha, I just experienced some sort of vision outside that window. First, I felt shivery all over, as if my blood had turned to ice, like those junks we saw high up in that mountain stream once. Then something falling outside caught my eye. It was white and the slow falling things fell on the ground and covered it and from the open window, I could feel a cold chill blow in. When you touched me, it broke the spell and now I am beginning to feel normal."

"Nickolas, do you think God was trying to tell you something?" Martha knew her husband needed to go but she knew Nathan would not hold it against his most faithful shepherd if he were a little late one time, especially when it came to matters of holy visions from their Creator.

"I cannot think of a better explanation Martha." Nickolas held tight to his tied-up package. "Since the things were white and falling to the ground, mounting up into a mystical scene, those white things could represent toys falling from heaven in plenty where all the good boys and girls would always find their special present."

"Or, suppose there really is a place like you described earlier. A special place for children where make believe can become real! A place where the ground is cold and white and toys are made to fill the hearts of children with joy in believing there will always be a Giver of Gifts just for them!" Martha touched his hand. "A place that is only meant for children who believe!"

Nickolas could not resist hugging Martha, knowing she not only knew how he felt about making the hearts of children filled with magical joy but wanting to keep their giving alive. He left for the night's watch, with plenty of smooth wood and a heart filled with a new kind of happiness unlike any known to man.

CHAPTER 6

Winter had finally arrived and another year would soon be over. The Kringle's list of children had now grown to over thirty-boys and twenty girls and along with the growth came a new title for the secret giver of gifts. The parents were now aware just who this generous man was and named him Kringle Jingle, the Giver of Gifts, since everyone recognized the shepherd by the bells he wore as he made his way up the slopes to guard sheep. So, to make his new title official, Nicolas would ring his bells every time he left the children their gift which made the adoring boys and girls simply call him, Kringle Jingle!

So, once again Nickolas had made his rounds just before dawn before heading home to sleep before he had to head back up the hills for another night watch. With a little time left, Nickolas sat at their small table packing his large leather bag filled with a new load of wood, perfect for carving. As he packed, Nickolas watched with interest as his wife sat quietly writing something on one of Kringle Jingle's children's: What do you want this winter, cards.

Martha glance up and gave her husband a smile before folding the card in half like the children always did for the Giver of Gifts to find. "There!" she chuckled at her husband's, confuse face. "What? Cannot grownup believers ask for what is in their heart Nickolas? I just wrote down the one thing I want Nickolas, but unlike the children asking Kringle Jingle for the gift I am asking the Lord for this special gift. He alone can deliver it."

"Martha, not another request for a baby, the one we have been told will never come?" Nickolas looked down expecting to find his beautiful wife 's sad face once more only to find her beaming with sheer hope. "Then, if it is not a baby of our own you wish for again, pray tell me what it is you want more than anything!"

"I bet it might be the one thing you want as well Nickolas, if you could ask the Lord for one special gift that only He could deliver." Martha reached into the Gifts Giver box and pulled out a blank card and handed it to her husband along with a quill pen. "Go ahead, write down your most precious wish gift, the one thing you could ask God for and miraculously receive it!"

"Alright! I will write down the one thing I would really like if by some miracle it could become a reality! What have I got to lose?" Without any hesitation, Nickolas wrote down the one thing he dream about then folded the paper like Martha had done and laid it next to Martha's. "Do we compare the notes now?"

"Not yet Nickolas. Like the children must wait for Kringle-Jingle and dawn to break, so must we wait for the Lord to collect our notes." Martha looked around for the perfect spot to leave the notes and smiled as she kneeled down and laid them under their large prayer plant. "We shall wait until you get home in the morning."

"I must admit they look very festive under the green leaves." Nickolas studied the white notes lying under the large green plant. "Since winter is such a barren time I been thinking how much livelier the appearance of the giver's gift if I had the children to put out some type of evergreen to find their toy under."

"I think that is a splendid ideal Nickolas! It would make the children's happiness more fulfilling if they had to get down and search underneath an evergreen to find their special gift." Martha hurriedly helped her husband, prepare for the long December night atop the Judean Hillside under the starry sky.

When Nickolas arrived home early the next morning, Martha instantly noticed an amazing difference in her usually exhausted husband. She could tell by his joyful movements and glowing happy face that something miraculous happened during the long-cold night watch on the hillside. Nickolas appeared to be bursting with news but the words seemed to be frozen inside his smiling lips.

"Nickolas, pray tell me what has happen to bring on such happiness and causes you to shine like the bright morning sun?"

"Great news Martha! He is here! I saw Him with my own eyes Martha!" Nickolas practically shouted out the good news, as though the frozen words finally melted into happy praise.

"He? Who is here my dear Nickolas?" Martha watched her husband in wonder. "Who has got you so excited?"

"Why, the MESSIAH, of course! Martha, the Lord has come down to earth to be among us, just as the prophets declared!" Nickolas slung her around laughing.

"You said you saw our Messiah, Nickolas? When? Where?"

"We had been tending the sheep as usual when we all noticed a very large star appeared in the sky and it shone down in a long stream on our little city! As we stared in wonder at the bright-brilliant star, suddenly an angel appeared in the heavens right above our heads and made a degree, just for us, humble shepherds." Nickolas could tell by Martha's wide-eyes and dropped jaw that she too was astounded that God would choose humble shepherds to announce His Sons birth.

"Nickolas, what were the angel's words? Can you remember what he said?"

"I can Martha, as I can hear them now still ringing through my head the good news." Nickolas moved to the window as the angelic words once again rang out. "Fear not, for behold, I bring you good tidings of great joy, which shall be to all people! For unto you is born this day in the city of David a Savior, which is Christ the Lord. And this shall be a sign unto you; ye shall find the babe wrapped in swaddling clothes and lying in a manger." Nickolas turned around to face his wife, now wiping tears that ran down her cheeks. "My dearest Martha, when the angel finished speaking, suddenly the entire heavens were filled with a host of angels, and the multitude sang out with a voice of one, praising God and saying, Glory to God in the highest and on earth peace, good will toward men." Nickolas reached for Martha's trembling hands. "The angels were gone away as quickly as they appeared and as we all stared down into the city, knowing the angel had gave us directions to go and see for ourselves this Holy child, God's-Own-Son! Martha, every shepherd there left the flock unattended, knowing the hand of God would protect them. We were just a bunch of humble shepherds but the Lord most-High had chosen us to tell the good news of His son's birth. Nathan made it official when he announced: 'Let us now go even unto Bethlehem, and see this thing which is come to pass, which the Lord hath made known unto us.'"

"And you found the babe lying in a manger?" Martha had been drawn into her husband's amazing visit."

"Oh yes Martha! We made with great haste down the hillside, our eyes never leaving the star that seemed to guide us straight to the tiny stable of Malcom, the innkeeper. As we entered into the warm stable we met the virgin mother whose name was Mary and her newlywed husband Joseph, both from Nazareth." Nickolas took

27

on a faraway look as he recalled his first glimpse of God's Son. "Then I saw the baby, God's little son, wrapped in swaddling clothes, lying in that manger. Mary, the boy's mother, nodded for us to move up to the manger and see her newborn baby, the Son of God. There we all stood, grown men frozen in our tracks but slowly, one-by-one we made our way forward, starting with our fearless leader Nathan." Nickolas gave a small sigh, recalling the reason he had got in back of their line. "While I waited my turn to see this incredible sight, I felt inside my robe pocket for the special trinket I had been making that very night. Dearest wife I had carved out the perfect angel, her wings spread in magnificent splendor. As I held it tightly in my shaking hand I kept telling myself, this tiny king is just a wee baby, not yet perfected into His heavenly glory."

"And is that what you found lying inside that manger stall my dear?" Martha had been drawn-up in her husband's fascinating story. "A sweet precious infant asleep on a bed of hay!"

"He was indeed only a newborn baby Martha, tiny and helpless looking lying sweetly on the bed of fresh hay, brought in for the animals but gladly given for our King!" Nickolas felt for a chair and sat down. "When I finally reach Jesus, my heart leaped for joy and I found my knees buckling under me as if some angelic force was slowly helping me down into a form of worship. I was too busy looking around for my invisible assistant to witness the Christ child open his eyes and stare up at me, sending forth my name in spirit language."

"Nickolas, are you telling me baby Jesus was conversing with you in words you understood instead of a baby's natural goo-goo's and ca-ca's?" Martha knew her husband had been serious over the entire heavenly experience.

"Although the baby never moved his lips and I was obviously the only one who could hear him, yes Martha, I heard every intelligent grownup word coming from my Savior's heart." Nickolas knew his Martha would never doubt what he told her, so he continued. "First, Jesus asked me if I liked the new Eastern Star created just for Him by His Father? The big-bright star whose top point stretched upward toward heaven, while just below it stretched its great arms and its long-pointed tail stretched down toward the earth, while rays shined out about and around it. Then the tiny King announced that it would be called, the Star of the East, the Star of

Bethlehem, and the Christmas Star." Nickolas gazed from the window, knowing the first rays of sunlight would soon appear and dim the star until nightfall. "Jesus told me His Holy Birth would be called Christmas, which translates into Christ-Messiah and Savior!" The weary shepherd got up and gathered his wife's hand in his and led her to the open door to show her the Star that God the Father placed above the stable to announce His Son's birth.

Martha gave a startled gasp as her eyes beheld the glory of God in His bright and morning star. "Even now it shines brighter than the sun. Oh Nickolas! O how happy our great Creator must be to bring forth, His only Son's announcement in such a magnificent way!" Martha looked up into her husband's radiant eyes. "What did he look like Nickolas, our little king?"

"I can tell you true, he was no ordinary baby Martha. Most babies are cute and cuddly and even though Jesus was both cute and cuddly, he actually glowed and His sweet face was overflowing with the breath of heaven. Suddenly the wooden carving did not feel good enough to give the Son of God so I nervously shoved it back inside my robe. That's when I noticed the two small hands held something clutched tightly inside each. Each little hand held a very familiar looking piece of white parchment paper, both folded in half."

CHAPTER 7

Martha was suddenly back inside the small house down on her knees, looking at the empty space she had laid their folded parchment request cards. She froze, finding the cards gone and Nickolas's decoration that he saw them in the Christ child's small hands. Martha's eyes met her husband's. "Nickolas, they are gone! Surely you are not trying to tell me Gods Son was actually holding 'our folded notes'?"

"I am my dear. Jesus, our Savior, knows what we both want more than anything." Nickolas helped Martha up from the floor. "I am also telling you that Jesus has ask to see you Martha, this day."

"See me?" Martha wandered around the house as she pondered her husband's last words. She was confused at how a newborn baby could let her faith-filled husband hear such a message, but this was no ordinary newborn infant he had seen. This Jesus was the Lord most high and nothing was impossible for Him to do. "Very well Nickolas, I truly believe you have seen our Messiah and being a woman of faith, I cannot doubt his asking to see me nor the amazing fact that Jesus now holds our cards written to Him. We must not tarry a moment longer, so I shall grab my long overwrap, strap up my shoes and follow my beloved husband up the streets of Bethlehem and down to Malcom's small stable."

The stable was warm and quiet except for a soft hum coming from the happy young mother. As Martha stepped inside she noticed the beautiful girl had a glowing radiance around her face as she gently rubbed her blessed baby's small cheeks. A sweet fragrance filled the morning air and somewhere overhead in the rafters a morning dove could be heard cooing over the manger bed where the holy child lay watching his mother as he listening to her sweet song.

Sensing a new presence, Mary turned to greet the early morning visitors with her angelic sweet smile as Joseph raised up to look over the stall wall that held their faithful little donkey that had traveled the dusty roads to Bethlehem carrying the virgin Mary and the unborn Son of God. Joseph stepped out after feeding the patient donkey and set the wooden bucket down to greet the special shepherd who Jesus had took an interest in.

"Nickolas, I see you brought your charming wife down to see baby Jesus." Joseph had easily stepped into his role as stepfather and the love he showed both the young mother and the holy child was overpowering. "Our little son has grown close to your husband from the moment he saw him."

"To both of you from what I heard between their conversation. "Mary had taken them both by surprise. "I never meant to listen in to your conversation with Jesus but since this was new to me as well, I felt the need to know what was being said between you since He is our responsibility."

"And you should know what is going on where your special son is concern." Nickolas heard the baby moving in His manger and watched as Mary reached in and lifted Him out and into her arms.

"Look son, see who has come to see you this morning."

Responding only in spiritual words, Jesus looked from Nickolas to Martha before smiling. "Good morning love ones. You both have ask me for a special gift, one that has never before been asked of us. This thing which concerns the happiness of little children proves your dream wish revolves around others, not your own rewards of recondition or riches." His heavenly blue-green eyes looked into Martha's blue ones. "Martha, I hold in my hand your written wish. I know what secret is inside that beautiful giving heart and when I become a man, you shall have your answer for this special wish you made." Jesus turned to Nickolas. "Your special wish is safe in my care and like Martha, you will know my answer after I have become a man."

"Then I shall wait with gladness in my heart, sweet Lord, for I know I shall see your blessed face again." Martha reached out and gently touched the face of her Messiah and felt the warm glow of heaven fill her heart. Nickolas stepped up behind Martha after he heard Jesus call him up.

"Yes Lord, I am here." The loyal shepherd knelled down at Mary's feet and smiled into the baby's loving eyes.

"Nickolas, I will see your carved angel you brought me last night then thought it not good enough." Jesus reached out his small hand, the notes had vanished.

Nickolas and Martha exchanged glances before the embarrassed shepherd took the carving out of his pocket. "Forgive my rash decision to take back what I was to give you dear child of God but found it inferior to your radiant beauty."

"This perfect angel is not for me my friend Nickolas. Please give it to Mary, my devoted mother, to keep as a reminder of the angel who came down with news of me. Gabriel looks very much like this angelic figure you carved."

Nickolas bow his head in reverence before handing the angel to Mary, who excepted it with total happiness and gratitude.

"This is very special Nickolas and I shall cherish it all my days along with the swaddling clothes wrapped around my special baby boy." Tears of joys shown clearly in Jesus's mother's eyes. "I believe my son knows of another carving you keep hidden inside your pocket Nickolas."

"Another carving?" Nickolas looked from Mary to Martha, confused and shaking his head until reality hit him. The very first thing he tried to make while learning the trade. A sad little colt with one short leg, a shaggy mane and short tail. He whispered into Martha's ear. "Perhaps I should have carved a white dove out of beech wood for my Lord. Surely he does not want my pitiful little colt."

"But I do Nickolas." The loving couple both heard the Lord's response. "The sad little colt that has been hidden away inside your pocket for fear someone might laugh at your first attempt at carving." They turned to see the newborn seated on Mary's lap and watching them closely. "My love ones, remember, I see all and I hear all."

Now red-face from embarrassed again, Nickolas reached deep inside his pocket and pulled out the wrapped-up colt. "I only kept it for a reminder of how far I have come since I started carving."

"This is what you were led to believe Nickolas, an ideal placed inside your head by us when in truth, we saw this mishap as a gift to us, not a failure from your gifted hand." Jesus held out his hand and took the wrapped gift before smiling. "As a small child, I now can feel how the children feel when the Giver of Gifts leave their asked-for present. There is a fluttering-world of make-believe living inside my heart in this land where children who believe go, the place that once you outgrow this belief the portals close and you can never return again." Jesus small hand unwrapped the gift and lifted up the sad, yet precious little colt up to admire. "One day this very colt will play a big part in my prophesied future and you both will be there to witness it. This is when you will learn of your own future and how your asked for gifts will be given."

"We shall happily wait for your answer Jesus." Martha had joined her husband on the stable floor at the feet of the Christ child.

"Even though my years are creeping up on me Lord, I believe I shall see you on the day you speak of." Nickolas could not resist his chuckle. "And, to see just how my sad little carved colt can be apart of any event concerning you is something worth seeing."

"Nickolas, you see a damaged little colt but I see a young colt made for the King of Kings to ride on as He makes His great entrance into Jerusalem." As soon as Jesus said the words and touched the carving, the plain wood was suddenly covered with brown fur, the face features now visible. "The prophets spoke of this Nickolas so you shall see me riding upon the colt of a donkey. This colt Nickolas, blessed with life from heaven and found tied up by my future followers." Jesus laid the donkey aside and held up the two folded notes. "Remember, on that day you both will get your answer to your secret wish."

Back at the North Pole

"Nickolas, I shall never forget knelling at our Lord's manger the last time we saw him as a baby, then seeing him thirty-three years later just as he told us. How he took time to be with us and how we received our long-awaited answer to our wish."

"It was the greatest experience in my entire life, to speak spiritually with the newborn Christ child after seeing the wander of the Christmas Star of Bethlehem, then witnessing the angel's message proclaiming the good news of His holy birth!" Nickolas felt a fresh rebirth of what made Christmas so special to him and Martha. "Then to see Jesus riding into Jerusalem on my colt! I shall never forget seeing the little misfit alive, yet still with its own distinct personality. One leg shorter than the rest, the mane shaggy and its tail, very stubby. Yet, the little colt walked proudly and gave our Lord a perfect ride." Nickolas remembered back. "Then the special invitation to sit with Jesus where He gave us our life-changing answer concerning our secret wishes."

"Did you see the twinkle in his bright eyes when he announced our secret wishes were for the exact same thing?" Martha smiled when her beloved Nickolas smiled and nodded in agreement.

"I can see it just like is just happened Martha." Nickolas pulled her into his arms as they stared out into the falling snow. "I can almost hear the crowds shouting their praises to the Lord as he rode our way and its been over 2,000 years.

CHAPTER 8

Jerusalem

The crowds had been excited as they followed along beside the young colt carrying Jesus to the holy city. Each voice was lifted up with praises and shouts of hallelujah as they waved palm branches singing; Blessed is He who comes in the name of the Lord!

Martha and Nickolas had made their yearly pilgrimage to Jerusalem for the Passover celebration and they were overjoyed to see Jesus there and riding on a colt that looked very familiar. As He grew nearer, they took hands and wondered if their longtime friend would look their way. As Jesus passed them in the courtyard just outside the temple walls, He turned to smile and promised to meet them in the temple gardens just outside the sacrificial platform were the priest stood receiving the Israelites offered sacrifices. Finding the spot just as the Lord had described, Martha and Nickolas sat down to wait for the one both had been anxious to see after almost thirty-one years since Joseph had taken the Son of God to Egypt for safety and await the passing of the evil King Herod.

There was a sweet sense of stillness that had settled around them and the air took on a sweet fragrance unlike any they had ever smelt at the exact moment the Lord appeared. Seeing the Lord brought the couple from their bench and down on the knees at the sacred feet of Jesus. Smiling down at the faith-filled couple, Jesus reached down and gently lifted them up.

"Come, let us sit in this pleasant garden and take in the Father's sweet peace and tranquility before I venture inside the noisy Temple Courts where jackals and sinners buy and sale sheep and doves and make the House of God a marketplace!" Jesus had taken a seat and with closed eyes continued with what he knew would happen. "Once inside the house of my Father my anger will be kindled and I will drive out the money changers and the ones selling live animals and birds to be used for sacrifices! The church leaders will find a time and place to have me arrested and the time for obeying my Father's will shall be at hand. To fulfill the prophecies, things will not be so pleasant for the Son of Man in a short while."

"Lord, this great pain you must endure, will it be worth all your suffering and the great sacrifice you will be making?" Nickolas could not contain his internal sadness over the horrible pain the Savior must endure on that Roman cross. "Jesus, can dying for the sins of mankind change the hearts of evil men?"

"Nickolas, I chose to leave my home in heaven and come down to earth to give my life for all of our children sins that they might be saved. We, the Three-in-One, chose to give mankind a living soul, just as we did the angels. Can my sacrifice on that cross change the hearts of evil men? This must be their choice to make but once made final their living soul lives on, either in heaven with us or in hell with Lucifer until judgement day." Jesus touched the hand of Nickolas before asking "Nickolas, your love for children does not waver from your Lord's love for all His children. As we love them so do you and just as I will give my life for them I know you would do so too."

"You know my heart well, my Lord. I could live my eternal life making the hearts of sweet children happy and if you asked me to become a sacrifice for them and give up any future personal life so they could remain happy, I would." Nickolas had laid open his heart to the One who knew it better than even he did. "Lord, what about Martha? She is a part of my heart as well."

"Martha is forever by your side Nickolas, for she too shares the same love and devotion to children and the desire to make them joyful throughout Eternity is her wish as well." Jesus laid his hands on their head. "As my life as been laid out from the earth's beginning so has the miracle of children's Christmas. Since I was to be born a child and my birth would become an annual celebration to welcome in the Messiah, Christmas was born! Christ-Messiah and Savior. Nickolas, you found the perfect mate, designed just for who and what you would become. The Giver of Gifts will take on many titles but there will always be just one man visiting children but only on Christmas Eve when God sent the world its first Christmas gift." The Lord took around the childless couple. "Martha, I know how much you and Nickolas wanted a child of your own but your Holy Creator chose to make you like parents for children all over the world. No matter how time changes the lives of our small ones and some even grow cold toward you, even lose their belief in the Giver of Gifts as well as their belief in me, there are many more who have found a place inside their pure hearts for Father and Mother Christmas."

"Jesus, you said we would be delivering gifts to children all over the world." Martha knew the Lord had made their visits to children just one day a year but would she and Nickolas be able to finish thousands of toys to hand out for so many? "Even if you supplied us with everything we needed to make that many toys, how could the two of us manage so many?"

"Martha does have a point Lord, not to mention how would we even know what every good little girl and boy wanted for Christmas?" Nickolas suddenly felt overwhelm by the task in front of them. "How would I get to every child even if I knew where they lived?"

Jesus could only chuckle at the couple who had been used to making toys for one small town. "Nickolas, Martha, you are thinking in human terms where this thing we give you cannot ever be done. Your time has not come yet to be Giver of Gifts to the world's children." Jesus looked down at the loving man. "Nickolas, you said you would sacrifice your life for these children. Did you mean those words my brother?"

"Yes Lord, every word." Nickolas looked over at his wife who he was completely devoted too and needed by his side to become Father Christmas. "Does Martha have to sacrifice her life as well to be beside me?"

"The sacrifice I speak of, yes Nickolas, but it must be her choice to make." The Lord looked lovingly at the beautiful woman listening. "It is your choice Martha. Are you willing to make a sacrifice to become Mother Christmas next to your husband?"

"Nickolas is my life Jesus and my choice is to be beside him for all eternity wherever that will be for us."

"You are wise to say wherever your eternity will be if you become Mother Christmas and Father Christmas." Jesus gathered both their hands in his. "My beloved, your eternity will not be in heaven for obvious reasons but this place we send you is a part of heaven, like Eden is. On the earths human map, it will be known as the North Pole, the highest point on our created earth and the closes place to heaven. Like heaven, there is continued daylight unless Father Christmas desires to see the enchanting Northern lights and wishes for night to fall. Nickolas, your vision of the white wintery landscape as snow drifted down and the chill of the North Pole swept inside your body, was only to alert you about your new home." Jesus watched them exchange glances. "Not to worry my brethren, you will instantly feel at home after seeing your very own village, complete with a giant toy factory and a neat street of charming cottages, both factory and homes suitable for your workers, which you will call elves. Father Christmas will feel warm and happy in his and Mother Christmas's big heavenly mansion."

"My heart is jumping with joy over the news you have shared with us Lord." Martha pulled in close to her husband. "Could you tell us more about the workers named elves? Will these be other humans who have loved children?"

"The excited elves will be some of the smaller angels who happily volunteered for the position years ago when we described a future Father Christmas." Jesus felt the joy the couple were feeling and was pleased. "You ask how you would know what the children would want. You will be receiving many letters, made out to Santa Claus, the children's choice name for you. They will write what they want and to answer how you would get to so many children all over the world, you shall possess a magical power and once you pass through the Portal of Mirrors, your image will change to Santa Claus and your giant sleigh will be waiting with a magic bag that can contain every toy asked for. Once your sleigh is air born, it will split up into many copies of you and fly off in every direction, being pulled by the nine-reindeer pulling you and your magical sleigh."

"So, that is how Nickolas can travel to every continent in the world on one night." Martha laughed merrily. "But then, why not! There is nothing impossible for God to do!" Martha grabbed her husband. "Dearest Nickolas, the Lord has made it possible for our impossible wishes to come true! The children will not be forgotten! They will never have to search for presents that aren't there!" Martha lifted the hand of Jesus and kissed it. "Thank you, Lord for giving us not just one child, but millions of children to share our love with!"

CHAPTER 9

Back At The North Pole: Present Time

"Nickolas, now you recall all that happened to bring us to where we are and why we chose to be here instead of heaven." Martha knew she too had been refreshed by their visit to their past and their time spent with Jesus. "It renewed all the reasons we chose this eternal mission to make sure all the good children would have their miracle of Christmas."

"It has certainly brought the spirit of Christmas back inside my heart." Nickolas felt revived after reliving all that happened on that first Christmas. "I was recalling the words Jesus spoke on His last visit with us and I marvel at how our Lord knew exactly what the future children would be like."

"Father Christmas, what beautiful words from our holy creator lifted your spirits from your deep despair?" Barnabas appeared with a large black bag bulging full of its contents and took the couple by surprise. "I must apologize for dropping in on your conversation about your time-travels back to your past life but Jupiter has just arrived with his first delivery of letters to Santa. I had sensed your return earlier but thought it best to give you some time to reflect on your little visit to Bethlehem."

"Barnabas, you know you are always welcomed in our home and by the looks of the letters arrivals, I'd say we have been away for quite a while." Nickolas had not stopped to think how long they had been away but he knew the Lord Most High would not make him late getting back in time for the Christmas rush. "You asked me about the beautiful words spoken to me from Jesus and although there were many, going all the way back to when He was an infant, I was just recalling the words said on our last visit, while in Jerusalem."

"Nickolas, you are referring to how Jesus knew exactly what the modern world children would be like, aren't you?" Martha knew her husband very well and the words Jesus had spoken touched on everything that had been bothering her husband regarding the new-age generation.

"I can still hear Jesus healing my aching soul with those words my dear Martha." Nickolas stepped over to the big window and gazed up into the heavens. "No matter how time changes the lives of our small ones and some even grow cold toward you and lose their belief in the Giver of Gifts as well as their belief in the Son of God, there are many more who have found a place inside their pure hearts for Father and Mother Christmas!"

Barnabas sat the heavy bag down and commenced to clapping, knowing the Christmas spirit had returned to Nickolas. "And these many letters are just the first to arrive and they were all postmarked the day after Thanksgiving which gives us just under one month to complete the long list and have you ready for that magic sleigh!"

"Barnabas, that sounds wonderful and perhaps all these children's letters to Santa will help stoke up the flame burning inside my beloved Nickolas." Martha gave a hardy chuckle as she declared. "Hot chocolate for everyone!"

"Sounds tempting Mother Christmas but I must get back to my toymakers!" The head elf started to walk away when he suddenly remembered the other reason he barged into the Kringle's large den. "Oh, I almost forgot the main reason for my interruption. You both have a visitor waiting to be announced."

"A visitor? Here, at Kringle Village?" Martha looked over at her husband with dismay. "Nickolas, are we expecting any visitors, besides Jupiter of course."

"I assure you wife I haven't the slightest ideal who could even penetrate the boundary of our hidden village." Nickolas stared at the smiling elf. "Don't just stand there Barnabas expecting us to read your bright mind. Who is waiting to see us?"

"Why, the boss man, of course!" Barnabas jumped when he felt a strong hand on his shoulder.

"Barnabas, how many times have told you to stop addressing me as 'boss-man!" The radiance of the Lord filled the room the moment Jesus appeared. "If you would not rattle on so then you would not have forgot about your creator waiting to be announced."

"Guilty as charged, my most high Creator." Barnabas blushed a bright red. "I must admit I did get caught up in Father Christmas new-found Christmas spirit and could not stop talking. I did mean well Lord."

"Very well Barnabas, you are forgiven. From now on just

announce me by my name?" Jesus waited as he watched the head elf scratch his head in confusion. "You do know what my name is, do you not? I've only had it for all eternity."

"True Lord, but you have many names and I am just confused which name you want me to use. Lord, Savior, Redeemer, Lamb of God, Emmanuel, Messiah. The Good Shepherd, Christ, King and many more." Barnabas wrinkled his brow when he noticed the frown on Jesus's face. "Did I fail to guess Jesus?"

Nickolas and Martha could not resist their laughter and Jesus joined in patting the blushing elf on the back. "You finally got it right without knowing you did Barnabas. Jesus is my given name Barnabas as you well know."

"Yes Jesus, this has been your name for as long as I have existed." The elf raised his shoulders in defeat. "I suppose it was too simple for me to figure out. I shall do better next visit I promise."

"I will expect nothing more Barnabas, now enough babbling, you have got a job to do." Jesus gave him a nod toward the door. "Your workers could use some of that hot chocolate about now so get Breanna to whip up her special brew and have a cup-break with your team."

"I'm off then! Enjoy your chat and Martha's great hot chocolate!" Barnabas walked out still speaking to himself. "Rich hot chocolate, double marshmallows sprinkled with peppermint and topped high with real-whipped cream! Cannot wait!" the three listening could hear Barnabas's running feet disappear down the hall, causing them to laugh again.

After Martha gave Jesus and Nickolas a big mug of her extra-great hot-chocolate, she joined them with her own mug.

"Thank you, Martha, this is a real Kringle Village treat." Jesus drank down a big gulp before speaking. "So, Nickolas you finally feel Christmas in your heart so we just deed to make sure the spirit remains after a few rude comments from the bad boys and girls.

"There is always a few each year who enjoy throwing off on Santa Claus Lord but most of them don't waste their time by writing, they just like to make the children that do believe feel bad by telling them I do not exist." Nickolas knew Jesus wasn't convinced that he was 100% back yet, so his visit was to assure him of his complete healing.

"I took the liberty to retrieve one such letter from this first bag which holds mostly good children's letters." Jesus produced a letter written on red paper. "This boy's choice of paper is already a bad sign that he is headed down the wide path." He handed the letter to Nickolas's outstretched hand.

Nickolas opened the red envelope and pulled out the red paper. "Greeting old fat one!" Nickolas read out loud so Martha and Jesus could hear what the rude boy wrote. He smiled when Martha mumbled, Fat, like a beanpole. "Look big boy, I, for one, don't think you exist but if you do, what's an old man like you doing still kicking? You should have been dust a long time ago! Your old memory can't be working and how do you keep from losing your stupid way. Why, you're so fat those poor old reindeer probably can't get your rear end off the ground! I bet you can't even remember their names to get them started and forget being led by Rudolph's red nose since your hands are probably to shaky to change his bulb anymore. But, just in case you are real, prove it by bringing me a red Corvette! And fat so, forget bringing it down my chimney, just park that baby in our drive way then hang the key over my red sock! Harty-ha ha! TOP GUN!" Nickolas glanced up and noticed both his listeners had serious faces. "This young man is as fresh as they come and kids like this one never get anything for Christmas. At least by me."

"And the little brat does not deserve anything but you can bet his parents give old top gun everything that he wants!" Martha sipped on her hot chocolate, made to stay hot. "What do you think about this rude boy Jesus? Does the young man stand a chance with his hateful attitude?"

"Not if things do not change for Morgan Matthews." Nickolas and Martha never questioned how the Lord knew the boy's real name because God knows all. "He is a spoiled young man and has only one sister, just five, named Annie. Morgan continues to tell the sweet girl there is no Santa and that she is wasting her time writing someone who does not exist. He claims all her gifts come from their parents and little five-year-old Annie still holds out hope that you are real. You will find her letter inside that bag and I know her doll is already made and waiting for the sweet girl."

"Annie Matthews, yes I remember her wish last year when she was four." Nickolas recalled the girls sweet writing.

"Dear Santa, I want a pretty tea set this Christmas, a big red ball, a princess outfit and some candy. I wuv you Santa. Your friend, Annie."

"What will happen to that sweet child as she grows older and her big bully brother keeps telling her there's no Santa?"

"If things aren't altered, you won't be getting a letter next year from six-year-old Annie Matthews." Jesus produced a model car of the red Corvette and handed it to Nickolas. "Nine-year-old Morgan cannot have a real car but this perfect copy of one might help convince the non-believer there really is a Santa Claus, created just for children who believe."

"He is sure to think his parents got it for him so how can he be made to believe Santa actually did get his hateful note and brought him something after all." Nickolas admired the perfect model in his hand.

"The parents have no knowledge of their son's hateful note to you. He would never want them to know he wrote Santa Claus in the first place." The Lord knew how this young boy could deceive his parents by acting innocent around them. "The Matthews do not know their nine-year-old son is telling his little sister there is no Santa Claus but I can tell you those children's parents do not have a lot of interest in their them when they think only about their own happiness and wealth."

"So, you think if Nickolas delivers this replica of the Corvette to Morgan Matthews the boy might have a change of heart were Santa Claus is concern?" Martha had a hard time imaging parents who were not interested in what was going on with their children. "Who knows, it might even bring a change to their parents to wake them up from their selfish-self-centered lifestyle."

"I do believe the young man will learn that sometimes believing is not seeing in what is real but feeling that special joy that makes it real and very much alive from within and without." Jesus produced something in a small square box that had a picture of a plane in flight. "You may lay this next to Morgan's Corvette model. It is a DVD he has secretly wished for consisting of his favorite movie and hero, Top Gun, his present pen-name.

"I get it, since no one knows about that secret wish, he finds that Santa Claus knew and left it for him." Nickolas smiled at the thought of this rude boy being blown away with the truth he had denied in front of five-year-old Annie. "Jesus, if Morgan kept telling his small sister there wasn't a Santa and her parents obviously never took any interest in helping her believe, where did this precious child learn to believe in me?"

"Annie learn everything there was to know about Nickolas Kristopher Kringle from her very best friend in Appalachia Elementary School in the small town of Appalachia, Kentucky. Annie Matthews, one very wealthy little five-year-old and Abby Asbury, a poor farmers daughter, the youngest of ten beautiful children."

"Ten children?" Martha sat up, the thoughts of having to take care of ten children on a poor father's income. "Tell me, does Mr. Asbury make enough to feed and clothed his big family?"

"Robert and his beloved wife Della has always managed to make ends meet on Robert's meager income from doing handyman work in the town below the mountains and the farm produced enough food in the spring and summer months to feed all the hungry mouths under the Asbury's loved-fill home in the deep coves of the Appalachian Mountains, one of the poorest spots in America."

"The Matthews cannot show their two children any love if they don't take interest in them, so how can the Asbury's work from sun-up to sun-down and find time to show their ten children love? Especially individual love, that means the most to all sons and daughters?" Martha knew no matter how many children she and Nickolas might have had, each child would be treated with the same love and devotion.

"It's true the Matthews relish in being rich but ignore their children's need for attention and love." Jesus smiled at the extreme difference between the parents. "On the other hand, the Asbury's are very close to each child and love them all equally and it all begins with the deep love and affection they have always shared with each other." Jesus sat down the empty mug, now clean by his touch, and stretched out his hands for them to come, follow. "We shall return to the past once again. The past where it all began for Robert Asbury and the very pretty daughter of his employer, the honorable Judge Nathan Daniels, the richest man in Riverside, California."

CHAPTER 10

Riverside, California Twenty-Seven Years Earlier

The Daniels's three-floor mansion stood proudly on Claremont Avenue in the old historic town of Riverside. The grand mansion was surrounded by three-hundred acres of the best land in the county. Both Nathan and his high society wife Doren came from wealthy parents and they had inherited millions between them and now that Nathan Daniels had become one of the states elected supreme court judges, Judge Daniels was now racking in an even bigger savings account for him, his wife Doren and their only child, eighteen-year-old Della, fresh out of high school and only one dream in her young heart. The love for one very special young man, two-years out of high school and working his way through the local text college in Riverside to get his master's degree in both building and landscaping. Robert Asbury had proved to be good at all kinds of carpentry skills as well as outside landscaping and the citizens of Riverside had found out about the young handyman's excellent skills and reasonable prices, and this kept him busy when he wasn't attending classes.

The wealthy judge found plenty of jobs around his grand estate to keep young Robert busy and Nathan Daniels was always please with the talented boy's work. It was on such a day as the judge worked happily inside his big home office where he could observe his handyman building him a much-needed book shelf for his new collection of law books, that everything changed for the wealthiest couple in the county and their daughter.

As usual, young Della met the mailman at the front door to offer him a kind word of praise for delivering the neighborhood mail on time every single day. She would then hand him a tip, give him her brilliant smile before waving then shutting the door. As she wandered slowly down the wide hallway to her father's office, Della went though the large stack of important-looking legal document. She was looking for one thing, college applications from three distinguish universities, Preston, Princeton or Harvard. The straight A student had no doubts about being excepted by all three and her assurance had nothing to do with her perfect grades or easily won scholarships from all three universities, she knew her father had intervened and his high standing with Harvard got her at the top of their list. Della thought about hiding the highly decorated accepted entries but she knew her father was waiting on those letters to arrive and if they didn't arrive on his desk that very day, he would have the innocent mail carriers job taken away from him. So, Della would have to face her father today with the truth about her and Robert's commitment to one another.

Della stopped at her father's big office door, building up her courage to face him with what she wanted for her life and not him or her mother. The eighteen-year-old reached for the cold doorknob and with shaking fingers gripped it tightly. She closed her eyes as she listening to the sound of soft hammering while the beautiful voice of her true love sang softly while he worked,

"Jesus is all the world to me, my life, my joy, my all! He is my strength from day to day, without him I would fall." Hearing her loves voice, Della softly sang along.

"When I am sad to Him I go, no other one can cheer me so. When I am sad, He makes me glad, He's my friend!" The words had given Della the strength she needed to confront her stubborn father. She lifted her small fist and gave the door a soft knock. "Father, I have the mail you've been waiting for."

Both men stopped what they were doing at Della's sweet announcement and watched the door open, then followed her movements to her father's side, where she handed him the large stack of mail. Della had deliberately left the three letters from the universities on the top and she waited for her father's big smile and joyful reaction she knew would be short lived.

Her eyes met Robert's when her father cried out. "Finally, oh happy day!" Nathan Daniels stood up to hug his daughter. "Baby girl, your mother and I are so proud of you! And, of course you will except Harvard most personal invitation." He stopped speaking long enough to noticed his wife standing in the open door. "Doren, you are just in time to join in this happy celebration! Our own little Della is going to Harvard this fall and study law just like her old man!"

"Going to Harvard, our precious child!" Doren pulled out a fancy lace handkerchief and wiped her eyes. "It just won't be the same around here without our baby girl"

"Father, I am sure Harvard is a fine university and I am well aware how happy you were when you attended it for eight-long-years but" Della was cut off by her excited father.

"And you will love it just as well, my darling daughter! It is what I have wanted for you ever since you were born."

"Della darling, your very clever father is right!" Doren joined them at the desk to see their daughter's name at the top of the Dene's list. "You have made us so proud Della and now you can get your law degree and with help from your highly ranking father, get promoted quickly to the top, just as we have always wanted!"

Robert had listened long enough to the Daniels bragging about what 'they' wanted without even considering what their daughter wanted to do with her life. Knowing her wants more than her arrogant parents, Robert climbed down and walked over by Della. "Excuse me Mr. and Mrs. Daniels, but aren't you going to ask Della what she wants to do with her life?" the strong young man of faith stood his ground when Nathan Daniels stared over at him angrily.

"No one ask you for any comments Asbury, so kindly get back to work and stay out of our private business.

"I am very sorry, sir, but I cannot stay out of this one-sided conversation." Before the judge could interrupt the young handyman, Robert held up his hand. "Sir, you are a man of the law, are you not? The way I see it everyone has a right to put up their side of a defense when they have not been given a fair chance to speak up and tell you what they want! Just give Della a chance to share with you, her parents, just what she wants to do with her life."

"Asbury, why are you so interested in our daughter?" Nathan made his way around the desk to get next to the brave young man. "Have you been making advances to Della behind our back? She is out of your league boy! You're just a poor disadvantage nobody from the sticks of the Appalachian Mountains in Kentucky! If it wasn't for me and my friends giving you employment, you would have to drop out of that sad little training school here and head back up to your pappy's fields!"

"Father, that will be enough! Stop speaking to Robert in such a fowl-hateful manner!" Della had come between her irritated father and her beloved Robert. "Robert came to my defense because you or mother have never asked me what I want to do with my life! I cannot live your life over at Harvard father! It's not what I want for myself! Neither do I want to be like you mother, always trying to out dress your friends at the country club or bragging about throwing the most lavish New Year's party for all your snobby friends! I want a simple life with the man I love! I want to have a lot of children to teach to be kind to each other and everyone around them. I want to bring them up in a loving home with parents who love each other so much it flows over into their children."

"Surely you cannot be referring to this young man Della darling?" Doren had been knocked down by her daughter's bold announcement. "I mean, Robert is a fine young man but he could never give you what you need."

"That is where you are wrong mother. Robert can and does give me everything I want and need. Love mother, Robert and I love one another and we want to spend our life together." Della did not need any words from her parents to know how they felt about her choice. Her proper mother grabbed her chest as she grew white from the shocking words that still stung her pride and vanity. Nathan Daniels grew red with anger as his fist went down slamming the large walnut desk that held his life's work.

"Are you so blindly stupid to choose this man who has absolutely nothing to offer you or are you trying to drive your mother and I to disowning you, sending you out of our lives for good?"

"If you cannot see what I want father, then go ahead, disinherit me! Live in your lavish lifestyle, keep climbing that latter you have been trying to push me up since I was born!" Tears laced the beautiful young woman's eyes knowing even with all their faults she would always love her mama and daddy, her cherished names for them when she was small and they always showed her love. "I see how it works now father, mother. As long as the child does things to please her parents, she is showered with praise and true love. But when she becomes a woman and discovers she does not have the same dream for me as you both do. I cannot be you anymore than you can be me. Can't you understand?"

"Understand? I understand you have chosen to listen to this boy that has nothing and in the end, your life will be one of suffering and misery!" Nathan swirled around to face Robert. "What did you offer my daughter to make her betray her parents?"

"Not to betray her parents I grant you sir." Robert had given Della the time she need to explain her choice, but it was pain to this hard-working young man, Nathan Daniels had closed his ears as well as his heart. "Mr. Daniels, we ask nothing from you, if it is your wealth you think I am after. You ask me what I offered Della, the answer is, I offered her my everlasting love and that she would always come first in my heart, second only to the Lord."

"Young man, love is a wonderful thing between two people, but it does not pay the bills and when you start out with nothing, the struggles can drive a wedge between a couple and that love will end up as hate." Doren had mixed feelings about her husband's breaking all ties with their daughter, so she thought some sensible advice might work.

"Mrs. Daniels, I can assure you I am not without an inheritance of my own and my parents have already excepted the two of us becoming one so one day the family farm will belong to me and Della." Robert knew Nathan Daniels would never except the fact that Della had chosen him for a mate but he knew the girl he had fallen in love with was more than willing to give up her entire inheritance to have a life with him. "We intend to be married in the near future and leave for Asbury Farm as soon as I finish my courses."

"You may intend all you like Asbury but you will not marry my daughter and as for finishing your pitiful courses, I will see to it that Mr. Craver, the head of the Text College will dismiss you instantly!" Nathan took a firm hold on the young man's arm and called for their guard. "Baxter, see this man out and make sure he leaves alone!"

"As you wish your honor." The beefy guard reached for Robert's arm and Della stepped between them, staring at her father angrily.

"You may not hold me against my will father! I have been taught the law since I could read and you made sure I understood every word! I am now eighteen and I can and will choose my own destiny. Maybe one day you will see the error of your actions toward your own flesh and blood." Della turned toward her mother. "Mother, I feel truly sorry for you having to remain with this selfish-arrogant man and I pray that one day you and father can feel the same love you had for me when I was a little girl." Tears now flooded her blue eyes as she took Robert's hand. "I hope your status in life makes you happy and all your wealth can comfort you when you grow old, with no grandchildren to liven up those lonely years. Will Christmas be the same for you daddy when you grow excited to take your only child to help pick out the perfect tree, then help you and mama decorate it." she noticed her father drop his eyes and felt some sorrow from her mother's tears. "The old piano will be silent, for I won't be here to play your favorite carol nor hear my voice again sing Silent Night, your favorite."

"Just leave then if that's what you want!" Nathan walked behind his desk and sat down. "If we want a tree for Christmas, we shall have one brought in, then we will let Deck the Halls decoration service come in to decorate the place."

"We shall miss hearing our sweet girl sing this year." Doren choked out the words.

"Don't be ridiculous Doren, you bought all those Christmas records years ago so we can hear all the famous singers from now on." Nathan glanced up to see everyone staring at him. "Look Doren we will be fine without our wandering daughter. In a few days you will get use to the new normal. Besides, Della will be entertaining her new hillbilly family. Maybe old Robert here can play the fiddle for her while she sings." He chuckled at his own sarcastic words.

"I will be more than happy to accompany my wife as she shares her beautiful voice this Christmas sir. My pastor told me that I had a God-given talent for playing the violin after receiving one from a retired concert violinist for building his wife a corner china cabinet for their anniversary. The kind Italian had been observing me while I labored on this beautiful old replica that belonged to his wife's departed mother. She had sketched her mother's old cabinet from memory and was overjoyed to receive this precious gift since her mothers had been destroyed in a bad fire." Robert looked down at his hand. "He said he could tell by my hands that I could play the violin and to my surprise, the moment he had me try this beautiful sound came out."

"So, you think you are good at playing the violin, do you?" Nathan laughed under his breath. "Play what Robert, Turkey in the Straw?"

"It's so like you to make fun of someone you hold under you, isn't it father? Well, we want stay where we are not wanted another second." Della stood straight. "We were hoping you would except my wishes father and give us your blessings. That was all we were asking of you and mother, just to be happy for me."

"Be happy for you? For what, ruining your entire life by running away with a loser!" Nathan mumbled.

"Robert is not a loser father! The fact is, Robert is twice the man you are!" Della squeezed Robert's hand when her father jerked his head up angrily. "Did I offend the mighty supreme court judge? The rich's man in Riverside?" Della jerked her own head up. "We don't want anything from you and all I am taking with me is my personal things, either gifts or bought and paid for from my own bank account!"

"If it was the pay from your simple job at the hospital this past summer, it couldn't be much." Her father sneered. "Just make sure you don't take anything from my house missy!"

"Yours and mother's house, or have you cut her off too?" She looked around the big office. "I hope you are very happy with your life father, laboring away over those old law books!" Della walked out, gathered her packed bags and started for the door to wait for Robert to collect his tools. Feeling a hand on her shoulder she jumped. "Mother, did father send you out here to check my bags for stolen things?"

"No darling, I would not stoop to degrading my own daughter's word." Doren pulled out an old familiar book and handed it to her only child. "If you are so sure about leaving with that young man, I've no doubt he'll want to have a lot of children, especially boys to help out on that farm, so this was always your favorite book when you were small. Since we won't be a part of your children's lives, please take this and share the story with them that your mama shared with you." Swallowing back her tears, Doren gave Della a quick hug, whispered for her to stay safe and take care of herself, then dash up the wide steps, leaving Della staring after her.

The three invisible witnesses had watched in silence, sad for the young eighteen-year-old for having to walk away from her parents, never knowing if she would ever see them again. But the sadness they felt for Nathan and Doren Daniels was the greatest. Not only had they lost their only child because of stubborn pride but for the fact that as the years went by they would regret their actions but neither one of them would bring it up or pray for another chance to be a part of their daughter's life again.

"Lord, did Della and Robert get married that day, knowing they couldn't wait as they had planned and Robert's apartment was their only home now as long as they were in Riverside, California." Martha could tell the young couple were strong in their Christian faith so living together out of wedlock was no option.

"Robert knew he would never get the degree he worked so hard for so he thought it best that he turned in his apartment key knowing he was paid up for the remainder of the year and most likely lose his rent money to his landlord. As luck would have it, the landlord was sympathetic over the young couple's situation and returned all the money Robert had paid for the last rent's bill and the kind man even paid Robert's truck repair bill off so he could get his 1950's Chevy truck out to get back to Asbury Mountain View Farm." Jesus smiled, knowing one kindness led to the other. "Mr. Preston had called on his young tenant more than once when an emergency arose in one of the other units. A broken shelf, a cracked wall, fallen light fixture, a hole in the floor and countless other mishaps. Needless to say, the landlord hated to see such a helpful-caring man go. All that work he had volunteered to help 'a friend with' had only required a thank you after he brushed away any payment while saying, 'glad to help a friend'" Jesus gathered their hands in his. "When Robert thanked him before leaving, Mr. Preston simply said; 'glad to help a friend.' We go now and see what life was like on the mountain."

CHAPTER 11

Asburys Mountain View Farm: Present Time

Jesus delivered the Kringle's to the mountains in Kentucky and pointed out all the small shanty houses and shacks along the Appalachians where poor families called home. Then they traveled to a large cove where the Lord pointed out a lovely old farm house with a wraparound porch and large windows aglow with soft lights. Nighttime had fallen on the mountain and the Asbury family were seated around the family's old harvest table that had been passed down from five-generations of Asbury's. The long benches on either side held all ten of Robert and Della's beautiful children while the loving parents sat on either end. Seated next to her mother was the youngest, little five-year-old Abby, the face of an angel, eyes blue as the eastern sky and hair as blonde as her mothers. The invisible visitors had arrived just as Robert Asbury was about to give the blessing. With every head bowed, he lifted his hand toward heaven.

"Blessed Lord, we give you thanks for allowing us to tend your mountain and sew winter harvest in the ground that you so lovingly blessed. This feast prepared by loving hands always seems to double by thy good graces so we can once again feed our most precious gift, these children, seated around the table. I give you thanks for them, the food, and most of all for my beloved Della. Amen."

As a round of amen could be heard around the table from the children and Della after she whispered "and for my beloved Robert." The family quietly passed around the bowls of greens and turnips. Every eye grew big when Della placed the hot cornbread in each plate. Watching it all was Nickolas, Martha, and Jesus, who was aware what would happen to make their Christmas brighter as well as richer.

Martha gave a sigh, knowing they couldn't hear her she said softly. "Such a small amount of food for such a big family, yet each child knew to dip only one spoon full."

"But the lack of food does not take away from the fellowship they are sharing." Nickolas added. "Its as if they are satisfied with their meager meal as long as they are all together. Listen how they share with each other their happy day, working in the fields with their father."

"Or the girls, singing praises about the day's work with their mother." Martha felt there was some hope for the modern generation after all. "I guess it is how the parents have raised their children, just like Della told her parents they would. To show kindness to one another as well as to strangers, just as Robert did with his landlord."

"Have you noticed Della's small dip and her small slice of cornbread?" Jesus watched his companions turn to see how little the young mother kept for herself. "She wishes to make sure her family has enough food to eat and there are days she goes without when the cupboard is almost bare."

"There's hardly anything on her plate." Martha suddenly wished she could present them with a real feast. "Is there nothing growing in their winter garden?"

"Very little this year. The usual rains were fewer this fall so much of the seed died before it could grow. The dear woman stretches what Robert brings in the best she can and even if she comes short, Robert lifts her up for making a feast for the family." The Lord turned his attention on the smallest member of the family and nodded his head toward her. "There is one that has noticed her mother's sacrifice and the precious child has kept back some of her food, like a biscuit or that cornbread, to give to her mother."

When it's just the two of them alone, Abby pretends she got full and gives her food to the starving mother."

Nickolas watched as Abby slipped half her cornbread in her napkin and held it in her lap, then waited for everyone to finish eating and go up to bed. After the older girls helped clear the table and finished washing the dishes, Della kissed them and sent them off to the rooms to finish their homework and get into bed for school the next day. Abby had waited behind and sat on the kitchen stool straighten out the silverware on the cabinet as she watched her mother putting the dishes away. Della turned to give her youngest a smile.

"Thank you, Abby, you are a good helper."

"I like doing my part mama. Someday I will be big enough to help with the clearing and washing the dishes." Abby opened the drawer beside her and placed the stacks inside before closing it. She looked up just as her mother grew dizzy and grabbed the cabinet to balance herself. The little girl puckered up, knowing her mother was hungry so she pulled out her half-piece of cornbread. "Mama?" she managed a smile as she held out the bread. "Mama, will you eat the rest of my cornbread? It was a real big piece and I got full, so I just couldn't finish it."

Della felt the urge to cry over such an unselfish act so she walked over and gave her daughter a hug. "That is very sweet Abby, but that is your cornbread. Mama wants you to eat it. You are a growing little girl and I know I gave you the same size as everyone else."

"Not everyone mama." Big drops of tears ran down Abby's cheeks. "Your plate was almost empty and you didn't have any oatmeal for breakfast after my big brothers were given big scoops in their bowl."

"I had plenty of oatmeal this morning sweet girl, besides your brothers need a hardy breakfast to help your daddy out in the fields all day." Della couldn't stand to think her baby girl thought she was starving herself,

"Mama, I know you didn't mean to make up a story about having oatmeal this morning, but I saw everything and after serving everyone else, you had to scrape the bottom of the pot to spoon me what was left." Abby's little hand took her mama's thin one. "Please mama, you got to eat something." She placed the bread in her hand. "I won't go to bed until you eat it mama! I don't want you to go away forever like Grandma Asbury!"

"Oh Abby, you have always been our little angel." Della couldn't watch her precious daughter cry another second so she lifted her dropped chin. "Don't cry baby girl, mama's not going away. I'll eat the cornbread."

After the first bite, Abby sat up smiling and after her mama had finished eating it, the little 'angel' gave her mama a big hug. "Mama, I know daddy is trying real hard to get food out of that frozen ground. I may be little but I can see, can feel. I can't explain it mama but I believe we are going to receive a miracle this Christmas."

"Abby?" Both daughter and Della turned when Robert walked up. "Looking into your angelic face I could almost believe we will receive that miracle." He exchanged glances with Della. "And thank you for sharing your bread with your mama."

"Abby, can you tell me and daddy why you believe this Christmas will bring us a miracle?" Della could see the seriousness in her daughter's blue eyes.

"Yes mama, I had a dream. I was standing in front of a really big house so I walked up on the wide porch." Her eyes were big as she recalled her dream. "The porch floor wasn't wood like our porch. It was a porch made of stone. Not round stone like the farm's wall but really big flat gray stones." Abby watched her parents look at each in wonder. "Do you know anyone that has a porch made with big flat gray rocks?"

"Maybe, but could you tell us what else you saw there?" Della knew her home in California had the exact porch her five-year-old just described. "Did you notice the front door? Did it have any markings?"

"Why yes mama, it did! The door was huge! Almost as big as one-side of our old barn doors only this door was a shiny brown color where our barn doors are red." Abby could see everything just like the night she dreamed about it. "When I walked up to the giant door I noticed a big letter took up the center of the door and the unusual doorlatch was gold."

"Abby darling, tell mama and daddy what the letter was." Robert's heart was pounding with the uncertain reason for their little girl to dream about Della's family home, miles from Kentucky. "Do you remember what letter you saw?"

"It was a large golden D." Abby grew concern when she noticed her mother turn white and waver back and forth. "Did I say something wrong mama? Do you know where I was?"

"Abby, did you see anyone in your dream darling?" Della needed to know if both her parents were still living.

"Somehow I found myself inside that big house. It was as silent as the night until I heard a gasped behind me and heard a lady's voice whisper, 'Della is it you baby?' then I woke up."

After they helped Abby get to sleep, Robert and Della sat up discussing Abby's dream and why she had been allowed to witnessed where Della grew up.

"God works in mysterious ways sweetheart." Robert sat up in bed, his arms wrapped around Della for comfort. "Maybe He used our precious daughter to let you know your mother still misses you."

"I suppose you're right, darling, but it all seems so strange. I haven't thought about mama and daddy for such a long while since the children take up much of my time. Maybe this is the Lord's way of reminding me to lift up some prayers for them, that they are well and as happy as I am."

"Are you still happy with your choice Della?" Robert stopped her when she started to object. "You are up before the sun and scape together enough breakfast to feed me and the children, leaving nothing for yourself. I did not bring you to this mountain to starve. Let me be the one to go without and start eating. Not just for yourself, but for me, for our children. Don't you know how much we need you my love?"

"And starve yourself Robert? Never would I let the man I love and the father of our children die from hunger!" Della realized she could not continue to starve herself. "Robert, I still have forty dollars left from those savings you wouldn't let me spend. Let me buy some more chickens along with feed for them. You can restore the hen house and make it fox-proof this time. If we get enough eggs, then I can work wanders with the meal flour, the bee's honey, the fruit trees and Bess's milk!"

"And they will make do until the real reason for Abby's Christmas miracle dream becomes a reality." Jesus announced after the couple kissed and cut the light out. "Now we wait for the beginning of the miracle that will save Christmas."

"Save Christmas?" Nickolas turned to look at the one who gave him the miracle of becoming Santa Claus, confused to the reason Christmas needed saving when it is celebrated every 25th of December with new-found love and joy. "What is the reason for our blessed holiday to be in jeopardy Lord? Has Lucifer done something to spoil it, besides turning some boys and girls to spoiled-hateful-kids?"

"Fortunately, my fallen arch-angel can do nothing against Christmas. That which has been written in the stars as well as the pages of my Holy Word can never be altered nor mired down to anything evil. Therefore, his powers are limited when it comes to interfering with Christmas CHRIST-Man and Savior."

"Forgive me from asking, but didn't you tell me Christmas stood for MESSIAH AND SON?" Nickolas knew the Lord never made mistakes so there had to be some logic behind His words.

"Does the mas stand for more than one thing?"

"Does not the Holy one, have many names and titles? Is not one meaning the same as the other." Jesus smiled as he patted his old friend's back. "Could it not stand for Manger and Stable? Magi and Star? Mother and Son? Messenger and Shepherd?"

"Alright then, if it is not the powerful Lucifer creating enough havoc to dislodge Christmas, then what other calamity will excel this most beautiful season?" Nickolas had no clue why Christmas needed saving nor did he know what the loving family had to do with.

Reading Nickolas's mind, Jesus went about answering his inward questions. "Christmas itself will not need saving because the first Christmas delivered Salvation to this sinful world in the form of a baby, the Son of God. Christmas will stand forever to be celebrated both on earth and in heaven! Now, as for why this family is involved with saving Christmas. We have chosen one small child to put love and the heart of Christmas back inside her grandparent's troubled souls and bring them back into the family, restoring a broken thread between them and their loving daughter. Thus, they will lose all guilt and sorrow which has robbed them of any Christmas spirit and replace their eternal hurt with real Christmas joy and it will mend their sad-lonely world with a heart filled with precious grandchildren, Della's children with her true love Robert."

They stood outside, looking up into the clear-cold-starry sky and the Lord began to speak again, Nickolas and Martha watched their Lord gazing up into the heavens. "We now wait until morning. The child will lead the way, so we shall follow. "His eyes met theirs. "She will be safe for she is never alone."

Chapter 12

The next day was the start of young Abby's heavenly adventure and she sat at the table consumed in her thoughts. The small child could not get her latest dream out of her pretty little head. It had seemed so real she could almost feel the warm stable she had entered with the tallest friend she ever had. Abby knew she had been with her magical friend many times before, she just couldn't remember when and where. She was certain he was the one who had led her to that big house with the flat rock porch and now, while sleeping last night, the tall handsome man took her back to Bethlehem. Abby closed her eyes and stiffed the air, trying to smell the fresh hay that Jesus had been laid on and the smell of the animals that had watched the holy baby in quiet wonder. She recalled how Mary smiled down at her newborn baby with so much love in her blue eyes Abby could almost feel it.

Abby had been staring at baby Jesus when a group of shepherds came in. They had been so still the young girl did not even know they were there until her tall companion turned her around and said softly. "There is the shepherd we came to observe Abby. Watch and see what happens when it becomes his turn to see the Christ Child the angels had told them about moments earlier." Abby had noticed the tears welling in the singled-out shepherd's eyes when he finally stepped up to see the Lord for himself. Her companion got down to whisper in her ear. "See what happens when Nickolas knells at the Kings manger and know this thing you see even this shepherd could not see."

As words passed between Nickolas and the Son of God, the humble shepherd dropped to his knees and young Abby Asbury watched in amazement as the shepherd was instantly transformed into Santa Claus.

Della had been observing her daughter's dreamy actions and reached for her hand, causing her to jump. "I never meant to startle you darling. You just seem to be in some faraway place and I was afraid your oatmeal might grow cold."

"Gee mama, I'm much too excited to eat!" Abby sat up to push her bowl over in front of her mama only to get it placed back in front of her. "Seriously mama, there's not enough room inside my tummy with all those butterflies floating around."

Robert had been listening and observing Della trying to convince their sweet daughter to eat her breakfast before heading off to school. "Abby, your mama is right. It's a long time till Lunch and to be able to learn properly, you must start out with a full stomach."

"But my stomach is full daddy! It's packed from the cellar to the attic with butterflies!" Abby heard her thirteen-year old brother snicker at her comment so she turned and narrowed her eyes at him. "Its not funny Jacob! Besides, I have got to get my project for the school's contest started when I get home so I can have it finished by Friday."

"Hey, little bit, have you come up with a winning theme?" Peter, the eldest, reached over to rub her head. "Would you like my help?"

"That's mighty thoughtful big brother but this is one project I must do all by myself." Abby gave her big brother a smile before turning to her father. "Daddy, may I have one of your smooth wooden squares to draw on? One that is thick enough to set up."

"Hey sis, are you making some kind of statue?" eleven-year-old Sarah piped up. "Maybe the first president?"

"Nowhere close Sarah, but I could not have made one of him anyway since our theme is something to do with Christmas." Abby's eyes were on her smiling father. "Well daddy, can you spare one of your birdhouse squares? The light wood would be better for my drawing."

"Abby, I will be glad to let you pick out any board in my garden shed. Just be sure one of your older brother's, are with you. My tools can be dangerous for someone your age, especially the jig-saw." Robert drank down his second cup of coffee and waved off a third when Della started to bring the pot over. "if you plan to have your Christmas item cut out, I'm afraid I must be the one to help you Abby. I will not let my baby girl near that jig-saw. I'm sure your teacher, Miss Johnson will except that kind of help for a five-year-old kindergartener."

"My teacher did say if you need help for anything that is too dangerous to do for yourselves, then you may ask a parent or older brother or sister to assist you." Abby blew her father a kiss, "Thanks daddy, I know you can do a great job with my project!" Abby turned to her mother. "Now, all I need mama is some paint and small paint brushes, like you use to use on those pretty pictures hanging all over the house."

"I'd love to loan you my paint set and art brushes, if they haven't dried out, if" Della handed her daughter her spoon. "you eat your breakfast for your mama!"

"Sure!" Abby put a spoonful inside her mouth and gave a happy "Mumm! This taste like a fair-trade mama!" Abby gave a wink up toward heaven. "My entry is going to be the very best ever!"

After School

Abby had drawn a sketch of her surprise Christmas theme and felt very pleased that it actually resembled the exact same thing she had seen in her dream. With careful and steady lines being applied, the exact scene began to come alive on the smooth wood. With the drawing completed, Abby would wait for the next afternoon to apply the color but for now, the little child would try to get the round bottle her mama had saved for some future use and Abby knew exactly what it was meant for.

"So, you want that old round bottle to use with your project?" Della shook her head in confusion. "This project gets more and more complicated to figure out darling. First you ask for wood to draw and paint a picture relating to Christmas. Then, instead of leaving it a painting, you asked your daddy to cut it out after it was finished." Della held the round glass bottle up. "I just cannot figure what my precious baby girl is making."

"It is a surprise mama, from heaven!" Abby knew she had her mama's attention so she would explain before the rest of the family came down for supper. "It was something I saw in my dream mama, the night the butterflies flew around my head and flew me and Simon far-far way!"

"Simon? Your imaginary friend you told me about?"

"Simon is not imaginary mama, he is my guardian angel and he took me to see the best Christmas gift ever!" she giggled "I couldn't remember his name in my dream." Abby took her mama's trembling hand. "You don't need to be afraid mama, I have known Simon all my life and he is very good to me. He is the one who saved me when I fell down that well at Uncle Burt's corn-shucking, remember?"

Della grabbed her lips and knelt down by her small daughter. "Abby, when we called and called and could not find you, everyone at the corn-shucking split up to look for you. Your daddy and I were frantic with worry after Burt reminded us about his old well, covered with old boards, most likely rotten after years of neglect. Uncle Burt led the way, mumbling to himself about it being his fault and if anything has happened to that precious baby he would never forgive himself. After thrashing though the fields, we finally found you, seated on the grass, wet from head to toe." The surprised mother reached for her precious girl. "Abby, we didn't know how you got drenched, but we were so grateful to find you alive we lifted you in our arms, thanked the Lord for watching over you and took you home."

"When I wandered off chasing a lightning bug, Simon chased off with me. When I finally caught the lightning bug I knew I was loss but I didn't know I had stopped on an old piece of wood. I heard it cracking under my feet and before you know it, it broke into, fell instantly down until it hit water, then I started falling but as soon as I hit the deep-dark bottom, Simon caught me and flew me back up and out, where we waited for you on the grass singing Jesus Loves Me."

"That's right! I remember now how we knew which way to go. I kept hearing what I thought was angels singing and they led me and your daddy to you." Della had tears in her eyes as she hugged her daughter. "Abby, I don't need to see what your surprise is until you want to share it with us. I know whatever your Christmas theme is has been heaven sent. After all, your guardian angel Simon is making sure my baby girl's entry will win."

CHAPTER 13

Abby had shut herself inside her room as she applied all her finished pieces inside the wide mouth round bottle, glue carefully brushed on to hold the manger adorned with hay which held the baby Jesus, whose hand was raise to the one kneeling in wonder. The kneeling figure had two different sides so looking from one side of the jar you saw a shepherd, holding tight to his staff. When you turn the jar around, you saw Santa Claus, holding a staff resembling a giant candy cane, adorned with a wreath of holly. Beside the shepherd lay a fluffy-white lamb and next to Santa Claus, lay a young reindeer, wearing bells around its neck and a garland of mistletoe around his antlers. Abby stepped back to look at her work and saw something was missing from the round glowing jar her angel had shown her in her dream. Speaking softly so her family could not hear her, Abby turned to look at the invisible being next to her.

"Simon, I have done everything you instructed me to do except making the miracle snow fall over the scene. I do not know how to make this magic snow so what do I do next or is this my finished project?"

"Abby, my cherished ward, your job is finished." The jar began to float as it drifted up to the tall handsome angel's hands. The little girl could finally see her friend again and raced over to welcome him with a hug, then stepped back to watch him check out her job. "Sweet girl, this is beautiful work. Talented enough to look exactly like we saw it happening and yet the sweetest artwork of a five-year-old artist. Which will prove to Miss Johnson, your teacher, that you alone made it except for the cutting part, of which your father will testify too."

"Simon, it isn't the same without the magic snow falling inside the bottle." Abby looked disappointed. "I guess that was just part of my dream and it cannot become real."

"Are you kidding? Snow globes not real?" Simon waved his hand over the wide opening as he smiled down at his big-eyed ward who watched in wonder as the bottle sealed tightly and a clear liquid filled it up, never disturbing Abby's real-life art work. "Now the good part, the magic snow that is as real as it appears." Another wave of Simon's wrist and the wintery flakes began to fall. Abby could not contain her happy squeals, then grabbed her mouth and turned to face the closed door, afraid someone had heard her. When no one came to check on her, Abby gave a long sigh.

"That was a close call Simon. I just knew I would alert the entire Asbury clan and they would rush up to check on me!"

"Knowing my excited ward was going to let out her happy shout I quickly sent a sudden breeze through the family's open dining room window causing your frantic family to chase after blowing napkins, candles, flowers and sliding china and it forbid them to hear your delightful squeals."

"It's just that I wanted to surprise them with my finished project." Abby looked up at her guardian angel with serious eyes. "Simon, what if my teacher asked me how I got the snow inside this jar? I cannot tell a lie and pretend I did it with magic."

"The rules were that no family member could help you unless there was danger involved, correct?" Simon knew but he needed the child to know the difference.

"That's right Simon. We could not enter anything into the Christmas Contest if someone in our family helped us make our project." Abby spoke up. "Not daddy or mama, nor any of my brothers and sisters."

"Did Miss Johnson say you couldn't ask God or an angel for help?" Simon asked with bright smiling eyes as Abby jumped up and down laughing.

"You are right Simon, not a single school leader said we could not get heavenly help!"

"So, if your teacher or one of the other judges asked you to tell them how, a little child like you managed to create a snow globe all by yourself, what will you tell them?" Simon knew his ward was far advanced in matters of the heart and if anyone can give them the perfect answer, it would be Abby Asbury.

"Simon, first I'll pray about what words to say but they must be true and honest, because I've been taught never to lie because in the end of every situation, truth wins out!"

Invisible to the young girl, the three visitors watched and listened and were moved by the wisdom on this one small child.

Nickolas had watched in wonder as the snow globe's characters came to life and he saw himself. First, as a humble-hardworking shepherd, adoring the Christ child the angel had just announced to them on the dark hillside and on the opposite side he saw himself as Santa Claus. As if the child knew everything about his transformation, a lamb lay by him as shepherd, holding a staff, then next to himself as Santa Claus, a festive reindeer. His voice came low as though he was afraid he might break the image before them.

"Lord, how could this beautiful smart child know so much about me?" Nickolas' attention remained on the young girl, now shaking the snow globe and delighting in the falling snow. "There was no record of me or any other shepherd's identity written in the Holy Bible. I lived on earth as a mortal man over 2,000-years-ago, long gone and long forgotten."

"That is where you are wrong my friend." Jesus gave his old friend a smile. "Do you recall me sending out two of my disciples into the village ahead of them to find the colt tied; whereon never a man sat; loose him and bring him. I told them, if any man say unto you, why do you do this? then you say the Lord hath need of him and straightway he will send the colt.

Nickolas thought back, recalling how he and Martha had watched Jesus riding on his first carving which had been miraculously changed into a living young donkey but that incident had not been written down. Knowing her husband was racking his head over this scripture and how it could have mentioned him, Martha had recalled being stopped by two men who looked as though they were desperately searching for something. Then reality hit her and she grabbed Nickolas by the arm.

"Nickolas, Jesus is right, you were mentioned in the Holy Scriptures!" Nickolas stared down, eyes wide with wonder. "If you remember back, before we reached the gates that led us outside where we saw the parade of people, worshiping and praises the Lord as King, you and I were stopped by two Galileans in the dwelling district and we noticed them looking around them untying a young colt!"

"Oh!" Nickolas turned toward Jesus, tears filling his eyes by the revelation as to who those men were, he assumed was stealing another man's young donkey and he had moved up to stop them. "Your words are true my Lord, for it was I that was passing their way when I noticed them looking around, most likely for the owner, and saw them untie the colt. Assuming they were thieves, I rushed over to stop them and I can still hear their words, that rang out like those of the angel hovering over us Shepherds the night you were born. Looking into my eyes, they spoke in unison and said: 'The Lord hath need of him!', then I did as it is recorded into your Holy Word, I sent them straightway to you by urging them to: Go, take the colt without delay! In my heart I knew the colt had been placed there just for this cause." Nickolas paused, suddenly recalling the other important reason he had no doubt this colt was heaven sent. "Yes Lord, now that my eyes have been open to thy truth, that beautiful little colt did walk with a limp, due to his one short leg, his mane and tail were cropped off, but even with all his misfortunes, that little donkey was the most handsome one this man had ever whittled!"

"So, you know that you are forever in my word, written for all God's children, both Jew and Gentile." Jesus smiled back at the precious scene unfolding in front of them. Little five-year-old Abby Asbury knew it was time to share her prize-winner to her waiting family, as the silent group watched the loving child make her way down the old farmhouse stairs with careful-slow steps.

"Nickolas, you asked how this little child knew so much about you." Keeping his eyes on Abby, Jesus revealed the beginnings of His new plan. "She knows what you were because We took her back 2,000-years to the town of Bethlehem and she witnessed what you became when you were altered into the Giver of Gifts, known to her as Santa Claus. Abby Asbury was given this special Dream because of her believing heart and she, my friend, will be the one to save Christmas, not just for her family but for every unbelieving child throughout Our earth."

CHAPTER 14

The Asbury family grew quiet when Abby stepped inside their big dinning room, where they had been waiting for her before setting the food out. Beaming a big smile, the little charmer marched over holding her prized box in front of her and sat it down gently on the table, in front of her father.

"Come on Abby, open the box so we can see your drawn cutout!" Jacob was growing anxious to start eating after having to wait on his baby sister to present her class entry for the Christmas Contest. "Let us see those round smile-lee faces decked out in red, green, and white!"

Peter, being more mature than his obnoxious twelve-year-old brother reached over toward him and playfully slapped his stomach. "Cool your heels brother and just be patient like we had to be to listen to your long presentation for making Christmas ornaments out of daddy's fishing bate."

"Peter is right Jacob." Robert gave his baby girl a wink before nodding. "Go ahead pumpkin, show what you made."

"Thanks daddy." Abby reached over to kiss his cheek before looking around at all the familiar faces watching her. "First, I wish to apologize to brother Jacob for missing his presentation, but my heavenly helper was putting in the final touches."

"Hey squirt, you cannot get any help with your project!" Jacob gave a sarcastic laugh, assuming he would win the contest. "That will be considered cheating."

"Jacob, maybe our Abby knows something we don't know concerning the school rules." Della gave her daughter a motherly look. "Can you explain what kind of heavenly help you received and why it's not considered breaking the rules."

"Nice way of saying, not cheating, young lady!" Jacob narrowed his eyes at Abby when she laughed softly. "Very well sweet talk your way out of this one! Although your drawing must look pretty bad if you needed a heavenly helper to fix it!"

"Jacob Asbury, that will be enough!" Robert called out. "Now, stay quiet or I'll send you out on your butt!"

"Good ideal!" words heard only by the three invisible visitors as they watched Jacob's chair slip out and over, dumping the twelve-year-old on the floor, right on his rear. As the family tried hard not to laugh, Simon winked at Abby causing her to giggle.

"See what happens brother Jacob when you question an angel's help?" her happy laughter brought out the hidden laughter from the other family members who could hold back at their outspoken brother's surprised face. "Now, if you will kindly get back in your seat and listen, I'll give my presentation to see how it sounds to you, my loyal family of whom I put my trust."

"With such a grownup statement Abby darling, I know all of the family are anxious to help by judging their little sister's presentation." Della looked around smiling at all the positive nodding. "Go ahead sweetheart, and show us what you have."

"Thanks mama. You may recall I had a very realistic dream the other night and it showed me what I needed to make to be the number one winner in the Christmas contest. Simon, my very charming guardian angel, took me on a long trip, back in time, over 2,000-years-ago, to the tiny town of Bethlehem." Knowing where this dream was leading their smallest family member, the family sat up, anxious to know what she saw that would become her project. "Yes, I found my myself inside a small stable, so real I could actually smell the fresh hay and the animals who stood silently watching the small baby who seemed to glow in the dim firelight. I heard the flutter of wings before seeing the swirling hay drift down around me from the rafters above. Hearing a soft goo, I looked up to see a large white dove and I knew it had to be the Holy Spirit because it was glowing just like baby Jesus. I didn't have to see the Christmas star shining over the stable for its great light lit up the stable like the sunrays of morning.

Then I heard Mary humming, it sounded like a lullaby and it brought out sweet laughter from her baby boy. Mary or Joseph couldn't see us watching and neither could the cow, sheep, or donkey. As Simon left me to check on some visiting shepherds speaking to Joseph, Jesus tuned his head and looked straight into my eyes and smiled. I cannot ever recall feeling that much love before. While my attention was on the baby Jesus, I hadn't noticed the shepherds coming in until Simon drew my attention to them.

The group of rugged shepherds stood back, staring at baby Jesus for some time. Finally, the one in the front stepped forward to pay his respect. As the others came forward, one at a time, Simon pointed out the last Shepherd and told me this shepherd was the one we were there to witness. I noticed how different this man was from the others. He was taller, strong built with a great beard and mustache and quite handsome. The other shepherds had been fascinated over the Christ Child and filled with respect, but this one shepherd was obviously moved from the moment he stepped inside the stable. Tears had filled his blue eyes from the first glance of the Lord and by the time he reached the manger, the tears were flooding down his face. I couldn't hear words being spoken, but this shepherd was communicating with the Christ Child. As they spoke, I knew a more mature voice was coming from within the Holy Child and whatever they discussed must have been powerful because the shepherd dropped to his knees. The moment he dropped down I saw why I was there to witness what had happened 2,000-years-ago. I can proclaim the truth for the very first time for I have witnessed it for myself! And before you laugh Jacob, hear me out! This humble man dropped to his knees a shepherd and was instantly transformed into Santa Claus!"

"Jesus transformed a poor lowly shepherd into the jolly old elf?" Jacob chuckled, then noticed how serious the rest of the family were. "Oh, come on guys! Surely you don't believe that fairy tale!"

"Jacob Asbury, the only reason you never got coal in your stocking was because you didn't write Santa a letter!" Abby turned to the rest of her family, who obviously knew their baby sister never told a lie, not even when she dropped the full gallon of milk and confessed after Peter told her he would take the blame. "I knew I would have problems with grow-ups and puffed-up bullies, like my brother Jacob and Annie's brother Morgan, but I believe in my heart that this dream was meant to reassure children all over the world." Abby looked around the table at all the loving faces laced with tears and she stopped at her brother, smiling cocky. "So, to help the children know what the shepherd's name was, I was privileged to hear the last words spoken by the Christ Child to the shepherd, now Santa Claus. Jesus spoke his name, just for me to hear. NICKOLAS KRISTOPHER KRINGLE!

Silence fell around the table as Abby lifted the lid off her box. "May I present my Christmas entry titled: The Christmas Miracle Snow globe!"

The instant they beheld the magical snow-globe with softly falling snow, they began to rise up from their chairs one at a time, in hopes of getting a closer glance. Robert, being the closest gently took the offered globe and peered inside at his daughter's fine artwork. Seeing the shepherd on one side and Santa on the opposite, Robert practically sang out.

"Abby, when I cut out these figures for you I couldn't imagine why you had drawn Santa Claus while all your other drawings were on the Christmas story." Tears laced his caring eyes. "Sweet girl, your perfect snow globe reflects everything you witnessed in your dream. After hearing you describe everything you saw, felt, and heard, how could anyone, adult or child, not believe there really is a Santa Claus! Why, if I weren't in my forties, I would find a way to write my own letter to Santa and asked him to bring me that Marvelous Master yo-yo I ask for when I was seven!"

"Are you telling us you believe in jolly ole St. Nickolas after he never paid you a visit down your chimney?" Jacob laughed, shaking his head. "I say, anyone who falls for a five-year-old's story is got a head of loose marbles!"

"To set the record straight young man, I never received my yo-yo because my letter came back, stating incorrect address." Robert looked over at his wife sheepishly. "I wasn't too bright to think the North Pole was in the U.S.A."

"Robert, you didn't!" Della laughed. "Well Jacob, I did place the correct address on my letter to Santa. To: Santa Claus, the North Pole, location: Unknown, and I received the exact thing I ask for when I was five like our Abby."

"And your mama and daddy read your letter to the phony fat man then on Christmas morning, five-year-old Della received her magic presents from the North Pole, location: unknown!" Jacob bent over double laughing.

"Go ahead and laugh son, but you see, like your little sister, I knew Santa was real, so I secretly wrote him and slipped my letter down the street to the mailbox." Della had recalled what happened on Christmas morning when she got up to check under the tree. How could time and age have hidden such a magical moment from her mind for all these years. "I had forgotten what childhood Christmas feels like until now." The ten-children watched as their mother's face lit up with a smile to match her youngest child.

"Mama?" Sarah broke the silence. "Please tell us what happened that Christmas morning. Was your letter answered? Did Santa pay you a visit?"

"Let me share that magical morning with you my darlings, especially Jacob." Della's face was aglow as she remembered back to her fifth Christmas. "I had woken up early, excited to see if Santa came, so I raced down the stairs. My excitement alerted my parents and they weren't far behind me. Mama and daddy stood back watching as I pulled out the presents they had gotten me. All lovely gifts but it wasn't the gift from Santa I wanted to find. I heard my mama ask me if I liked all the presents from Santa and they were surprised when I told them I had not found his present to me yet. Of course, they insisted the presents I had been opening was from Santa, but I just thanked them for getting me those things when my eyes spotted Chatty-Kathy, the doll I had asked Santa for. I practically screamed with joy when I reached for the pretty doll and gave it a big hug. I heard my parents give a gasp and glanced up to see them debating where the doll came from and demanding each other to confess to buying her. I simply stood up and carried my doll over and said, "I found my doll from Santa! He got my secret letter!"

"Don't you see Abby daring, not only does your heavenly gift lift the hearts of children but it brings the child-like Christmas spirit back into the hearts of adults, who had been children like you once and felt the magical unexplained feeling that comes from believing."

As the family gathered around the heavenly snow-globe, the three invisible visitors looked on. Jesus smiled at the young child who had brought Christmas memories back into her parent's hearts.

"Nickolas, now you are aware how Abby knows about you and her beautiful heart wants to wake-up the Christmas Spirit in the hearts of all those she knows. This will be the start of her saving Christmas and with your help, help the unbelievers to believe. There are many past gifts to deliver and many hidden things wished for but never asked for."

"From children like Jacob and Mason? Adults like Nathan Daniels?" Nickolas knew there were many more unbelievers, not only those who didn't believe in him but those poor lost souls who did not believe in Jesus, their Savior and only hope. "May the love of this one small child light the way for everyone to return to Bethlehem and feel the true meaning of Christmas once more, where children can believe that Santa Claus is real and a special part of Christmas created just for them."

CHAPTER 15

Appalachia Elementary School

The excited students had gathered in their auditorium to watch the forty contestants tell about their project then present it. An older student would then carry the Christmas entry down to the six judges to score. The student with the highest score would be declared the winner. There were entries from all six elementary levels, from the Kindergarten class to the fifth-grade classes. The judges consisted of two highly educated parents, two teachers, the principal, and the Appalachia Journal's renown art critic. All the judges were experts at judging fine works of art and new talent.

Theodore Threadwell, the art critic had been chosen as spokesman for the group and chose to begin with the ten fifth graders, each one choosing their own take on this-years Christmas theme. The first young man presented the tree of lighted jewelry stones where he had taken various sizes of stone-studded brooches and glued them on a cutout Christmas tree made of wood. The talented fifth grader bored small holes around each stone to place a single light through from a long strand of white lights. When the silver cedar was plugged up the stones glistened in a rainbow of colors. As he held it up to a loud applause, the boy proclaimed:

"If you choose my entry, this year's Christmas theme will be called, Rainbow Christmas!" He smiled when the Judges seemed impressed with his ideal and talent.

Many other great ideals were shown from the other nine fifth graders. The forth, third, and second grades had very different projects, although many chose making a special ornament to represent the Christmas theme, like pinecones covered in glitter become Sparkling Pines Christmas or candy-cane sleigh Christmas, by making egg white glue to glue two-upside down candy canes down under a full-size Hershey bar. There were ornaments of paper stars, sprinkled with gold or silver glitter, for Christmas Star Christmas, and bells, bows, holly filled homemade vases. When the judges got down to the nine first graders and saw their entries, they noticed one small child left, the only one from the Kindergarten class.

Mr. Threadwell glanced up, expecting to find the small girl nervous but received a big smile instead. The serious face broke into a slight smile as he called her up to the front. "Abby Asbury, from Miss Gladys Johnson's Kindergarten class."

Everyone watched in amazement as the small five-year-old marched to the front, pulled up a foot board, and stepped up to the mic. "Good afternoon everyone. Most students would get nervous to have to be the last one up but watching all my fellow older classmates present their terrific projects has really lifted up my Christmas spirit. I sure wouldn't want to be one of the judges, having to decide which entry is the very best for this year's theme. I keep my entry inside it's carrier due to it's delicate design. I learned from an amazing-realistic dream just what my project was suppose to be and why. The Lord wanted me to come to Bethlehem to witness for my self the most marvelous gift He made just for children." Abby heard several older boys snicker and knew Annie's brother Morgan was one of them. "I am aware there are children here who do not believe in Santa Claus and that breaks my heart, but not as much as it does Nickolas Kristopher Kringle. I gave the judges my written witness as I recalled my dream. I can tell you I heard the Christ Child say his full name so I could hear it. I witness a very humble shepherd dropped down in worship and instantly he turned into Santa Claus." Abby reached in her box and took out the heavenly snow globe. I named my entry: The Christmas Miracle Snow Globe." The entire student body as well as teachers and judges gasp out at the magnificent snow globe that actually glowed from within as the very-real-like snow fell softly. Somewhere in the stunned audience came a loud burst of laughter.

"Hey kid, you can't expect the judges to except your entry! No kid born could make a magical snow-globe like that one!" Morgan Matthews stirred up his gang as they joined in with laughing and condemning the small child for cheating in front of the entire school.

"Hey, Morgan is right! I bet the little poor loser stole it from a retail store!" the fifth grader called out.

"Abby did no such thing!" Annie narrowed her eyes at her obnoxious brother. "My friend would never take nothing that didn't belong to her! I bet she can explain how her cutouts look so real, just like the falling snow and the heavenly glow!" Annie and Abby exchanged smiles and watched the art critic stand up and turned to the rude boys.

"Young men, if you cannot refrain from making rude remarks to this very talented young lady, I will have you ushered out! Understand." Theodore Threadwell walked up on the stage and took the snow-globe for a closer look. "Abby, we are aware your daddy cut out your lovely drawings with his jig-saw." He held up Robert Asbury's statement for using the sharp saw. "We have Mr. Asbury's statement for cutting the pieces to assure his daughter's safety." The friendly man looked at the snow with wonder and searched the inside for the bulb creating the glowing light. "Abby, can you tell us how you made the snow and your secret for hiding the light bulb inside the globe?"

"Sir, if I had known how to make my own snow for my snow-globe, I would be happy to tell you." Abby looked up with her angelic face and blinked her big eyes. "I assure you neither of my parents would know how, nor my sisters or brothers. I would never steal a single thing from anyone sir. It wasn't magic that filled my art globe with snow, it was Simon, my very talented guardian angel. He simply waved his hands in front of the jar and Zap, then real snow began falling instantly!" Her eyes fell on the glow. "As for the glow, my guess would be an added gift from the Lord, the only thing missing from what I saw in my dream!"

"Mr. Threadwell, Abby did not break any rules sir. We never mentioned heavenly help could not be used, now did we?" Abby's teacher gave her a wink. "I do believe this Christmas Miracle Snow-Globe just went to the top of our entries!"

"Gee wiz Miss Johnson, that makes me as proud as Grandpa Asbury's lucky old turkey who always struct around the barnyard spreading his big fan!" Abby laughed along with the entire student body. "He fancied himself lucky being the only Tom Turkey on the farm and not just because he had a lot of wives. He was always spared when we chose our thanksgiving turkey to join us at the harvest table." Another round of laughter while the three invisible visitors joined in, enjoying the innocent description on their family farm.

"Well Abby, you have a very good chance in this school contest. You're not only a talented young lady but remarkably intelligent for five-years-old." The art critic patted her head and led her back down the steps to take a seat on the end of the front row that held all forty contestants. "Students, as soon as we, the judges, have looked over Abby's entry, we will tally up our votes and announce the winners for runner-up and first place. Please remain in your seats. This should not take long."

"It is obvious who must win this Christmas contest." Martha felt anxious for the sweet-precious girl who sat swinging her legs nervously, as she waited for the judge's results. "I mean, the other students did an outstanding job and I would instantly interview anyone of them to work as elves, if possible, but Abby Asbury's snow globe has the kiss of heaven all over it! The winter-wonderland inside the bottle brought back being there the night you were born Lord."

"Martha is right Jesus. Looking at it puts the enchanting-magical-feeling reeling back inside my heart!" Nickolas lit up with wonder recalling that first Noel and the Silence of the Night. How peaceful the air felt inside the tiny stable and the incredible scent of heaven showering down around them. "All those wonderous feelings that cover you in Christmas Spirit! I recall every little detail, except" Nickolas turned to the Lord. "except transforming from a shepherd into Santa Claus."

"This was not meant for you to see at that time my brother. I was the only one, besides the Holy Spirit, who could see the transformation." Jesus patted his old friend's back before turning his attention on the small girl. "That is until it was the right time to bring the chosen child to witness your change." Jesus nodded at the art critic. "The judges have made their decision. Try to relax Martha, the right child will win."

Theodore Threadwell walked back up to the microphone and got everyone's attention. The soft rumble of voices grew silent, everyone anxious to hear who had won and the big majority of the student body rooting for Abby Asbury.

"Students and teachers, the judges have made a decision on the final two students who have won runner-up and this year's contest winner. The remainder of the contestants will receive one of the twenty-dollar gifts on the table next to the teachers." The head judge looked down at the excited group as he called out for the two, finalist to come up on the stage. "Jason Berry, fifth grade and Abby Asbury, Kindergarten class, congratulations for reaching the last phase of the Christmas contest." The art critic looked out at the large group of students as he stated: "Now I will tell what these talented and gifted winners will receive for the first and runner-up prize. I was just made aware when I arrived that some students took it upon themselves to change the cash amount as a prank. Unfortunately, this ugly stunt could have caused some students second thoughts about making an entry this year. The number of students entering for the past ten-years dropped from 100 to only 40 this year. Mrs. Clark, the teacher who has organized this contest for the past eleven years has always placed posters around the school's classrooms describing the rules and what to base the theme on. At the bottom is the winner's prize amount. It simply states: the first-place winner will receive a cash prize for 100 and the runner-up gets 50. The clever-jealous leader of the prank managed to place a dot with a magic marker after the 1 making it 1.00 and before the fifty he placed the magic marker dot before the 5: .50." his attention was on Morgan Matthew as he spoke then he looked down at the two winners and noticed Abby's dropped jaw. Knowing the sweet child had assumed the winner would get one dollar and to learn the prize was for one-hundred-dollars instead gave her a shock.

"Jason, for a ten-year-old young man, the judges were very impressed with your Rainbow Christmas Tree. It was truly a sparkling-original, unlike anything we have seen before. You received a perfect nine score out of ten and this won you runner-up. Congratulations!" Theodore handed the fifth-grader a fifty-dollar bill inside a small box.

"I would like to thank all the judges for this special award and I would like to say, I am truly happy that first place went to Abby Asbury. She most certainly deserves top prize for such an amazing snow globe! I have two snow globes my parents bought me in New York City, but mine pales to this heavenly one Abby made." Jason's eyes were on the smiling girl as he finished with "Abby, I was rooting for you to win the whole time! Great going!"

"Thanks Jason, I was up against some very blessed artist and I really love your rainbow Christmas tree. It is like a symbol of God wrapping his promised rainbow around every Christmas tree, that whenever we look at the colorful lights sparking on our own trees we are reminded of the baby Jesus and why we celebrate Christmas on His birthday!"

"That was a beautiful message young lady and I'm certain that most of us will recall your words when we put up our own Christmas tree and see God's promised rainbow gracing our tree." The head judge looked out at the listening group. "Right people?" an uproar of praises went up from the students and teachers until the art critic held up his hand smiling. "It's easy to get into the Christmas spirit with this little child's loving words but it is time to give Abby her first-place award of $100! The judges were once again unanimous, giving Abby straight tens for her Christmas Miracle Snow Globe! Congrats Abby, for making the most incredible snow-globe ever made by human hands with a little needed help from a caring father and a heavenly presence. For me personally, you and your miracle globe have brought Christmas spirit back into my heart, that has been without it far too long. Bless you child."

"All praise and glory, goes to the Lord for without Him there would be no Christmas, therefor no snow-globe and no Santa Claus to brighten the hearts of children all over the world!" Abby took the small box that held her prize and hugged it to her chest. "This prize really means a lot to me. Since it's 99 dollars more than I had thought previous, my gift can go a lot further."

"Do you mind sharing with the audience what you are going to get with your prize money Abby?" Miss Johnson, Abby's Kindergarten teacher call up from her seat.

"I would love to share with you what I want for myself." Abby was cut off by Morgan Matthew's big mouth.

"What kid, a big-new bike, shiny and red, top of the line with mag wheels?" He chuckled. "I hate to pop your fantasy bubble Shirley Temple or is it Alice in Wonderland who fell down into the rabbit's hold and hit her head?" Morgan howled along with his friends. "You won't find a shiny new bike anywhere for 100 bucks unless you look at Goodwill or in the county dump!"

"Young man, this is your final warning!" Theodore Threadwell called loudly over the mic. "Now, you and your friends refrain from speaking again or I make you leave and wait outside for your principal!" he noticed the rude boy slide down in his seat when other students turned around to see his reaction. "Go ahead Abby, you may tell us if you like. Just ignore those losers. They are just jealous."

"I know sir, jealous and lost!" Abby glanced back to see Morgan's squinted eyes staring up at her. "Sometimes it takes some of God's children a little longer to live in the light of Jesus. I'll lift up a prayer for him tonight but now I promised to tell you what I am going to get for myself, then give the remainder to my mama and daddy." Abby heard a snicker but continued on. "I just want to buy a stamp, a sheet of writing paper and one envelope."

"Abby, is that all you're going to buy with your money? A book of stamps, a box of stationary and a box of envelopes?" the judge asked surprised at the child's request.

"Just one stamp! Just one sheet of writing paper and one envelope!" Abby looked up innocently. "That's all I need to write a letter to Santa Claus."

"A letter? You want to write Santa Claus?" Mr. Threadwell wasn't expecting such an unusual gift from such a small child who had never gotten much, he was certain of that.

"That's right sir. I have never got anything from the dear man before because I didn't have any stamps or envelopes to send my letter in." Abby looked around and noticed everyone had tears in their eyes. "I never meant to make you sad. I did have the paper my mama cut off the grocery bag. I can't use mama's stamps because there's just enough for the bills to be mailed."

"Why do you plan to give the rest of your money to your parents, Abby?" someone called up from the judges table.

"So, my mama and daddy can buy some much needed food for the whole family." Abby spoke, from her little heart. "Daddy tries real hard to grow things in the winter and my mama stretches whatever she has to feed the family." Abby stopped and sniffed back her tears. "There are days when my mama doesn't get much to eat herself because she loves all of us so much, she makes sure our plates have food in them first. Sometimes she is so hungry she gets dizzy and almost falls. This money will really help feed all my family, including my precious mama." Abby wiped away her tears and looked out at Morgan and his gang. "I suppose many of you might be wondering why a little girl who has never had a doll or a tea-set of her very own would throw away a chance to finally have what other little girls brag about having, but I have never needed what I couldn't get so I see no reason to start now. I live everyday with my tummy empty but I never show it to my mama because even though the little bit she gives me is never enough, I know that everyone seated around our table pretends to be full then goes to bed hungry, just so mama and daddy won't feel bad. So, most of my money will go for food and I will be proud as punch to get my stamp, my writing paper and my envelope, to write Santa Claus."

"Abby, saved the money for a stamp." Theodore Threadwell reached inside his jacket and pulled out a new book of Christmas stamps. "This is my Christmas gift to you Abby, for helping me get Christmas back into my heart and soul."

"And I just happen to have two new boxes of envelopes and I wish to share one box with you Abby." Miss Johnson walked up and handed her sweet young student the box of envelopes. "My gift to you sweet girl, for filling my heart with Christmas."

"You couldn't very well send your first letter to Santa on a heavy-brown grocery bag Abby so I have this used writing tablet and after counting the sheets of paper, you now have twelve sheets to write on." Mrs. Clark, the teacher over the contest, had been moved by all the special givers, so she needed to feel Christmas as well. "Thank you for waking up the adults in the room to remember how it felt to be a child like you at Christmas."

"Gee-wiz, this is the best Christmas every." Abby gave all three givers a loving grateful hug. "You gave me everything I ask for and more! Twelve sheets will be enough for the entire family to write a letter to Santa!"

Unable to resist a rude remark after Abby's comment about her family writing Santa Claus, Morgan Matthews laughed out. "That kid is living in a fairy tale if she believes her mama and daddy will write the non-existent fat man living at the chilly North Pole a stupid letter!"

"I warned you young man about rudely speaking out so you may leave and take a seat outside in the hallway." Mr. Threadwell had enough of this obnoxious boy's comments to this innocent little angel.

"Hey, what happen to freedom of speech?" Morgan reared back in his seat, propping his arms behind his head. "Can't anyone tell the real facts about this phony legend little Miss muffin keeps bragging about?" before the head judge could speak, Abby took the mic.

"You don't believe Morgan because you never got anything from

Santa Claus! He doesn't visit naughty children! You can make fun all you like, but the truth is, Nickolas Kristopher Kringle is as real as you are! I know because I saw him change from a shepherd! My mama knows he's real as well because she told us when she was five she wrote Santa a secret letter, then slipped out the house and walked by herself to the corner mailbox to mail it. On Christmas morning Della, my mama's name, got up early and raced down the stairs to find her doll only she and Santa knew about! She said her mama and daddy watched her pull out the presents they had bought and she opened them first but she kept searching under the tree for her gift from Santa. When her parents knew that was all the presents from them they asked her how she liked her gifts from Santa and she replied she had not gotten Santa's present yet. While her parents discussed their child's behavior Della saw her gift and reached under and pulled out her Chatty-Kathy doll to her mama and daddy's surprised. She noticed them accusing each of secretly buying the doll when mama stood up to inform them, she really liked the gifts they had giving her but Santa Claus had read her secret letter she had mailed herself and delivered the Chatty Kathy doll she asked for!"

Jason moved over, obvious moved by Abby's revelation. "Abby, I have been thinking about your family not having enough food for the winter so I have decided to give you my fifty-dollars, a gift to a very beautiful and unselfish daughter and sister." The ten-year-old's voice cracked with emotion. "Morgan was wrong to make fun of your beliefs Abby. He and I are from a wealthy family and no one in our families have ever gone to bed hungry, so, please except my gift to help buy your family more food to help fill up your mama's pantry."

"Jason, that is a most thoughtful-unselfish gift and my young heart is feeling real gratitude in an overwhelming way!" Abby spoke between sniffs as she fought the tears that could not be retained inside. "I feel real swell being your friend and I know Jesus is very proud of you for helping the less fortunate."

"You are welcome Abby Asbury and I'm proud to call you my friend." The ten-year-old fifth grader looked out at the big group listening. "My hope is that those with more than they need will help those who are without this holiday season. We cannot expect Santa Claus to bring everything our neighbors on the mountains are in want of this winter."

The art critic had been taking in the caring actions of the two winners and he felt moved by their Christ-like actions. "All you students and teachers, this day has shown us two remarkable loving children with hearts as pure as the gold of heaven." His eyes met the troubled young man who had been rude throughout the contest. "Morgan, you and your friends could take a lesson from these children's Christ-like actions." He looked out over the many faces, most in tears. "We all can take a lesson from Jason and Abby's behavior. Sometimes, the greatest lessons learned come from a sweet innocent child. Abby, you have brought the heart of Christmas back into many a life this day. I am certain both Jesus and Nickolas Kristopher Kringle are very proud of you."

"Theo is absolutely right, I never have witness a nicer child." Nickolas gazed at the small girl wiping her wet eyes. "I look forward in receiving Abby's letter in the mail."

"Nickolas, I knew there was something familiar about the art critic. He was little shy Theodore Treadwell from Atlanta Georgia who only asked for a box a cracker's and a paddle-ball." Martha tried to snaffle her laugh. "How you managed to get the cracker's there in one piece is beyond me after Packer placed them on the bottom of the magic bag."

"There's the answer my dear, my magic bag can perform wonders on Christmas Eve." Nickolas thought a moment, pondering, recalling pulling out another gift for the shy boy. One he had not asked for. "One of the only times I was stumped on my deliveries was when I slid down Theo's chimney and pulled out a third present for him I wasn't aware of. Do you remember what I told you I found in my bag for Theo?"

"Oh yes, now I recall that mysterious gift that just showed up in your bag." Martha looked back up at the grown-up Theodore and noticed the paint on his hands for the first time. "It was a paint-set, complete with canvas-paper for the beginner. "Now how would that magic bag know shy-little Theo would become a famous painter, own his own art store and work for the local paper as its art critic?"

"Nickolas, Martha, have you forgotten, I know everything before it happens." Jesus laughed softly at their blushed faces. "It was the Holy-Three-in-One that gave Theodore his gift for creating beautiful-real-life paintings as well as the talent to look at art and see what it was meant to be and if it passed the test." Jesus could not only feel what was being felt by all those seated in the small auditorium in front of them, but He could see what lay ahead for them and just how many had found the real Christmas Spirit and the reason we celebrate it every 25th of December. As for those whose heart had been convinced by little Abby Asbury that Santa Claus was really real, they might help bring the faith back into Nickolas' heart. "Nickolas, you might want to prepare yourself for an influx of letters, addressed to Santa Claus, the North Pole, Address Unknown!"

CHAPTER 16

Everyone in the Asbury family were happy to learn of Abby's first-place win and were seated around the harvest table listening to Abby retell everything thing that happened. Everyone grew quiet when their youngest told what her winnings would be spent on.

"I learned today that there are some really good people in our town and their giving hearts were as joyful and meaningful as my winning first place." Abby dipped her spoon down in her vegetable stew and enjoyed the great taste. "Mumm, that's good mama!"

"I wanted to make us something extra special to celebrate your big win Abby." Della reached over to caress her daughter's face. "We are all so proud of you sweetheart."

"Thanks mama!" Abby stared down at her full bowl of stew, then checked out the other eleven bowls, each filled completely up, even her mama's bowl. "Gee whiz Mama, you really outdone your magic today! I haven't seen that many vegetables in our bend since summer crops started coming in!"

"Abby is right Mama." Sarah had been too excited over her baby sister winning $100 to wonder where her mama had found that many winter vegetables to fill ever bowl full. "Where did all these good vegetables come from? I haven't noticed our winter garden springing to life and never growing all these kinds of vegetables in the cold of winter!"

"Sarah has a point daddy." Jacob said with a mouthful, then swallowed before he was fussed at. "I noticed the big pot was full for the first time ever and I'm super happy for the yeast rolls but I recall mama asking me to check the meal bend and see if there was enough flour left for gravy. I scape the bottom to get her enough. So, where did all this come from?"

Peter glanced at his mother smiling. "Mama, may I tell my inquisitive brothers and sister where all this blessed harvest came from?"

"Please share with the family just how wonderful the hearts of our town citizens have been moved by one small girl who shared her Christmas story with her entire school and place the real

Christmas spirit back into the majority listening." Della smiled down at Abby whose eyes were glistening with tears.

"Daddy and I had drove the old truck down to repair Fannie Randle's porch that had caused the eighty-six-year-old spencer to fall, by stepping through a rotten plank just outside her door. You all know daddy does not ask anyone who is living alone, like Miss Fannie, to pay, but the rich widow always insist on giving us $100.00 or more if the job requires more material and time. We finished the job and started back through town when Mr. Preston came running out from his big grocery store to stop us. He had a huge stack of crates set out on the sidewalk and asked up to please take them and distribute the produce to the families listed on each box. He declared that a new shipment of produce had arrive and was unloading in the back of the store. With a kind expression, he said with good conscious he could not let the older produce go to waste when people were hungry."

"That is when Pennie Parker dashed across the street waving a large bag." Robert took up their encounter with the town merchants. "She had brought over a Pennie's Sweet Treat bag filled with fresh baked rolls and her young helper Toby James rolled out a cart filled with matching bags and one big white box." He smiled, recalling her gracious words. "My dear Mr. Asbury, I went a bit crazy this morning baking my hot rolls and ended up with more than I needed. I have placed a family name on each bag so if you can deliver the rolls with Mr. Preston's things, I would much appreciate it." Suddenly remembering the box, the baker and owner of the only bakery in the small town, snapped her fingers and asked for the cake box. "My daughter Annie is a dear friend to your little Abby and she called from school all excited about Abby winning first place for; in my daughter's words, making a miracle snow globe that actually had real snow. Annie said everyone arrived to watch forty contestant's showoff what they had made for the Christmas theme contest but almost everyone watching thought Abby's Christmas Miracle Globe was the very best entry ever made. Annie told me, despite Morgan's rude remarks and actions toward her best friend, Abby stood her ground and remained loyal to both Santa Claus and Jesus. My daughter told me Abby had everyone in tears and warmed their hearts so much, the Spirit of Christmas jump right back into their cold hearts." Pennie took a big breath. "I was so proud of your

Little Abby I wanted to make her something special so I baked her this cake to congratulate her for not only coming in first place for her entry, but helping save Christmas for so many students and teachers!" Robert got up to get the large-three-layer cake covered in creamy buttercream icing and saying: Congrats Abby! God's smallest witnessing angel! "My precious daughter, you will get the first big piece after we finish our wonderful stew!"

"Sounds yummy daddy!" Abby licked her lips as she observed the 'mile-high' cake in front of her mama. "This feast reminds me of Thanksgiving and Christmas! A very special meal with the family to celebrate a special event!"

"And it is special Abby. Today, you brought the feeling of Christmas is the hearts of the Appalachia community and opened the doors to all those shut-off hearts so now they can walk by faith, not by sight. They witnessed how families on the mountains above them suffer from the lack of food, medicines, heating oil and many other things they have and take for granted. Their hearts were touched today through the words of a little child. One, strong in her belief in both God and Nickolas Kristopher Kringle. "Della smiled down at her precious little girl. "I knew about the cake, long before Peter or your daddy did. Pennie called me the minute she hung up from speaking to her Annie, and asked if she could bake you a special cake. After expressing my hardly thanks, knowing I had ran out of flour and egg custard pie just didn't sound festive enough for our big winner, she asked me what Abby's favorite cake flavor was, and I told her"

"CHOCOLATE!" Abby nearly jumped from her seat with excitement, hearing her brothers and sister clapped with the same excitement. "That's great mama! We all love chocolate, our one-time Christmas dessert!"

"Abby is right mama, Christmas is the only time you, spurge and make your great chocolate cake!" Jacob could not take his eyes off the cake. "You are still planning to bake your chocolate cake this year again, right mama?"

Robert knew Della wouldn't break tradition and change her desert just because Pennie Parker sent one to Abby, but their daddy like to pick with his children whenever the time arose and after Jacob's bad behavior toward his younger sister, now seemed appropriate. "You know Jacob, this may be the perfect Christmas for your mama to try that coconut cake she has been checking out from my mama's old recipe box." Robert gave a playful wink to his wife and she read into what her husband was up to. "What cake would you like to bake this Christmas sweetheart? If the children get the taste for two chocolate cakes so close together, it may spoil them."

"Oh, come on daddy! Surely you can't be serious about us getting spoiled by having our favorite dessert twice just one year!" Jacob grew tense, excited over the prospect of having chocolate cake twice instead of just one time and now his daddy might mess-up their chances. "Come on mama! You make the best chocolate cake on the planet!"

"Gee Jacob, your daddy has a point." Della played along with Robert's mischief. "I have had my eye on grandma Grace's coconut cake for some time. She always made one every Christmas until she past the cooking over to me. I recall it had five layers with fluffy whipped cream in between, then topped around with the thick fluffy whipped cream and covered with fresh shredded coconut then topped with candied cherries!"

"Gosh mama, that cake sounds as yummy as your chocolate." Abby gave both parents her bright smile. "I've got it, why can't you bake the chocolate cake for Christmas and the Coconut cake for Easter! After all, it sounds like a big-fluffy Easter basket filled with coconut grass and candied cherry eggs!" she giggled when everyone laughed, agreeing with her bright ideal.

"Thanks pee-wee, you saved the Christmas dessert too!" Jacob lend over to kiss her. "I just might write jolly ole St Nickolas myself, if I can decide which treasure I want the most."

Abby gave her thirteen-year-old brother a big grin. "That will make Santa Claus really happy brother, just don't asked him for something impossible to bring down our chimney or that cost tons of money."

"No kidding!" Jacob laughed. "I would have thought Kris Kringle was loaded with money, being able to take millions of presents to kids all over the world. Surely his magical elves can't make everything. Take batteries for instant, lots of kid's toys require batteries and I'm sure the North Pole don't have a factory for everything they need."

"Abby, daddy can answer that question from your skeptical

brother." Robert reached for another roll and took a bite. "Son, Santa does not supply the batteries required for certain toys. Parents make sure any toy that needs a battery gets one placed inside it, either before or after their little tot's dash down the stairs to see what Santa brought them."

"Jacob, there are also whined-up toys that don't require batteries, like a top or a jack in the box." Della noticed Abby's hand go up for a question, so the loving mother reached over and gave her a loving pat on her head. "You wish to ask me a question sweet girl?"

"Mama, why aren't there any Jill's in a box?" she heard her family laughed. "Well, my book is about Jack and Jill!"

"That is true Abby, the little children that ran down the hill to fetch a pal of water." Della smiled. "That is a different Jack, Abby. The one in the box that jumps out is a clown, preforming a circus act!"

"Oh! I have never seen the clown name Jack mama. What makes him jump from his box? Is he afraid of something?"

"Abby, a toy clown cannot get afraid! They are not real pee-wee!" Jacob finished his stew and longed for the cake to be cut. "There is this handle attached to the side of the box. The clown is down inside the box and the box lid is closed while you turn the handle. There is a little tune that starts playing until suddenly the clown pops up, making you jump."

As the family were enjoying the cake, Abby told them about her personal gifts and what she was going to do with the money. "Mr. Threadwell started the chain of giving after I told everyone about all the families on the mountain not having enough to eat due to a bad winter crop. So, instead of giving me one stamp, the nice man gave me a whole book of stamps!" Abby said cheerfully. "Then, my teacher, Miss Johnson, gave me a whole box of envelopes!" She continued to smiled as she listened to the excited whispers circling the table. "Mrs. Clark, the fifth-grade teacher who is over the contest, gave me her writing tablet that had exactly twelve sheets left, enough for everyone one in our family to write a letter to Santa!" Abby practically jumped from her seat with excitement. "Now I can give mama and daddy all the money to buy food and fill up the pantry!"

"Abby, sweet girl, your little heart is so generous to want to give the family all your winnings, but darling, that money is yours and I'm sure there must be something you want for yourself." Robert, being the head of the home, spoke for the family. "We all know how much you love us baby girl, but you worked so hard on this beautiful snow globe, just having it be the center of our Christmas table is the only gift we need."

"Abby, your daddy is right. We are very proud of you and you deserve to have something you want." Della took Robert's hand when he stepped up beside her. "I have seen you admire that adorable doll in the Carter's Department Store, the one with the Christmas dress on and holly in her long blonde curls."

"Mama, are you talking about the one setting in the big store window, priced at $140.00?" Sarah sat up, knowing sales tax would make up the other $10. She forced a smile at her baby sister. "She is a very special doll Abby. Holly is the doll's name and she is this year's Christmas doll!"

"Daddy, surely you aren't going to allow your little girl to waste $150.00 on a stupid doll she'll outgrow!" Jacob stood up, feeling anxious over being left out. "Abby, if you have to buy something for yourself, make it a game-set so all the family can play!"

"Brother Jacob, the prize was given to Abby, so she can choose anything her little heart wants." Peter gave his baby sister a wink. "Jacob, you might have won your own prize if you would have tried harder to make something a little more Christmas!"

"I know it was a stupid ideal to make ornaments out of daddy's old fishing lures." Jacob dropped his head feeling downtrodden. "How did I know my theme was so funny."

Sarah couldn't resist her laughter as she looked around to find the twins, also in middle school, trying to hide their stickering. "You should have seen Jacob when he held up his red, green and white rubber worms and announced proudly: My Christmas theme is Worm In-to Christmas. Everyone watching burst into laughter over the corny theme and I think it livened up the students, who seemed bored up to that point."

"They must have been totally entertained then!" Jacob sunk down in his seat. "They laughed at my stupid worm ornaments for five-long-minutes!"

Abby giggled at the thought of hanging up red, green, and white, worms on the tree. "I'm sorry you, loss Jacob. Maybe next year you can use daddy's old fishing hooks instead to hang some really winning ornaments made out of gum berries or big-pinecones." Abby turned to her father. "Daddy, you said I could have anything I wanted, right?" she watched him smile and nod. "I know what I really want, so promise me there will be no argument over my choice."

"Abby, no one at the table will speak ill of the choice you make." Robert knew his beautiful wife stood with his ideals and agreed that their youngest deserved to choose her gift."

"Very well then, I want, more than anything, to give my $150.00 to my mama and daddy to buy food for the pantry so we all can have food for the winter month." Abby held up her small hand when she noticed her parents came close to speaking up. "It is mine to give and this is my choice! Since the whole sum stayed in tac due to the generous hearts of Mr. Threadwell, Miss Johnson, and Mrs. Clark, supplying me with stamps, envelopes, and writing paper, everything I wanted for myself was supplied and more. The exact amount of paper was a God-given sign that there would be enough writing paper for each member of my family." Abby's bright eyes lit up. "Then another revelation hit me! I would have enough stamps left to give the other ten children living on this mountain, plus envelopes and if our family's four middle and four high school graders could supply the ten-sheets of notebook paper between them, they could write Santa as well."

"I can manage one sheet pee-wee." Jacob raised his shoulders in defeat. "Mrs. Larson gives us a lot of lessons and she is giving us notes to write down all the time."

"I'll be happy to share three sheets Abby." Sarah gave her brother a smile. "I write smaller than brother Jacob so my paper goes a lot further."

By the time the twins, Robby and Bobby, Frank, Mary, Clara, and James gave their amount, Abby had her ten sheets of paper. Peter had been listening to his brothers and sisters offering what they could and he wanted to do his part. Since graduating last year, the eldest son worked alongside his father, doing odd jobs, but mostly carpenter work Robert's specialty. Peter raised his 6'4" frame and smiled down at his small sister.

"Abby, I had no paper to offer since I no longer attend school but if you would permit me, I would love to play your delivery boy and take all letters to Santa Claus, The North Pole, Destination Unknown, down to the town's post office and mail them for everyone." Peter glanced at his father. "That is, daddy allows me to drive the truck."

"Since it's such an important mission Peter, I will be happy to let you take the truck to town." Robert winked at his wife and she knew there would be a cute remark to follow. "Just as long as you don't paint Delivery Truck on the side of my old Chevy!" Laughter spilled out around the room and Abby had never felt happier as she waited for everyone to settle back down.

"May we go around the room and find out what everyone wants Santa to bring them?"

"If they all know what they want." Della looked around at the happy faces of her children. "Just remember, Santa Claus doesn't bring really big presents, like that new car you've been dreaming about Peter." Della smiled when her oldest son laughed, obviously knowing his wants had to be reasonable. "I'll start! I am going to ask for a new Sunday dress to wear to church since mine is rather faded and thin. Nothing fancy, just a nice dress."

Robert lend over and gave his wife a gentle hug. "Nice request sweetheart. As for what I want for Christmas, that great-Yo-yo I missed out on when I was a stupid kid!"

Peter laughed and looked around at his anxious brothers and sisters. "I am going to ask Santa for a badminton set, a tennis-like game played with a shuttlecock, sometimes called birdies." Peter gave a high-five to James, just two-years under him. "We can all try our hand at playing the game."

"I've seen some of the kids play a similar game at school called volley ball. Since your set comes with a net, I ask for a volley ball and we can have two different games to compete at!" James threw his glance on his sister Clara, seated next to him. "You're next, Miss senior."

"Thank you, Mr. Junior!" she laughed and gave her mother a smile. "Since I'm too grown up for toys, I will ask Nickolas Kringle for a new dress, same as mama. Pretty but simple."

"That's a great choice for you Clara." The Asbury's forth child Mary was in the ninth grade and had loved to read since she was very small. "I am asking Santa to bring me the first set of Nancy Drew Mysteries! I have always dreamed about having my very own set instead of taking books from the library."

"That, young lady, is a very wise choice, especially for such an avid reader." Della knew all her children well, so she knew the next son loved anything to do with trains. "O.K. Frank, what are you asking for?"

"I really would like a train set! They come with two trains and a winding train track, two controls and some landscape with hills, trees and a depot!"

"Gosh Frank, that sounds swell brother!" Bobby and Robby said in unison, causing everyone to laugh.

"Bobby, what to you want for Christmas, son?" Robert had pulled a chair up by the woman he loved so dearly.

"Actually, Robby and I would like to ask Santa for very similar things." He gave his twin a playful slap on the back. "I am asking Santa for a catcher's mitt and a baseball."

"And I am asking for a catcher's mitt and a bat." Robby winked at his tomboy sister, seated by Jacob, knowing what she wanted.

"I want a soft ball and a catcher's mitt as well!" She gave the twins her toothy grin. "The twins told me I could use my ball with their bat for roller bat and they would play toss with me! Isn't that grand?"

"It sounds like someone in this family wants to try out as pitcher for their school's soft ball team." Peter tease the eight-child causing her to nod her head in agreement. "You can count on me to be there to root on you winning!"

"Of course, if Babe Ruth Sarah makes it to the team's pitcher's mound, you can bet the entire Asbury clan will be there rooting for her to strike 'em out!" Jacob teased. "I guess the thing I really-truly want more than anything, will be a wasted stamp after the Jolly ole St. Nickolas reads, laughs and tosses my dreams in the trash!"

"Jacob, if what you ask for isn't a car or a horse wearing a saddle, you might be surprise to find your dream under the tree." Abby looked over sincere. "But you cannot be pretending to believe Jacob, Nickolas Kristopher Kringle knows all phony letters when he reads them and you're placed on the naughty list, winding up with a chunk of coal!"

"Well, little miss perfect, even though I'm smart enough to know I cannot ask for a car or a horse, ready for riding, the thing I want cannot be place 'under' the tree and less Santa lays it over."

Jacob felt hot under his collar with everyone watching and waiting for what he would ask for. Abby suddenly picked up on what he wanted.

"You want Santa Claus to bring you a bike for Christmas, don't you?"

"Not just any bike Abby, that red stinger I saw in Carter's showplace window!" Jacob looked out, suddenly thinking about the bike he had wanted ever since he laid eyes on it. "I guess that expensive bike doesn't exist in Santa's workshop, so I will settle for any bike as long as it's a boy's bike and has two good wheels." His eyes met Abby's. "Tell me the truth Buttercup, am I asking for too much? Should I ask for something smaller?"

"Jacob, if you sincerely want a bike and you truly believe in Nickolas Kringle, I believe in my heart that you will find a red bike under our big tree on Christmas morning." Abby thought she saw tears in her brother's eyes, so she thought to change to what she wanted. "I really like everything everyone chose for Christmas, so now all you have to do is write Santa and tell him. It might be a kind jester if you thank him for making girls and boys happy all over the world or whatever personal statement you wish to tell him. The thing I want the most for Christmas cannot be wrapped or even brought down the chimney, but I feel that by believing in this thing I want with all my heart, somehow, someway, Santa can deliver it this Christmas."

Robert and Della exchanged glances, then Della reached for her little girl's hand. "Abby, there must be something you want Santa to put under the tree for Christmas morning. The rest of us have asked for a gift from Santa and we would feel bad if you were left out sweetheart, without nothing."

"Mama, the thing I want is far better than a gift under the tree from Santa." Abby looked up, her small serious face too precious to argue against. "Don't ask me how I know but, Santa knows all my childish wants, like that doll and the glass tea set with red roses on it. He also knows how much I love Christmas and my family. Nickolas knows I am a child of God and there's no one I love more than my Lord! I feel like I have a mission to help put Christmas back into the hearts of the sad and sorrowful. I cannot tell you what I want because it hasn't been made clear to me yet, but it has something to do with this family and my snow globe." Abby noticed her parents looking concerned over her words. "Please don't worry Mama, daddy. This thing is good for it is blessed by Jesus. Remember when I told you baby Jesus looked at me in my realistic dream?"

"Abby darling, did Jesus speak to you? Did he mention something happening at Christmas that involved you?" Della gripped Robert's hand.

"Jesus was just a baby mama but the voice I heard coming from his silent lips was the voice of a man. He said:

"Abby, my bright loving child, you will mend broken hearts and renew that which is lost. We have waited for you Abby, to be born and save Christmas through your love in the cold hearts of-the one's lost to your family."

"Baby girl, whether yours was just a dream or one as real as that of Joseph from Gabriel, you shall know by Christmas." Robert knew Abby could never lie so he and Della would watch over their youngest child throughout the holiday season and keep close. "Just write Santa what is in your heart Abby, but it will be alright to ask for a second gift should the first be too difficult for Santa at his busy time."

CHAPTER 17

Back at the North Pole

Nickolas and Martha had arrived back at Kringle Village right after watching the school contest and settled back down into their normal routine. Christmas was only two-weeks away and Santa's village was busy, dashing from homes to the Toy factory, to the stables to care for the reindeer, and the Mail Deliverer had grown very busy collecting large bags of mail every day from every corner of the globe, from the scattering collectors, flurrying around to and throw.

Nickolas's power to be a speed reader sped up the process of sorting the good little children from the bad little children, but his attitude had changed back to his old self. No more did he feel depressed over the modern-world children's bad behavior after witnessing children like five-year-old Abby Asbury and ten-year-old Jason Berry, who had given his $50.00 winnings to the poor mountain girl for food.

Martha found her husband humming Jingle Bells as he read the large stack. She walked over with a large mug of her famous hot chocolate. "Care for some hot chocolate while you dive into that new stack." She pointed to the bulging bag that had just been set inside the door.

"I would love some of your festive hot chocolate dear." Nickolas gave his wife a wink after taking a big gulp. "Mumm, another successful recipe, rich, creamy, and loaded with milk chocolate and lots of marshmallows!" he finished the last letter in the bag on his desk and waved the other bag over. It floated across the room and lit softly on his desk, opened up, and dipped over for easy reaching.

"Now, if you could only train your letter bags to help you read all that mail they carry." Martha pulled a chair up by the desk and reached for a letter to read.

"Who needs a third reader Martha dear when I have you?" Nickolas reached for her hand, lifted it, then planted a kiss on her palm. "Besides, I enjoy hearing from the children and reading what they want for Christmas." He paused, then smiled. "The gift of seeing each precious face while reading is my favorite reason for reading each and every letter and my reason for having you hold up your letter before placing it in the good or bad basket."

"That is truly a beautiful gift the Lord blessed you with Nickolas." Martha had thought many times how nice it would be to see the face that went with the letter to Santa. "I'm sure it has helped you on occasions when a child gets up, hoping for a glimpse of you. By the gift of recall, you instantly can say the child's name and send them back up to bed after a nod of your head and a wink of your eye."

Nickolas gave her a smile before nodding and giving her another wink. "It works with the curious child all the time. They believe in me, yet for some children, believing is simply not enough, they have to see Santa Claus for themselves." Nickolas chuckled recalling the children's startled faces when they are caught spying on Santa Claus. "It's really quite humorous Martha. Santa Claus is also equipped with the gift of sharp hearing, so even the slightest creak of the floor or the soft gasp from the child alerts me that I am being observed by a hidden being, sometimes a parent, but mostly an inquisitive child. I turn and softly call out their name, child or adult, who used to be one of my children. The parents are too frozen to bother my quick work and the children run back to their room after I warn them that their mama or daddy might find them up and make them wait to get their presents. It works every time."

"Your job sound like fun Nickolas. Busy but a lot of exciting adventures and endless towns and houses!"

Martha noticed her husband suddenly grew still, his eyes focused on the letter in his hand. "Nickolas, who's letter has you so serious all of a sudden?"

"It's the letter from Abby Asbury." Nickolas glanced up and gave Martha a slight smile. "I saw her precious face the moment I lifted the letter up, before seeing her words to me."

"This is the first time you have witnessed the face before reading the letter?" Martha thought for a second. "Perhaps it is because you just saw this sweet child and heard her very grownup words. Witnessed how she brought the Christmas spirit back inside so many people's heart and helped them remember why they celebrated Christmas in the first place."

"Yes Martha, I am certain it was because of everything you just said and more." Nickolas walked to the window, Abby's letter still in his hand. "Before we departed from the Lord, He pulled me to one side to inform me of a mission I was to make with this very child."

"A mission?" Martha let his words sent in. "Nickolas, why would the Lord need Santa Claus to perform a mission with Abby Asbury. Has it got something to do with that snow globe that has you clearly becoming Santa Claus?"

"The snow globe may play a small part of the Lord's request." Nickolas took Martha's hand when she joined him at the big picture window. "Do you recall what happen to Della and Robert when they confronted her parents about getting married?"

"How utterly cruel and deceitful her father was toward their relationship? Never have a witness a more selfish and spiteful man like Nathan Randle Daniels, who deliberately ran his only child out of his house! Della's mother, Doren could have intervened, but she chose to stand by her husband and their great wealth!"

"The mission the Lord-God wants to send me on with their smallest grandchild is in hopes of turning their sad and sorrowful lives around so they can come to life with a renewed Christmas miracle. Once they are touched by the love and faith of that one small child, new hope will spring up inside their cold-shutoff hearts and family ties can once again be rekindled." Nickolas looked into his wife's caring eyes and knew a question was coming. "You have a question my love?"

"This thing you speak of is very moving and I am certain that if anyone can accomplish this beautiful blessing, it is Abby Asbury." Her attention fell on yet another full bag of letters being set inside the office door. "Nickolas, why must this mission be on Christmas? The Lord knows this is your busiest time of the year. Even with the magic mirror splitting you into four clones, the night is long and tiring for your four selves!" Martha looked worried. "Nickolas, I am here to welcome you back from your long night's journey. I can see how exhausted and worn out you are and how you nod off to sleep the moment you sat down in your comfortable chair. Many Christmas mornings you sleep in and I must enjoy my Christmas cup alone. How can you possibly deliver all the children's presents and go on this mission with little Abby?"

"For myself, it would be impossible dearest wife. But for God, all things are possible." He delighted in seeing her relax and smile. "The Lord can have me at all places at all times, even without His presence."

"Jesus will not be with you and Abby then?" Martha knew in her heart, even though the Lord would not be there in person He would be there in Spirit, for He is ever present. "Will it be just you and Abby, to go and convince Nathan and Doren Daniel to believe again?"

"Just the child will be seen Martha but Abby's guardian Angel will be present with us to help me work the wonders and miracles from Jesus that will aid in placing Christmas back in their shutoff hearts."

"What does Abby's letter say Nickolas? What did she asked Santa to bring her for Christmas?" Martha watched her husband scan the letter and she noticed tears forming in his brilliant blue eyes. "I can see this child has touched your heart. Can you share her words with me?"

Nickolas lend over to give his loving wife a kiss. "Gladly will I share the words of this precious young child." Nickolas led her over to the sofa and they sat down. Abby writes:

"Dear Nickolas Kristopher Kringle, my name is Abby Asbury. I am five-years-old, the youngest of ten children to Della and Robert Asbury, my mama and daddy. I would have written you sooner Santa but up until now I did not have a stamp, or an envelope. I did write you twice before on some of my mama's grocery bag but I had no way of sending it. Santa, I know most little girls ask for pretty dolls or tea sets, and even though I really like them I want to ask you for something completely different from toys. Santa, I need your help to bring love back into my Grandpa and Grandma Daniels hearts so they can love my mama again. I have caught my mama crying on Christmas morning before the rest of the family wakes up. I asked my mama what made her so sad that she would cry on one of the happiest days of the year. Mama told me she missed being with her own mama and daddy at Christmas, so I asked her if they had gone up to heaven like Grandma and Grandpa Asbury had. Mama said I was too little to understand why her parents ran her and my daddy out of their lives and told them they never wanted to see them again. Mama explained that she never stopped loving them but it was always the hardest on Christmas morning when she remembered how much they loved her when she was my age and they always made Christmas morning so special by being there with her when she opened the presents you brought her. Please Santa, I know this is a very unusual request but if I do not try to bring some hope back inside their troubled and sorrowful hearts when I am the same age my mama was when she was the happiest with them, there might not be another chance to save Christmas for my grandparents and love my mama again. Maybe they would surprise mama again on Christmas morning and put happiness back into mama's eyes when she goes down first to remember.

My daddy told me I should give you a second choice in case what I'm asking for is too impossible for you since it will be Christmas Eve. I wouldn't want to sound selfish, wanting so much of your loving time, but it's not just for me Santa. I feel in my heart that this is what Jesus is asking me to do and it's obvious I cannot do it by myself. I don't have your magic Santa so I know the Lord can help you managed to be at all places on one night. If you can't, I will understand and if you plan to give me a gift instead, could you give it to Cindy Holder, a new student in my kindergarten class who doesn't have much because she wears a worn-out coat to school and has crackers for her lunch. She didn't even have enough money to buy milk and had to take a cup of water. I felt really sorry for her but mama gave me just a nickel for my own milk. I have decided tomorrow at school, I'll give her my milk and drink her water. She looks puny and pale, so I figure she needs milk and old Bess, our big milk cow gives me all the milk I need.

Well, I'll be waiting and if you can help me save my mama's parents so me and my brothers and sisters can have grandparents again, just appear to sweep me away by magic. Will you be bringing your sleigh? I had better dress warm. If I don't see you on Christmas Eve, I still love you Santa Claus. I wanted to send you a special gift for Christmas, a Miracle Snow Globe, but I couldn't afford stamps! Love, Abby."

CHAPTER 18

Nickolas smiled at the other eleven letters address to him from the rest of Abby's big family. It was obvious to Santa Claus that Abby's childlike belief had spilled over into every member of her family, including her parents and Jacob, who had made fun of her belief for such a long time. He had given Martha Jacob's letter to read and get her take on his belief in Santa.

"Nickolas, isn't this the brother that always made fun if you, much like Morgan Matthews." After reading his letter she noticed he asked for the biggest gift. "He sounds sincere enough but children today can put on an act when they want something."

"I agree Martha and this brother has been a non-believer for quite some time. Maybe he chose to disbelieve because he knew he could never write me and see if I would deliver." Nickolas took the letter back. "Jacob has the kind of face that gives him away instead of his writing, which is hanging on the border. This is what I see. Jacob has a hard time really believing in a person who can deliver so many presents in just one night."

"That's because Jacob does not know Santa Claus is no ordinary human. Santa Claus is eternal and connected to heaven, the place one can do anything they choose as long as it is approved by God." Martha knew many children had the same reason for not believing. "Jacob is seeing you as an ordinary man, not the Giver of Gifts turned into Santa Claus and made able by the Almighty to do the impossible." Martha laughed. "If these skeptical children watched you on Christmas Eve transform into Santa Claus the way I have for over a thousand years, I am certain you would become one of their greatest hero's, Nickolas Kristopher Kringle."

"Well, since Jacob cannot see my miracle transformation, I will have to prove to him I do exist my dear." Nickolas folded the empty bag and gave her a wink. "When the doubting Thomas comes down on Christmas morning, he will find a red Zinger Bike, waiting for him under the tree from Santa Claus."

"Oh, I see what you're doing." Martha laughed. "Since Della and Robert could never afford such a luxury, Jacob would be blown away, like the kids say, when he spots his dream waiting for him under the tree."

"And Mason will get the model Corvette, Jesus gave me, just to set him straight about Santa being real." Nickolas winked at Martha before starting the new bag of letters.

TWO DAYS BEFORE DECEMBER 24th

"Well Barnabas, it looks like we are right on schedule. The toys requested are coming out as fast as the children asked for them." Nickolas had been making his rounds and was pleased with the elves progress.

"It is easy to get the toys out on time Father Christmas when Christmas spirit fills the air! It energizes the workers and they grow all the more-merry in their singing." Barnabas gave a hardy laugh, happy to see their leader in a happy mood again.

"Well, I'm off to the stables to check on my sleighs for Christmas eve." Nickolas gave the busy elves a thumb's up for a job well done and started for door, Barnabas right behind him reading the lastiest list.

"Father Christmas, before you leave for the stables, could you tell me where I might find this unusual named Yo-yo for a Robert Asbury? I do think someone erred in writing his age sir. It states 41. Shouldn't that be 14 Santa?"

"The age is correct Barnabas." Nickolas smiled. "You see, when Robert was small he sent me a letter asking for this Yo-yo, popular for that time. I recall sending thousands of the Yo-yo but poor Robert put the wrong address on his envelope and it did not arrive at the North Pole, Destination Unknown. "

"Well, that was bad luck Santa, but why now, a grown man? Surely he doesn't still believe in you after his childhood ended and the door to wonderland was closed on him forever." Barnabas couldn't understand why Father Christmas was taking this request serious. "Maybe it is his son that wants the Yo-yo after hearing his father talk about it. Maybe his name is Robert too, named after his father and he is 14."

"And maybe Robert's youngest child believed so deeply that she convinced the entire family to write me." Nickolas chuckled at Barnabas's blushing face. You will Find Robert's wife's name down that list, where twelve straight last names are the same. By the way, the little girl's mother was Della Daniels."

"The five-year-old cutie that got Chatty Kathy for Christmas?" Barnabas finally smiled. "So, this little five-year-old Abby is her little girl."

"She is and you'll notice she asked for no kind of toy for Christmas for herself but for a classmate named Cindy." Nickolas grew serious. "See that Cindy gets a warm coat plus a doll. As for Abby, see that she has Holly, Christmas Doll and the red-rose china tea-set, for being a little angel this year."

"It shall be done as requested Father Christmas. And the Yo-yo, where might this yesteryear item be hiding?" Barnabas checked off the list after checking it twice.

"Wall West left, top shelf, box 717, bend 1200, package Marvelous Master Yo-Yo!" Nickolas gave a nod, pointing to the sliding giant ladder. "Now, I am off to make sure my five sleighs are being made ready for light speed."

"Excuse me sir, but did you say, five sleighs?" Barnabas knew Santa always took out four sleighs on Christmas eve to head North-South-East and West, at the same time. "What is the fifth sleigh for? Is Mother Christmas going out for a Christmas Eve ride through the snow while you are away delivering presents?"

"Martha will remain safe inside as usual Barnabas. The fifth sleigh is for me." He knew this inquisitive elf could hold him there all evening if he'd let him, so, he would nip the situation in the bud. "I will say this only one-time Barnabas then you head up that ladder for package Marvelous Master Yo-Yo! While I'm away delivering packages in my four-clone stage, I will head out on a mission for the Lord, in my single stage, using the fifth sleigh." Nickolas turned him around. "Now scoot up that ladder, then get Marcy to whipped up two beautiful dresses for Sunday go meeting clothing. One for the mother and one for the oldest daughter. Sizes and colors will appear for Marcy in the sewing room. I'm off now, keep up the good work!" Nickolas hurried out the door and gave a flash, and appeared in the Reindeer stable.

After arranging for a fifth sleigh, Nicolas returned to his house to put an ideal he wanted in front of his understanding wife. He knew she would be compassionate about his motives for desiring his one wish. Recognizing the look on her husband, Martha gave him a smile and took his hand.

"There is something weighing heavy on your mind Nickolas, I

can see it clearly. Please share this thing you must want pretty bad."

"Martha, you know me so well. It's as though you can look into my soul, my heart." Nickolas led her to the sofa. "Christmas eve is drawing near so this thing I wish for must happen soon."

"Does this have anything to do with Abby Asbury, Nickolas?" Martha knew this child had touched both their hearts and she knew Nickolas had a heart full of love for children.

"My wife is wise as well." Nickolas caressed her face. "You are aware we have never had a living human come to Kringle Village because it is connected to heaven, like Eden was."

"Nickolas, you wish for Abby to come to the North Pole?" Martha knew this was something a higher power must permit. "Have you spoken to Jesus about this desire to have the sweet child come here?"

"Not as yet Martha. I wanted to run the ideal by you first." Nickolas paused, taking a breath. "The Lord has asked me to take this child on Christmas eve to California, U.S.A. It would be far easier for me to cross over through the magic mirror with her beside me when I am transformed into five Santa's. The same four of me will journey to the four winds while the fifth of me will transport Abby and Simon, her guardian angel, to the West-end of the United States, destination Riverside, California, 727 Claremont Avenue."

"That sounds reasonable Nickolas but how do you expect to get the child to the North Pole, if it is even possible for a live child to step through the portals of Wonderland when it is blocked by an invincible shield and angels stationed around its borders to keep intruders out?" Martha could see how strongly her husband wanted the child to come to their domain and the thoughts of having a real child there made her heart leap also with joy. "It would be beautiful to have Abby come and see where you live, my love, since she knows so much about you."

"That precious little girl has melted the heart of many adult, from all the letters I have received lately." Nickolas got up and walked to the fireplace, looking in at the flickering flames. "Most of them just give me thanks for keeping children happy, a few asked for something useful or a toy they recall having as a child."

"Abby was the first that wanted to give you a gift Nickolas. And her prize Miracle Snow Globe at that." Martha gave a soft laugh. "I bet she did not share that with her parents."

"I am sure of it." Nickolas smiled, recalling the sweet letter. "I can tell you true, if I can get the child up here on Christmas eve, she will have the snow globe with her."

"It would surely break her parent's heart, not to mention her family and the town's people, who has grown to love Abby and the snow-globe that snows real snow." Martha watched her husband produce at big box out of the air. "I see you have a gift Nickolas. Would it be a special present for a special five-year-old girl?"

"It would not seem fair to take Abby's precious gift without giving her something just as special in return, now would it my dear?" Nickolas glanced down and winked at the woman who had stolen his heart many years ago and his love for her was just as strong as the first day he met her. "I wanted to create Abby's same snow globe but with something containing heavenly magic from both here and in Bethlehem's stable." When Nickolas held up his perfect gift for this special little girl, Martha arose from the seat slowly, her attention never leaving the magical gift.

"Nickolas, this is the most enchanting snow globe ever made. One large enough to hold two scenes that tell of who you were and how you became the eternal giver of gifts to the wonderous place called the North Pole by children everywhere! The Christmas magic of the joyous season, with live evergreens adorned with lights and ornaments, garland and tinsel! A large stone fireplace a blazed with a warm fire where above a mantle covered with lighted garland drenched in holly and berries, surrounded by glowing candles. Hanging in their usual place, a pair of festive stockings, for Father Christmas and Mother Christmas. Above the mantel is a large wreath, loaded with white lights and wearing a big-red-bow on the top!" Martha sighed. And standing in front of the fireplace holding a present is Santa Claus, moving as though he were alive. Just outside the large picture window, the snow is falling and Mrs. Claus is gazing out at the waving elves surrounded by twelve reindeer, hooked to a big red sleigh." Martha thought, not only had Nickolas created Kringle Village exactly as it was in the snow globe, but also those living there seemed to be captured inside the magical gift.

Nickolas turned the snow globe around for Martha to see the other scene and it brought instant tears seeing baby Jesus again awake and smiling at all who came to worship Him. "Nickolas, this is truly a miracle. Your globe has swept back time to the night our

Messiah was born. It's as though time has stood still and Mary and Joseph are once again alive on the earth and watch with love the baby Mary just bore. The Christmas star shines brighter than any stars we see in the dark skies at night. You would have to put them all together to make that one special star! The Father in heaven was proclaiming to the world, MY SON HAS BEEN BORN ON THE EARTH!" Martha took out her handkerchief to wipe her eyes. "The donkey and cow are real again, and the sheep that followed you and your friends, all there, moving as though it were all recorded but there were no camera's then."

"Yes Martha, it is indeed moving, the way I felt when the Lord let me return to my becoming Santa Claus and I saw over 2,000 years had melted away and I was back in Bethlehem, as though I had never left." Nickolas pointed in the round globe at his fellow shepherds. "Look Martha, it is my good friend Nathan, and Ruben and young Mark! It's as if they are alive again and I can almost hear them speak."

"There is another difference in your snow globe Nickolas, there is no snow over the manger scene like the one Abby made." Martha looked closer and smelled the hay, the animals and an overwhelming, distinct smell of heaven. "This one is alive with the smells we smelt that night. I can hear the cooing of the dove that rest above baby Jesus. So, both the Holy Spirit and Jesus is present in your snow globe."

"Did you notice how you can feel the warmth of the stable and the cold breezes from the night air when the doors are opened for us to enter?" Nickolas wrapped his arm around his wife after setting the precious heavenly gift down. "Martha, this was my first time seeing what was inside the box too." He nodded when she glanced up confused. "You really don't believe that I could create something this majestic and powerful, do you? I prayed that the Lord would give me the perfect gift for the little girl that helped me as well. I was renewed with Christmas spirit when I was taken back to remember how it all begin. I was lost Martha and I needed to find myself, find the real Nickolas Kristopher Kringle. Jesus helped me recall my becoming Santa Claus and why. Abby Asbury helped me see that there are still precious loving children in the world who believe with a pure heart."

"Nickolas, my beloved brother, you are now complete, for you have healed from within and without." Jesus appeared before them. "The miracle snow globe will be Abby Asbury's greatest treasure from her friend, Nickolas Kristopher Kringle. Your wish for Abby to be brought here will be granted and by the miracle of My time and space, she will arrive in time to be treated to a grand tour of Kringle Village before you stepped through the magic mirror to become Santa Claus once again. You and Abby will watch your four selves fly off into the four winds, then on your fifth sleigh, nine magic reindeer will race through the clouds and set down behind Nathan and Doren Daniels home." Jesus smiled down, waiting for the question to come.

"How will Abby get here Lord?" Martha was always the practical one and she had the same sensible questions that a parent would have. "She cannot be taken away without her parent's knowledge. We would never want them to worry about their little girl going missing. Not knowing where or why we took her! Why, I would feel like a kidnapper if they missed her and grew anxious that something bad might happen to her!"

"Martha, you may relax from your worries, dear one. Robert and Della will know nothing of their daughter's absence. We shall wait until the family goes to sleep on Christmas Eve, then whisk Abby away, where she will be here in the blink of an eye." Jesus assured the serious woman. "Martha, Is your God still not in charge of this world?"

"Why, of course you are Lord." Martha took a relieved breath.

"Does Time obey My command?" she blushed at the Lord's words and nodded. "Can the Lord demand night to be day for one small child, if He so chooses?" Jesus smiled when Martha finally gave him a smile. "Martha, to the people living on Appalachia Mountain, Christmas morning will arrive on time. For Abby Asbury, she will leave their time and arrive at the North Pole on my time, Christmas Eve, 6:00p.m. with Simon, her guardian angel!"

CHAPTER 19

Back On Appalachia Mountain

The Asbury family had returned home from Christmas Eve church service and were seated together in the large parlor in front of their annual Christmas tree, found on their farm. The old Christmas lights had been stringed on a few days earlier when the family had gathered around it hanging on their homemade ornaments, now sentimental from other past Christmases when the first children were born.

Being a close-loving family, they all enjoyed doing traditional things as a family and gathering around Robert's grandmother's old Spinet piano singing carols was just one tradition they did every year on Christmas Eve, after church services and on Christmas morning, after the presents had been opened. As they gathered around their mother seated at the old piano setting out their favorite Christmas carols, the Asbury children discussed the program at church.

"I think Clara made the best Mary ever!" Sarah piped up, admiring her older sister's performance. "Dress in that period style blue robe and wearing the lighter blue headwrap, it was like watching the picture from our family bible magically jumped from the page!"

"Your sister did portray the mother of Jesus wonderfully." Robert winked at his pretty seventeen-year-old daughter. "Her daddy and mama were very proud of her this night."

"Thank you, daddy." Clara looked down shyly. "I felt blessed to play the part of the blessed Mother of our Lord. How truly amazed she must have felt to find herself the chosen one out of every woman born."

"I guess the Almighty didn't have many 'virgins' to choose from with all the loose values in our society!" Jacob noticed no one laughing but himself. "Ah, come on guys, I heard most teenage girls are always flirting and willing to make out on a first date!"

"You are talking about now, Buddy boy!" Peter frowned at his youngest brother. "Over two-thousand-years-ago, things were a whole lot different than they are today. Like our family, children were brought up to worship God and make Him first in their lives always! Like us. Mary was taught from a very young age to obey all of God's rules and like most young women in her day, remain a virgin until she got married."

"Brother Jacob, all four girls in this family have been taught to wait, just like our mama had done before she married daddy." Mary spoke up. "So, this new generation still have young ladies that respect God and His laws."

"I think Lance Taylor made a very handsome Joseph! He was totally perfect in his costume!" Sarah said dreamily.

"Forget it kid, old blue eyes Taylor won't give a middle schooler a second glance." Jacob kidded around with his six-grade sister. "Now, Clara might have a better advantage being a straight-A senior and wearing a glamorous face!" Jacob looked over at his attractive sister and gave a goofy-middle-school-laugh. "I say by the coo-coo eyes they were making at one-another, the sparks are already flying! Soon we will see they made the senior classes Best-Looking-Couple, then read their wedding announcement in the local paper!"

"Jacob, don't be ridiculous!" Clara lifted a piece of sheet music from the pile and placed it in front of her mother. "Mama, can we sing this one first and dedicate it to our dear brother Jacob? The little cut-up in this family!"

When Della saw the song Clara had chosen, she gave a hardy laugh and asked for everyone to draw in close to sing "I'm Getting Nothing for Christmas. Jacob behaved himself for the remainder of the evening. So, after a few more carols, and some of Della's great hot chocolate, the Asbury's headed upstairs to get ready for bed.

No one seem to notice how quiet Abby had been throughout the evening, nor the fact that she kept staring at the fireplace, a blazed with a warm fire. Only until Robert called out for everyone to say their goodnights and head up for bedtime did Abby finally say something.

"Daddy, will the fire be burned out before Santa comes? We wouldn't want to catch his pants on fire." Abby asked so innocently, Robert could only catch his laugh and give her a smile of reassurance.

"I promise you baby girl, not one ember will be glowing when your special friend slips down the chimney."

"That's good, Daddy because Nickolas might have to swoop down early and pick me up to fulfill my dream wish!"

Again, Robert thought, such a serious face for one so small. I mustn't let her hopes be so high she will be heartbroken when Nickolas Kringle don't show up to get her. "Abby, sometimes we want something so bad it makes us anxious and get butterflies inside our tummy. Your mama and I can tell you want something very much, so badly that whatever it is tops getting a great gift from Santa. Suppose this thing is too big for Santa to take on sweetheart? Maybe what you have asked him is impossible for Santa to perform." Robert knelt down by her. "All I am trying to say Abby is, don't get your hopes up too high! It's alright to believe in Santa Claus, just don't loose that belief if your friend fails to help you."

"Daddy, this thing I asked my friend Nickolas to help me with is far greater than any ideal a little girl like me could dream-up. I truly believe the Lord is asking me to save Christmas for someone near and dear to our hearts. I simply cannot let Jesus down daddy and if Nicolas does not take me this Christmas Eve, this thing cannot happen and Christmas will be lost for them forever."

"Well baby girl, I guess all you can do is wait and see." Robert lifted his small daughter up into his arms and gave her a warm hug. "Sweetheart, sometimes things don't work out like we hope they will, but our compassionate Lord will always make things right." Della had been listening as she kissed her other children goodnight, then came over beside them.

"Abby, your daddy is right precious. The best thing for you to do is go up to your bedroom and get into your nighty, then get ready for bed." Della lovingly touched her daughter's sad face. "Cheer up Abby. Santa Claus is coming tonight and I am sure if he can manage whatever you asked him he will deliver it for you. But, you must not lose any sleep over worrying whether or not he can deliver your beautiful wish. He still loves you very much."

"I know Nickolas loves me mama." Abby gave both her parents a big hug. "After I get ready for bed, will you come upstairs and tuck me in? Maybe read, Twas the night before Christmas, so I can get sleepy?"

"Abby, daddy would be more than happy to come up and read your favorite book so you can get to sleep." Della smiled when the small girl got down and walked up the steps, turning to looked back at the fireplace. "If Santa has plans with you darling, he will awake you and let you know." Della called up.

"Thanks mama." Abby stopped at the top of the stairs and gave her mama a smile. "Don't forget to put out Santa's cookies and milk. You make the best cookies mama and old Bess gives the best fresh milk around." Feeling disappointed from not hearing anything from Nickolas Kristopher Kringle, the small child walked inside her bedroom and shut the door. After brushing her teeth and using the toilet, Abby slipped her long white gown over her head and placed her bedroom slippers by the unmade twin bed, then climbed under the cover to wait for her loving daddy. A soft wrap on the door brought out a sweet "Come in daddy."

Robert saw his young daughter sitting up holding her favorite storybook, giving him her sweetest smile. He walked over and sat down at his usual spot, the side of Abby's small bed, then took the book. "I see you picked your mama favorite bedtime storybook baby girl."

"Mama said it was one of the books she packed when she left her mama and daddy's house." Abby recalled how sad her mother looked when she spoke about being Abby's age and receiving 'Twas the Night Before Christmas'. "Mama told me her parents always made Christmas special for her and they had taken turns reading her favorite book. Mama said she would lay there listening to the familiar words and imagine it was their house the story was about and her daddy that woke when he heard the prancing and pawing of each little hoof." Abby giggled. "Mama said every time they read the part that says, 'ma-ma in her kerchief and I in my cap had just settled down for a long winter's nap' she would try to picture her mama wearing the kerchief and her daddy wearing a cap."

"I imagine that image was rather comical." Robert laughed at the thought of those high-society snobs dressed like an ole world couple. He glanced down at his sweet daughter. "Is that the way you imagine me and your mama when we read that part?"

Abby giggled and reached over to open the book. "I haven't yet daddy, but I might tonight."

Robert reached over and rubbed her head laughing. "Let me begin. Twas the night before Christmas when all through the house, not a creature was stirring, not even a mouse." After reading the book to the end, he noticed Abby had drifted off to sleep. The loving father silently closed the book, lend over to kiss his small child then stood, lying the book on the night table. He slowly switched out the light and walked over to the open door where Della waited.

"My beloved, I don't think we have anything to worry about where that sweet child is concern." Robert gently put his arm around his sweetheart. "If God does have a plan for our baby, she will be in good hands."

"I just don't want her little heart to get broken if things don't happen where Nickolas is concern." Della couldn't take her eyes off her sleeping daughter. "Oh Robert, our precious little girl is so innocent and if things don't turn out as she has expected, her Christmas will feel empty."

"Della, we must hold out hope that whatever this saving Christmas means, will be another miracle from God and what better messenger to deliver the gift of Christmas spirit than that beautiful angelic child our love made." Robert felt his wife relax. "Miracles come on Christmas morning with renewed love!"

CHAPTER 20

Silence had fallen on the old farmhouse as each child and parent lay in restful sleep. Despite most of their ages, that long-loss magical feeling they once felt on Christmas Eve had once again invaded their hearts and there seemed to be a happy smile on each sleeping face.

Unable to sleep since he was created, Simon looked on until the last Asbury finally went to sleep. Knowing no one but Abby could hear him when he spoke, the charming guardian angel could not resist his chuckle over the childlike smiles on each face. "I do believe they are all dreaming about sugar-plums over their heads." Tilting his head, he vanished and reappeared in Abby's bedroom.

"Abby, sweet one, wake from your sleep." The patient angel smiled when the little girl tried to open her heavy eyes. "If we do not go soon, Nickolas will start to wonder if you are coming for your visit to the North Pole."

Abby's eyes sprang open and she sat up to find her guardian standing by her bed holding her coat. "Simon, it really was you talking to me about a visit to the North Pole!" she blinked her big blue eyes. "I thought I was dreaming."

"This is no dream Abby. Nickolas Kristopher Kringle is expecting you and I whenever it is safe for us to make our exit without a lot of drama." Simon helped her get out of the bed and into her coat, hat, and gloves. "Even though we will not be in the cold elements for a long period, it doesn't take but seconds in that frigid high place to give a person frost bite when they are not use to it." he smiled when Abby stared down at her bedroom slippers turning to furry-line boots on her feet.

"Simon, don't I need to change from my nighty?" Abby had learned like all the Asbury children to wear proper clothes when they left the house. "Nickolas might ask me to remove my coat and I might look pretty silly wearing my gown instead of my overalls."

"Abby, your mission requires that you be wearing your granny gown, the very same thing your mama would have worn when she was your age." Simon had been given the Lord's demands earlier and the reasons for each. "When the time comes for you to know, I will tell you God's reasons."

"Simon. What if mama or daddy come to my room and check on me, to make sure I am in bed asleep?" Abby felt anxious about her parents finding her missing and start worrying.

"No one will find you missing Abby, I promise. Your daddy checked on you one last time around twelve midnight and found you fast asleep, so he finally felt safe to close his eyes until Christmas morning." Simon noticed another anxious look cloud the small face. "You are worried about Santa having to leave on his sleigh before we arrive, are you not?"

"Santa Claus has billions and trillions of kids to visit tonight Simon!" Abby began to worry. "We can never make it on time!"

"Abby, we can when God is in control! With God, everything is possible!" Simon needed to reassure Abby so she would relax for the quick transfer from her room to the Kringle's front door. "Jesus has altered time thrice-twice and between, so if we leave now it is three plus three more hours before midnight at the North Pole, making it six p.m."

"I will be ready as soon as I get my present for Santa Claus!" Abby gave Simon a big smile.

Simon looked down at his sweet ward, his strong right hand holding hers tightly while his left hand lovingly carried the cherished snow globe wrapped as only a small child could. "Hold on tight Abby and keep those beautiful eyes close until I say open them. You don't have to be afraid to fly with me."

"I'm not afraid Simon so let's go, I'm ready!" Abby gave her guardian angel one last smile, then squeezed her eyes shut while her tiny fingers gripped Simons strong hand tightly. In a flash, they were standing at Nickolas and Martha's front door.

Kringle Village: The North Pole

Simon smiled down at his trusting ward, her eyes still closed tight as ordered by her guardian angel. "Alright Abby, you may open your eyes baby girl, we have arrived at Kringle Village."

"Already?" Abby's eyes flew open and she looked up at the big door then around at the village square, that was alive with five funny looking men featuring a set of pointed ears sticking out from their green and red felt caps. Each man was leading twelve reindeer around the large center. Christmas lights hung from twelve high light poles to one huge pole in the very center of the circle. Written in red and green letters down the large white pole, the name of the place to let visitors know where they were, THE NORTH POLE. "Wow! Simon, we're really at the North Pole!" Abby gazed up at her loving angel. "I never dreamed an angel's wings could fly that fast! You asked me to close my eyes and before I could think one thought, you said I could open them!"

"That's because I did not use my gifted wings this time Abby." Simon patted her cheek and found it freezing. "I keep forgetting humans get cold fast in a frozen land. We must get you inside Santa's warm home." The faithful angel took hold of the doorknocker and gave it three bangs. "We got to the North Pole with lighting speed Abby. One might call it, in a flash!"

"We moved like lighting." Abby was repeating the magic journey when the door opened and Barnabas smiled at the visitors. Abby noticed this person resembled the men leading the reindeer, but somewhat taller. "Are you Santa Claus?"

Barnabas chuckled, patted her head and motioned them inside. "Simon, my brother, I have not seen you in decades! I still see you are entertaining the young."

"And I see you are still performing as Nickolas Kristopher Kringle's head elf." Simon was interrupted by his wards giggles.

"So, that's what those short men were with the reindeer! Elves really do have pointed ears!"

"That is correct young lady. Santa's elves have a look that no other human can possess." Barnabas gave the very special invited guest his polite smile. "Before the great Jehovah sent us here to the North Pole to prepare a place for Father Christmas and his lovely bride, we were busy working for the Holy Three-in-one in Zion. We were a part of the Cherub angels and each order had leaders and ranks. The group chosen for Santa's helpers were known as Children's Prayer listeners and after hearing a child's beautiful-innocent prayer, we would record all the words inside our head and deliver what we heard to whomever it was directed, either Jesus or the Father-Creator-God. Knowing our love for children, the Lord Jesus created a special look for our class and assigned to us our new position called Elves whose job it was to make glad the heart of Children every Christmas morning by making toys, asked for by the good girls and boys." Barnabas titled his head proudly. "Such is the life of a short, pointed ear angel turned elf!"

"And I hear you enjoy every minute being the head elf, keeping those brother and sister elves busy working under your authority, Barnabas." Simon knew the slightly taller cherub had been over these toymakers in heaven and carried his titled here with him. The caring guardian noticed his ward shivering and snapped alert, recalling humans were not like God's angels, who never felt any difference in hot and cold. "Barnabas, may we come inside and get my adorable freezing ward out of the cold outside?"

"Do except my apologies Miss Abby." Barnabas took her by the hand and gently led her in and shut the large door. "I, like your dashing guardian, forget sometimes that God's earthly children are not as adapt to colder climates as His angels are." He reached down and touched her red nose. "With those red cheeks and cherry-red nose, you, my dear, could almost pass for Father Christmas's own daughter!"

"Why, thank you Barnabas, that was a lovely compliment." Abby said with a shivering voice. "Is Nickolas here or is he getting ready for his big night?"

"What a cute kid!" Barnabas chuckled, winking at his angel brother. "Your friend Nicolas is waiting for you in his and Miss Martha's large den. Do follow me." The dramatic elf waved toward the twelve-foot double doors and led the two visitors in. "Father Christmas, your very charming quest has arrived."

Nickolas had been placing another yule log on the fire for his young guest, knowing she would grow cold the moment they arrived. He swirled around and laughed happily, not the jolly HO-HO-HO, Abby expected. Neither did the exceptional child expect to find her friend so young and handsome. Not seeing the young woman resting in the oversize-high-back rocker that faced the fireplace, Abby's eyes grew even bigger when Mother Christmas swiveled around to face their visitor. Instead of seeing a slightly tubby older lady with snow-white hair and a bonnet made out of white lace trimmed with a red and green ribbon, Abby admired the same fine-figure her mama had, along with a similar smile that graced her dear mama. Nickolas took a step toward the surprised child.

"Abby, were you expecting a jolly-old fat man with white hair and a fluffy white beard?"

"That is the way I had you pictured Nickolas." Abby gave the friendly man a sweet smile. "I never expected you to look exactly like you did in my dream when you were a shepherd."

"Oh yes, you did dream about me visiting the baby Jesus when I was a shepherd living in the small town of Bethlehem." Nickolas waved her over by the warm fire. "Come and warm yourself child. You appear to be a frozen lollipop."

Abby giggled and walked over next to the tall man she had assumed was short, fat, and jolly. "I had a lollipop once Nickolas, at my friend Annie's house. Annie said it tasted like bubblegum. I wouldn't know, I never had any."

"That makes two of us Abby. There was no bubblegum around when I lived a human life." Nickolas lit a good smelling pipe and Abby searched for the smoke that circled his head like a wreath. "I guess that wreath made from your smoke was just in my favorite story book."

"Wreath, from smoke?" Nickolas pondered the statement while glancing at his wife when she chuckled. "Martha, I take it you understood Abby's statement."

"As will you Nickolas when I remind you why it sounds so familiar to you." Martha went to the bookshelf and collected a very old book. "Abby was referring to Santa Claus's description from your favorite story book."

"Is 'Twas the Night Before Christmas' your favorite book too Nickolas?" Abby asked with excitement. "First, the fact that neither of us have had bubblegum and now we have two things in common, my friend. That is my very favorite story book, as it was my mama's when she was a little girl."

"So, that is where you got the smoky wreath!" Nickolas laughed.

"The stump of a pipe he held tight in his teeth and the smoke from the pipe circled his head like a wreath!" Abby smiled then grew serious. "Nickolas, how did it feel to be one of the first to see the baby Jesus?"

"Abby, it has been over 2,000 years since I knelt down at that manger and looked into my Lord's eyes for the first time, but in my heart, soul, and mind, the beautiful moments with that Holy Infant changed by whole life. Mine and my dearest wife, Martha and I will remember it for all eternity." Nickolas reached down and patted her head. "I hear you saw me transform from a lowly shepherd into Santa Claus."

"It was a beautiful dream, more like a vision." Abby reached for Nickolas's hand. "You said you would remember those beautiful moments in your heart, soul, and mind forever." Abby glanced behind her to make sure Simon still had her gift for Santa. "I remembered to bring you the present I promised. Because it is very special to me, my family, and even my school, I knew it was special enough to give to you Nickolas. I wrapped it so you could place it under your tree and open it on Christmas morning." Abby paused a moment. "Maybe you're want to rest a spell, being all tuckered out from delivering toys all night, then open your present."

Nickolas and Martha had tears in their eyes as they both felt the need to hug the angelic child. Nickolas sat down and pulled Abby in his lap. "Abby, do you realize you have already given me and Martha the second-best gift we have ever received? Just a few weeks back I was ready to hand my position over to another giver because I had lost all faith in the modern-day children. I could see their behavior had grown into selfish, rude, and bossy brats with the need to rule their family. The letters to Santa had dwindled down and even some of those contain ugly remarks from mocking bad girls and boys. Children's belief in me had dropped to only a few. I was so depressed over the situation I had lost my Christmas Spirit completely." Nickolas choked up and Martha came to his rescue, settling down by his feet.

"My beloved husband was in a bad way Abby, so bad he could not hide it from two of us who love him dearly. Myself and Barnabas. We noticed his unusual words and actions so everyone in Kringle Village started lifting up prayers to the only One that could help Nickolas find himself." Martha could see her Nickolas had relaxed and was ready to take up the story. "You can tell Abby what the Lord did, my darling."

The handsome man lovingly caressed his wife's face. "Abby, just like your vision, Jesus took me and Martha back to when we lived in the little town of Bethlehem. I once again was making toys for the poorer children who were playing by the road with either sticks or rocks for their donkey, sheep or shepherd. I began secretly hiding the gift at the child's door for them to find in the morning.

Martha, helped me by sewing rag dolls for the girls and by painting faces on the people and animals. Pretty soon, parents and children were calling me the Giver of Gifts and at last, Kringle Jingle, due to the bells I wore as a shepherd. I was on the hillside when the angels came and announced the Lord's birth. We made our way down to the stable led by the bright-morning star sent from God, the Father, to announce His Son's birth. You witnessed the rest, as I knelt down to worship my Messiah, that is when He recognized me as the one who would become Santa Claus." Nickolas gave his little friend a smile. "That is when you witnessed what I could not see, my transformation. My Christmas Spirit had been renewed."

"That is wonderful Nickolas! Our Lord can work wanders." Abby considered his previous comment about her. "Nickolas, you said I gave you the second-best gift, but I have just arrived here, so how could I have given my friend a gift I cannot remember giving?"

"Abby, remember when I told you my depression started because of the change in children, those once innocent boys and girls who believed in me had turned into rebellious bad girls and boys? Then you came into our life Abby, with more faith that many adults cannot possess. You taught me that I had been wrong to place all children into the bad category when this world still had millions more who still had childlike belief in me, and better still, in our Lord. Sweet child, it was your faith in the Lord Jesus and your deep belief in me that healed my broken spirit, so now I am completely healed and more-ready for Christmas than I have ever been!"

"Dearest friends, I am just glad that I was a part of helping you find the real Nickolas Kristopher Kringle and I am super proud that you will help me get that same Christmas Spirit back inside my grandparent's heart so they can make their little girl's Christmas happy like she remembers."

"Abby, you always think of others. Such a pure heart, not asking Santa for anything for yourself." Martha could feel the joy of having this little girl come to pay them a visit. "Abby, Santa Claus will not let you go without a gift under that fabulous tree you and your family put up this year."

Before Abby could reject, Nickolas held up his hand, "Abby, Santa wants to place a special gift under your sweet-smelling cedar and I will not take no, sweet one." Nickolas sat her down and gave her another pat on the head. "And before I drop you and Simon off at your house on my last stop for this Christmas Eve, your two loving friends, Nickolas and Martha has a gift to give you."

"You are giving me two gifts?" Abby blinked her big eyes. "Listen, I know you both love me, same as I love you, but shouldn't you give one of those gifts to another needy child?"

"See Abby, that is why we give you two presents." Martha kissed her soft cheek. "You have given so many gifts already just by being you. Consider your gifts are from two different sources. One is from Santa Claus, the jolly man wearing a red suit, the other gift is from two friends who have found the love and joy of knowing you, like the child we never had."

"My heart is filled with love for both of you as well, so, if it makes you both happy to give me the presents, then I except them with great joy." Abby felt her tears slowly rolling down her pink cheeks. "Thank you."

Nickolas thought it best to cheer up their small visitor. "My good little friend, how would you like to take a tour of Kringle Village?"

"Wow! That would be swell, Nickolas!" Abby's eyes lit up. "Will we visit the Toyshop and watch the elves making toys?"

"That will certainly be on our list young lady but first we need to get you properly dressed for the North Pole." Nickolas waved his hand over his small friend and like magic, Abby stood wearing her own Kringle Village attire, woolens from the undergarments to the long red coat that was made just for her. "It's not too heavy on you, is it?"

"It appears heavy Nicolas, but it feels perfectly wonderful and warm!" Abby looked down checking out the wool pants and sweater underneath the rich red coat. She then happily thrust out her foot to admire the green fuzzy-wool socks inside a very handsome back boot. "Nickolas, I could pass as one of your elves or" her bright eyes found his. "or your very own little girl, preparing to escort you tonight in your sleigh!"

"Abby, Martha and I would proudly pretend you are our very own little girl, if just for tonight." Nickolas caught his emotional wife's positive nod as she wiped away a falling tear. "Isn't that right my dearest Martha?"

"To have such a sweet and loving little girl, even though a short time, will be an answered prayer made many years ago." Martha knelt down to hug Abby. "Thank you for helping Nickolas find Christmas again."

"It was what the Lord ask of me mama Martha and I will be forever grateful." Abby felt Nickolas take her hand and noticed a wool hat and fluffy wool gloves in his other hand.

"Put these on and we can begin our walking tour." Nickolas enjoyed her giggles then turned and extended his hand to Martha. "My dear, would you like to go with me, Abby, and Simon?"

"That sounds very tempting but I was thinking how lovely it would be if I had some of my special hot chocolate made ready when you return, needing a good hot mug to warm you up." Martha laughed at Abby's happy face as she licked her little lips. "I hope 'our little daughter' likes double chocolate and lots of marshmallows!"

"Mama Martha, I love chocolate and marshmallows, but at home we cannot afford a lot of either. My mama bakes one chocolate cake a year, every Christmas, and she fixes twelve cups of hot chocolate with six marshmallows a piece, on Christmas Eve after church service's." Abby looked up with wide eyes as she wondered just how many marshmallows mama Martha was referring to. "I will have the same amount as you and daddy Nickolas."

Martha had been touched by the poor child's honesty over her family's poverty. As she promised them it would be ready and waiting at their return, Martha was making her own Christmas list for Santa's sleigh. A box filled with tins of her hot chocolate mix and bags of fresh-soft marshmallows, delivered to: Della Asbury, from: Martha Kringle.

CHAPTER 21

Nickolas led his special visitors up around the village square and Abby's eyes danced as she watched the colorful snowmen playing in the freshly falling snow, stopping to wave at the cute child walking with Father Christmas. Nickolas and Simon could not resist their laughter when Abby gave them a wave back. Hearing the big barns doors open, Nickolas stopped to point out the five elves bringing the reindeer back out one last time before preparing them for the nights flight. As the parade of reindeer circled past the three watching, each elf would acknowledge them with a tip of his head.

Abby was busy counting the reindeer as they passed by and gave a confused face before asking. "Nickolas, I count 45 reindeer prancing around the circle. If a sleigh needs only 9 reindeer to pull it, what's the other 36 for?" Abby glanced up to find her friend smiling.

"What would your guess be Abby?" Nickolas gave Simon a playful wink.

"I can think of two reasons, but whatever the reason is, it cannot be like our favorite storybook about where you had 9 reindeer with names and the lead reindeer had a shining his red nose."

Nickolas chuckled as he proudly announced all his reindeer had names. "I will tell you little friend, but please entertain Simon and me with your ideals."

"First ideal: Since there are way too many children to visit in one night and each child expects you to have the time to munch a bunch of cookies followed with milk that has probably grown warm setting there ever since they went to bed, you chose four of your elves to help you deliver and drink down all the milk as well as munch those cookies set out for you." Abby could tell by their happy laughing she was no where close. "This one is probably closer. Santa makes all the delivers, starting out in the places it grows darker sooner, then returns to change out his team of reindeer. Sort of like a pit crew does in a car race when the tires run out and they put on new tires." Abby noticed their serious faces and assumed she had guessed right. "So, Santa Claus just flies back in for a pit stop and the elves unhook the warn out reindeer and hook up the fresh ones up before taking back off!" She giggled. "I got it, right?"

"No where close Abby, but that was another great solution if this one wasn't faster." Nickolas reached down and rubbed her little red nose. "We best get you inside young lady before you become an ice sickle. To the Toy Factory!"

"Yip-e!" Abby grabbed both their hands and marched happily down the Candy Cane Lane until they reached Toyland. With eyes big as a saucer, the small farm girl could not believe she was actually walking through Santa's workshop. "I have never seen so many toys before in one place like this! Why, Christmas Eve night is almost here and all these happy elves are still joyfully making toys." She smiled up at her guarding angel. "Look Simon, listen how happy they are as they make all those toys for us children! They know every single carol by heart and their singing fills this very big room with angelic voices!"

"Sweet girl, it is the singing of angels you hear. These cherubs are all my brothers and sisters and like me the heavenly Creator created them to have love for all God's small ones. This is why they do their work with joy in their hearts and as Christmas is the celebration of our Lord Jesus's birth as Messiah, Savior, and King, this Christmas Spirit lives inside our hearts year-round!" Simon noticed Nickolas waving them on down the long row. "We must hurry this tour along Abby, for Nickolas has to prepare for tonight's journey."

Martha was waiting inside with four mugs, smelling of rich hot chocolate and topped high with fluffy white topping. She gave a happy laughed when she noticed the sparkling eyes staring at the rich treat waiting in front of them.

"Abby, let me help you out of your coat, hat and gloves." Nickolas laid them aside till later, when she once again would dress warm for her cold ride through the air. "Now, let us enjoy my sweet Martha's great recipe!" He helped Abby take her small chair in front of the warm fireplace, then handed her one of the mugs, thick enough as not to burn the fingers while holding it.

After everyone was seated and enjoying the hot chocolate, Nickolas knew it was time to tell Abby how the magic night would work. "Remember out in the village square I told you I would let you know why I need 45-reindeer?" He chuckled when she nodded after taking a big sip of her hot chocolate and looked up with a marshmallow mustache. "I have 45 reindeer this year to make nine for five sleighs instead of my usual four. I could tell by your four elves theory taking out four sleighs, plus mine, that you had counted exactly nine reindeer per sleigh, meant for five sleighs." Nickolas gave her a wink when she gave him a smile. "Let me start with that big mirror I noticed you observing before we went out for our tour."

"It is a very unusual mirror, Nickolas." Abby's attention went to the floor to ceiling mirror. "Why, that large mirror is tall enough for a giant to look in! I have never seen a mirror that did not reflect the things in front of it. Both you and Simon, as well as I were standing directly in front of it when we were at the front door getting ready to leave, but neither one of us could be seen inside that weird mirror." Abby pointed at the bookcases directly in it's view and they too were vacant. "See, nothing! It's as if there's another room on the other side of that mirror."

Martha gave her husband a knowing smile as she picked up the tray to gather the empty mugs. "Abby, I can assure you sweet girl, that mirror is real." Martha walked passed it at a closer range and her reflection was easily spotted. "This is another gift from the Lord Abby. This mirror is a magical entrance into an enchanting world where the same transforming you witness when Nickolas was a shepherd and the Lord made him into Santa Claus has become a reality."

"What's this place called that waits just on the other side of that magic mirror?" Abby could not take her eyes off the incredible mirror she had been afraid of earlier.

"It is a place you have heard people sing about, never really knowing it actually exited." Nickolas walked up in front of the large mirror and instantly a swirl of white started floating behind the glass. "It is called, WONDERLAND OF ZION!"

Simon took his ward's hand and led her over beside Nickolas. "Abby, once through that looking glass, you can see how Nickolas becomes Santa Claus and how he can miraculously visit every single child that wrote him or sat on one of Santa's helper's lap."

"Simon, Nickolas changed my clothes and you said I needed to stay in my nighty because Jesus ask me to." Abby didn't know what happen to her clothes and she remembered her guardian's words before they left for the North Pole.

"The clothes you wear now are for traveling through the cold air on Santa's sleigh. I promise Abby, you will be back inside your granny gown when the time comes." Simon gave her a reassuring smile. "Now, we go through the mirror with Nickolas, Abby. Just listen to everything he tells you. I shall be right beside you sweet girl."

"Simon is right Abby. We will be beside you and help you know what to do when we arrive at your grandparent's home." Nickolas assured the small girl and heard her gasp when she noticed a large Santa suit floating in the air through the mirror. "It is time for my transfer." Martha had been standing beside her husband, holding his hand, preparing to see another Christmas miracle. He turned to hug her tightly before giving her the traditional Christmas Eve kiss before leaving. "Alright Abby, once inside, I become the Santa Claus you came up to see!"

The moment Nickolas stepped through the magic shield, he transformed into the Jolly fat man with white hair and a perfect white beard.

As Simon held Abby back for the next phase, the young girl watched in amazement as Santa Claus suddenly separated into five Santa's and the one in the middle sent the other four to four waiting sleighs, harnessed to nine reindeer each, all facing different directions. A voice could be heard over a loud speaker. Prepare to fly! North! South! East! And West! Away you go!" the sleighs left in a flash of light.

"Now Abby, you see how I manage to pay each and every good child on this earth a visit on Christmas Eve." St. Nickolas waved them over as the fifth sleigh appeared. "I had to clone an extra Santa this year so I could take you to save Christmas for those grandparents living a sad, miserable life. Just hop in the middle of the sleigh and after we cover up with heaven's blanket, we will be off like a thistle as soon as I give my team a whistle!"

Hearing Abby laugh St' Nickolas gave a loud HO-HO-HO and left in a flash!

CHAPTER 22

Nighttime had just fallen in Riverside, California due to the time zone. The little girl recognized the big 3 floor mansion on Claremont Avenue from her dream she had months before. Seeing the lights of the town from the sleigh, the three in flight could see everyone in town and throughout the neighborhoods were decked out with Christmas displays and lights. Everyone that is, except the couple living at the end mansion, setting on 300 acres, whose home was completely dark.

Growing discontent over their loss of their only child, Nathan and Doren Daniels had all but given up on trying to pretend to feel any form of Christmas spirit. The first few years the couple tried to decorate their house as they had when their daughter was at home, but the holidays just wasn't the same without their Della. Slowly, the decorations grew less, the happy carols, were fewer, the need for presents reduced to nothing.

Della had moved out and at first, they blamed Robert Asbury for ruining her life. Along with the anger and hate came the need to block out any memory of their misguided daughter, so they took down all her pictures, packed her favorite books away, locked the Christmas Carols sheet music away before locking the lid down on the piano keys, never to be played again, as long as they lived. Absolutely nothing to remind them of Della, thinking she would be forgotten one day.

At least that is what Della's father wanted, to wipe all thoughts of having her gone, forgotten! Doren had a harder time letting go of the precious little girl she remembered when the holidays grew close with the passing of each year. Nathan had been so harsh and demanding over everything connected to Della, being either done away with or packed away permanently! Playing along to keep her husband's contented while holding on to a part of her daughter, Doren asked to have Della old room to turn into her own private office. So, after promising Nathan she would clean out all Della's things and get them out of her sight, her big act paid off. Knowing there was still a part of her sweet daughter still there, where she could slip off to, lock herself inside Della's old bedroom with all of her things still there, the mother inside the sad woman could let out her grief and just miss the perfect girl she had help send away.

As time past, all thoughts of Christmas had been replaced with two very lonely people, each one living in their own world of hopelessness, gilt, and complete solitude. The couple barely spoke to each other anymore and they blamed each other for letting the best thing in their life walk away. Nathan had beat himself up in the privacy of his rooms since the once loving couple chose to have their own space, apart from each other. Outwardly he blamed Doren for not stopping their daughter from leaving, but inside his solitude world, Nathan knew he was really the one to blame for losing their beautiful precious girl.

Doren had stopped slipping away into her daughter's old room due to the overpowering sadness she felt while inside her little Della's quiet-empty room. The brokenhearted mother would weep for hours as she lifted familiar things she had watched her daughter use in happier times. After ten-years of unhappy decorating their big den that held their most memories of five-year-old Della's secret gift from Santa, hidden under the tree and the once beautiful Christmas carols being played on the grand piano by their talented daughter, gone silent, Doren blew out the last single candle she had placed on the mantel, never to plan for another Christmas again.

So, like many other Christmas eves, Nathan and Doren had set apart as they had their dinner, softly bid one another goodnight, and went their separate ways to bed. While the rest of the town and neighborhood celebrated the joys of Christmas, two broken parents tossed and turned until they cried themselves to sleep.

Just behind the large mansion, away from the hustle and bustle of Christmas activities throughout Claremont Avenue, Santa Claus brought down the nine reindeer in an open meadow. Taking Abby's hands, Simon and Santa had the small girl standing at the front door, just like she was in her dream.

"Well, since it is dark inside my mama's homeplace, I better not knock or ring that bell like I did in my dream, right?" Abby had noticed there was not a single light burning in her grandparent's large home. Yet the rest of the neighbors had their houses completely decorated for Christmas.

"We don't need to be let in Abby, I've got other means in getting in homes and creating my own light when needed." Santa laughed softly when Abby stepped away to stare up at the very high roof with four huge chimneys. "Now do not start worrying about me taking you up on that high roof to go down a chimney."

"Well Santa, that is the way you get inside with that magic bag of toys, right?" Abby blinked her big eyes.

"Yes Abby, when I deliver toys, but I am delivering a very charming little lady tonight." Nickolas enjoyed Abby's relieved smile. "Take our hands again and once we are inside, stay still until I give us some light." With another flash, the three unexpected visitors were standing in the big den. As promised, Santa Claus magically brought forth a very high evergreen with sparkling colorful lights and endless amounts of ornaments, then topped with a bright angel. To Abby's delight, the mantle was magically covered with garland, braided with white lights and covered with red berries. Candles set on either end of the fireplace mantel and a set of three dominated the center. All the clutter that had filled the top of the grand piano had disappeared and was replaced with sheet music of favorite Christmas carols. And hanging just above the mantle in a large frame was the exact copy of the decorated den and as Abby stared up at the Christmas photo obviously taking several years ago due to date plainly visible in the corner. As she looked, something amazing happened. She could see herself standing at the big Christmas tree, her back turned as she appeared to be looking under the tree.

"Excuse me Santa, but how come there is a portrait of me standing at the tree you just sapped there?"

"I can see why you are confused sweet girl but if you look real close at the gown's bottom." Simon knew Abby thought the little girl had to be her wearing the white granny gown. She was the exact same size and had the very same hair. "That precious girl is wearing a gown with double lace at the bottom. Yours has a single row of lace. That was all your mama could afford to buy you precious. Your mama had rich parents and they thought nothing about buying the very best for their precious five-year-old."

"Oh! So, that is my mama in that portrait! Wow! I bet her face looked just like mine!" Abby looked down and noticed she had on her gown. "You're right Simon, my gown didn't disappear after all. It has been on me the entire time."

"Now Abby, everything has been set up sweet girl. I believe you must know what Jesus needs for you to do to help put Christmas back inside your grandparent's heart." Santa watched Abby glanced up the lighted banister then back up at him.

"Jesus wants me to save Christmas in their sad-shut-off hearts Santa." Abby looked up at both her friends and knowing they would be there for her, even though her grandparents might not see them, she would listen in her innocent heart for the guiding light of Jesus to help her words. "I'm ready Santa! The night is fading and they must find Christmas before it is too late."

"Then it shall be done." Santa waved his hand up toward the left upstairs and gave Abby a wink. Simon and I will be right beside you and Jesus will speak through the Holy Spirit that lives inside that loving heart of yours. Now, turn and look toward the tree Abby, just like your mama did when she was five. This your grandmother will see first and the renewal will begin to heal inside her troubled heart."

Upstairs, Doren Daniels had been awakened by a soft voice calling her name. She had been dreaming once again about her happiest memory of Christmas, when Della was five. Doren sat up when she noticed a colorful light under her door. "Now, what could that be?" she climbed from her warm covers and reached for her robe, aggravated for being woke up. Thinking Nathan had forgot his medicine again and went back downstairs only to forget to cut back off the down stairs lights, she mumbled to herself as she opened the door and gasp when she saw the staircase flowing down in Colorful Christmas lights. Confused as to how the banister got decorated, she spoke softly to herself as she descended the high-flight on steps, mainly to break the silence of the house. "Now who on earth managed to hang all those lights and garland without me hearing them?"

When Doren finally reached the bottom she instantly noticed lights coming from the big den. Suddenly it flooded back inside her memories of her and Nathan in a happier time following their little Della down the steps to find her standing looking under the huge lighted tree. Always ready to capture their little daughter in a keepsake photo, Doren was ready with her expensive camera and snapped the perfect Christmas memory, only to have it taken down by her angry husband and boxed away in the hot attic. Suddenly thinking her husband was trying to rub the hurt in deeper by making her hope she would find Della waiting at the big tree, the upset woman started to return to her room when she heard the soft voice call out again.

"Dorine, you must never stop believing in Christmas. If you want to find Christmas again, just walk inside that room that holds your favorite memories and you will receive much more than you lost."

"What do I have to lose?" she thought. "Things cannot get any worse for me than they already are and the One leading me forward has filled me with some hope." Doren stepped into the wide threshold and froze at what she saw. "Am I still dreaming?" she whispered, afraid her daughter's image would disappear. Her fingers reached up and traced the wet tears that ran down her face. "If I am dreaming, why does it feel so real." Doren swallowed, knowing there was only one way to find out. Call out to her baby girl. "Della, sweetheart, it's mama."

Abby sniffed back her own tears and turned around. Hearing her grandmother gasp again seeing who she thought was her own little girl, the goodhearted child took a step toward her grandmother and softly said "Merry Christmas grandma."

CHAPTER 23

Doren Daniels could only stare at the mirror image of her daughter when she was five years old and she felt too stunned to speak as she watched the small child walk up and take her hand. "My name is Abby, grandma Doren and I have come to save Christmas for you and grandpa Nathan."

"Abby, you have to be our precious granddaughter." Doren finally felt like smiling, something she had not done for many-years. "You are the smitten image of Della, our beautiful daughter who has been gone from us for way too long."

"Yes ma'am. I know. I walked up on my mama one day and she was crying, just staring down at our favorite story book, 'Twas the Night Before Christmas'. I asked her why she was so sad and she told me she had been remembering when she was my age and how her mama and daddy would take turns reading her the story about Santa Claus. Then she told me about getting thrown out of the home she grew up in by her parents because they couldn't except my daddy to be her husband."

"Sweet baby, you know all of that about your grandparents and yet, you came here to help save Christmas for us?" Realizing the child was in the big room alone, Doren glanced around the large room, searching for the ones who accompanied her there. "Abby, the only one who could possibly have a key to our home would be our daughter." Doren grew hopeful as she frantically scanned the far corners of the room, only to find them empty. She gave a nervous laugh. "Abby, you may tell your mama and daddy to stop hiding. They are more than welcome now."

"Grandma Doren, when I left my house, my mama and daddy were fast asleep with the rest of my family." Abby looked up, a loving sincere expression filling her cherub face. "Two of my very favorite people in the whole world escorted me here so I could do what Jesus ask of me. Grandma, I, being a Christian and little lamb of Jesus, could never hold any hard feelings for the two-beautiful people who brought my mama into this God given world and gave her life. After Jesus planted her loving soul inside her. You and grandpa might have broken my mama's heart, but it's never too late to mend it back together again and start loving the wonderful daughter who has never stopped loving you." Abby heard Nickolas and Simon say amen and she giggled when she looked their way.

Doren glanced over to the vacant spot and turned back to find her granddaughter smiling up at her. "My companions are invisible to you grandma. My very personal-lifelong companion will remain invisible but my other very best friend will appear when he is ready."

"Well, alright Abby, tell your 'very best friends' they are very welcome and my deepest thanks for delivering you here safely." Doren felt strange smiling at a blank space, then quickly turned back to her granddaughter. "Did your friends do all this decorating Abby?"

"Oh yes, one of them grandma and he made it exactly like the big picture over the fireplace mantle, see" Abby turned and pointed to the precious photo that caught Della on Christmas Eve when she was five. "Your house looked pretty barren for the Christmas season grandma, so my friend just brought it back like your favorite Christmas."

"Abby, who is this magical friend that can recall that Christmas so long ago?" She stared up at the portrait, long gone from it's rightful place and hidden away in the dark attic.

"The same one that is going to find the cookie plate empty and the milk glass bare." Abby giggled when her grandmother turned white and whispered close to her granddaughter's ear.

"Your very best friend is Santa Claus?"

"Isn't Christmas a magical wonderland, grandma!" Abby laughed. Now that you know, we better find some cookies and store-bought milk."

"Store bought? Is there any other kind of milk Abby?' Doren chuckled, feeling alive for the first time in years as they made their way to the kitchen.

"Yes ma'am, if you live on a farm like we do." Abby held up the glass for her grandmother to pour some milk in. "Make it just half full and two small cookies. Poor Santa eats more cookies than a cookie factory bakes in a year! He really likes old Bessie's milk."

"Does he?" Doren gave the sweet child a smile as she gathered the plate carrying two small cookies. "Which brand of milk does this Bessie buy?"

Abby burst into giggles. "Bessie don't buy her milk grandma, she gives it! Bessie is our family milk cow."

"Well, I'm just glad I could scratch up a couple of fresh cookies. Between me and your grandpa, we don't eat many."

"I guess it's a good thing you found two then grandma. I'd sure hate to make Santa create his own cookie."

Upstairs Other End of the Hallway

Nathan Daniels had been having a most unusual dream. He had watched his sad wife making her way down a lighted staircase, its rail alive with Christmas garland ablaze in colorful lights. As he dreamed he felt as though he were walking behind her invisible and he appeared to notice the twinkling lights dancing through the great room's arch entrance at the exact moment his wife had, for they both stopped walking in secants. Pausing only for a moment, the connected pair walked inside the brightly decorated room and instantly thought they had been taken back to a more happier time. When Christmas was something special to the whole family. But it wasn't the identical Christmas tree they had put up together, or the mantle alive with garland and lights. It was the presents of one small child, standing with her back toward them while her precious eyes searched for Santa's gifts.

In his sleep Nathan called his little girls name out. "Della, its daddy." Then his heart melted when she turned around to give him a smile. Before he could speak another word, he suddenly awoke from a soft voice calling out his name. For a few moments, Nathan just assumed the voice he heard was a part of his very realistic dream about his baby girl. Nathan's first thoughts were going back to sleep in hopes of taking up were he left off in his beautiful dream, the only thing he had left of his loving daughter he had ran from their lives.

After trying for several minutes, Nathan knew it was hopeless, so he sat up, noticing the flickering lights under his door, somewhere down the hallway. Checking his clock, he noticed it was 11:00 p.m. and concluded that it must be Doren, out of bed unable to sleep. After putting on his winter robe and bedroom slippers, he stepped into the hallway, seeing the Christmas decorations dancing down the stairsteps.

"Good Lord, my wife has gone off the deep end." Thinking

Doren put up all the decorations after he went up to bed, the tired man stumbled down the long flight of steps until he reached the bottom and stopped, dead in his tracks from what he was hearing.

Somewhere within the well-lit room, the sound of a piano could be heard and one small, sweet voice singing Silent Night. Nathan knew the instant he heard her angelic voice who was singing his favorite carol. The same carol he had enjoyed hearing his own mama sing when he was small and filled with love for his own big family. The emotional father all but whispered her name.

"Della, daddy's precious baby girl. I know you are singing that carol just for me."

"That precious little girl is singing her heart out for you Nathan Daniels." The voice that had woken him from the realistic dream. "Yes, my brother, it was I that brought you out of the vision I placed before you so you could see and hear the words spoken by my smalless witness sent to save you, so by, saving Christmas as well. Remember these, my words, spoken for times such as these: And a little child will lead them. Many of her words to you are mine, through her. Many more of her words come from her own pure loving heart."

"Then, this child I hear singing and sounding just like my own little Della is a heavenly being, sent down by you to help Doren and I heal our broken lives?"

"Nathan, you will learn this child is much more than you ever hoped for." The voice grew softer as it began to fade. "Go now and meet this child who can save Christmas in your shut-off heart and by putting me first in all you do, there is no mountain to high to climb."

Silence fell around Nathan Daniels and like his wife before him, he mumbled. "What have I got to lose if there is just the slightest chance I can find peace at last!" Lifting up his head, he stepped forward to noticed the one playing the piano while she sang. It was as though the weight of a thousand-pound stone had been lifted off his chest and the shut-up heart perked up with new life as laughter fell from his recent snarling lips. Nathan found himself moving toward the piano, humming along with the clear high voice of the angelic girl setting where his little girl had sat, performing that very song, years before.

Abby looked up into her grandfather's eyes for the very first time and gave him her beautiful smile. Doren had been turning the pages for Abby while she played, just the way her mama had taught her.

"Hello grandpa Nathan!" she giggled when his eyes grew surprised with her way of addressing him. "My name is Abby, your little girl's youngest daughter." Seeing her words had taken him by surprise, the caring child reached up and patted his face. "Are you surprise to see me here grandpa?"

"Well Abby, it did come as quite a shock, to learn I have such a beautiful granddaughter that is the smitten image of her dear mother." Nathan could feel himself smiling and although it had been ages since he had anything to smile about, the sight and voice of this one small child had melted his cold heart. "Tell me child, where is Della hiding? I am certain her and Robert, I mean, your daddy, must have brought you here. No one else has a key to our house."

"I'm sorry to disappoint you grandpa, but when I left my home to go to my very best friend's village, mama and daddy were in bed fast asleep, like the rest of my family." Abby gave him an innocent smile.

"Then, who took you to your very best friend's 'village'? Nathan suddenly thought he might still be dreaming. "Were your parents aware of your late-night plans sweetheart?"

"My mama and daddy knew I had been waiting to go with my very special friend if he excepted my gift wish. So, when they checked on me a midnight, I was still in bed fast asleep and they assumed my gift had been turndown." Abby felt Simon pat her head and she looked up to see him smiling so she blew him a kiss.

"Abby, who did you blew that kiss to? Someone on the ceiling?" Nathan turned toward his wife when she chuckled softly.

"Nathan, you will learn that our little granddaughter has very special friends in high places."

"Grandma Doren is right grandpa. You asked me who took me to the North Pole and that's who I blew a kiss at. Simon, my guardian angel." Abby giggled when Nathan's jaw dropped.

"Your guardian angel took you all the way to the North Pole, still in your nightgown?" Nathan stared at the empty space that obviously had an angel standing there. "Can Simon make himself visible for me and your grandma?"

"I am afraid he cannot Nathan." Santa appeared on the other

side of Abby. "You see Nathan, Abby needed someone who could get her to Kringle Village in a flash, which he did, after placing her wool coat on her along with the child's boots, hat, and gloves. When my very special friend arrived at the coldest spot on the planet, I presented her with Kringle wear to keep our important child extra warm while visiting and riding here in my sleigh."

Nathan absentmindedly rolled his eyes up toward the roof. "Are there 9 reindeer presently standing high above our head St. Nick?"

"We decided it best to park the sleigh this time around back in the flat green meadow, due to your neighbors becoming suspicious as to why Santa Claus chose your house where no children lived. A dark depressing house, whose occupants had simply forgotten the real meaning of Christmas!"

"That's why I'm here grandpa Nathan, grandma Doren, to save Christmas, that got lost deep inside both your hearts the day you ran away the one thing that made you both the happiest at Christmas." Abby young face had grown serious. "Jesus asked me to come here and bring peace back in this home. Deliver light instead of darkness. To help mend your broken hearts so you can renew the love you have always felt for your daughter, my sweet mama." Abby walked up, little in size but strong with her Christ-like faith, that reflected more love than they had witnessed since losing their most precious gift from God.

"Abby, our precious grand baby, if your mama could forgive our horrible behavior toward her and your dear daddy, your grandma and I would keep Christmas in our hearts every day of the year!" Nathan knew his tears were flowing non-stop but he considered each tear drop a bad choice melting away from him.

"Abby, your grandpa is right. We have been living a sad-lonely life far too long and you, along with your very special friends, Santa and Simon, and with the mighty grace of our Lord Jesus, have truly brought the real Christmas spirit back into our hearts." Doren's tears were also falling as she said softly "The Lord's truth is our blessing Abby, for a little child has led us back."

"Mama has been sad too, over her loss. Believe me, she has missed her mama and daddy and thinks about her happier memories with you both." Abby turned and pointed at the painting of her mama standing at the large Christmas tree. "She has told me about that Christmas morning, when I found her crying. She cries every

135

time she reads me our favorite book because she remembers both of you reading it to her at bedtime."

"Twas the Night Before Christmas, I remember how much little Della loved that storybook about you Santa." Doren could vision reading the book to five-year-old Della. "How that child would giggle when Nathan read it at the part, 'Ma-ma in her kerchief and I in my cap"

Abby giggled, recalling why her mama laughed. "Mama told me why she laughed at those words. She said she would imagine her mama wearing a kerchief and her daddy wearing a cap in bed."

"And how your daughter wrote me in secret asking for a Chatty Kathy doll and when she found it where I tucked it back for her, she surprised you both into believing in me." Nickolas winked at a smiling Abby. "I do not wish to rush you Abby, but our time is slipping away quickly. We must finish with this visit soon. My-selves will be returning back to the Wonderland of Zion soon and although they know my special mission, I cannot keep my other four waiting to reunite, so I can return to Martha, who waits up for me."

"We must not keep mama Martha waiting daddy Nickolas." Abby looked up tearfully, dreading when she would be separated from her dearest friend. The young girl fought her tears as she smiled up at her grandparents. "I must be going back home soon. The Lord has held time back so I could come and still wake up with my big family on Christmas morning."

"Your big family?" Nathan glanced at his wife, never considering Della and Robert might have more children. "How many brothers and sisters do you have baby girl?"

"I have six brothers and three sisters, one big happy family!" Abby smiled as she took Simon and Santa's hands. "I wish you both could come tomorrow morning and surprise mama, but we live on a farm in the Appalachian mountain of Kentucky. Unless your angels can flash you there in light speed, it will take a miracle."

"Our baby has ten children!" Doren couldn't get pass Della and Roberts big brood.

"Doren, our granddaughter has given us the best Christmas gift we could have possibly needed and her wish is for us to give our Della her parent's love back by showing up tomorrow on Christmas." Nathan smiled down at Abby. "Abby has taught us that by believing with a child-like faith, miracles can happen."

"That's right grandpa, believing is seeing! It was the Lord's will that I put Christmas back inside your hearts and seeing the one thing that has still been missing in your Christmas renewal has been replaced to its rightful spot." Abby turned her grandparents around so they could see the large manger scene had appeared in a glowing light. "Now your Christmas is complete! Merry Christmas grandpa, grandma! I will be looking for that Christmas miracle tomorrow!" with that, Abby and her two most favorite friends were gone.

CHAPTER 24

Abby was delivered back to her home by Simon due to the need for Santa to return to the North Pole and reconnect to his other four-selves before daybreak. Nickolas had explained why he could not delay the transformation. Should daylight come in while any of the separated Santa's were still out, the magic from the Wonderland of Zion mirror would be shut down until the following Christmas Eve and the separated Santa's would have to remain behind the dark mirror until then. Simon had assured the worried child that her friend would make it back in plenty of time to make the magic transfer.

The tired little witness barely hit the pillow with her head before she fell asleep to dream of being with Nickolas and Martha, making her rounds with them in the Kringle Village Square.

Riverside, California: Claremont Avenue

Nathan Daniels had been on the phone ever since Abby and her magical friends disappeared, trying to rent a private jet to take him and Doren to Appalachia, Kentucky.

"I am truly sorry Mr. Daniels, but every one has left for Christmas Eve. Tomorrow being Christmas is totally booked up." The airport operator, a friend of their daughter, had checked over the private plane rental's log and found them booked except for one spot the day after Christmas. "I can fill that space in for you Mr. Daniels if you like, so, unless we have a cancellation tomorrow you can at least get to your meeting by noon the day after Christmas."

"I am afraid the day after would never workout." For the first time since becoming a well-known face in California, the Honorable Nathan T. Daniels, felt like a failure. "I want to surprise my daughter and her beautiful big family on Christmas morning. Doren and I miss our little girl and we must let her know this Christmas. An angelic child told us so and it brought Christmas back into our shutoff hearts. We want to beg Della and Robert's forgiveness and tell them along with our grandchildren, just how much we love them and need them in our lives!"

"Praise God, for that beautiful angelic child who stole inside your cold hearts and radiated them with the warm light of the Christ Child!" The airport operator spoke with sincere compassion. "I wish there was a jet available for you and Mrs. Daniels this night of miracles, your Honor and if I had my own pilot licenses, I would take you this moment, had I a plane to take up in. We can shoot for day after Christmas sir, what do you think?"

"I think you are a very loving and considerate young woman Colene, but it must be Christmas morning when we surprise them, so we must find a fast way there now." Nathan caught his wife's attention and shook his head negative. "We cannot wait for the day after Christmas nor depart sometime tomorrow and find ourselves there late in the day. We must leave tonight."

"My dear Mr. Daniels, that will require that night of Miracles I spoke of earlier." Colene Edwards had just graduated high school with her best Della when the heated argument between father and daughter erupted before the irate judge ordered his only child out of their lives, along with Robert, the young man Della had chosen to marry instead of attending the same law school her father attended. "If one small child could change your heart sir, somehow I know you will get that Christmas miracle tonight."

Switching the phone to speaker so his wife could hear Colene Edwards response, he could only smile at the young lady's words. "Colene, I can see why you refer to this night as a night of miracles, which it is. My wife Doren and I had become worse than Scrooge was in the Christmas classic, A Christmas Carol. Not only did we refuse to practice our faith anymore and simply forget Christmas existed, we blamed each other for the loss of our only child until we grew too cold inside to make conversation with each other." Nathan looked apologetic toward his tearful wife. "Colene, we both got a second chance tonight to start over with our daughter and all it took to change our heart was our five-year-old granddaughter." They both heard the listener gasp, never realizing the angelic girl was her dear friend's little daughter. "We cannot go into details right now my dear, but by help from heaven Abby Asbury was able to pay us a very memorable visit with two very special friends."

"Then I feel confident that you will get that miracle tonight Nathan. The one you and Doren have inwardly been searching for ever since Della walked out of your lives." There was no doubt about the young lady's emotional feelings. It was obvious she was crying over the miraculous renewal in these, two lost people. "If our Lord sent his sweet messenger to help you find Christmas so you could reunite with Della and Robert, then He will send someone to help get you to the Appalachian Mountains tonight."

"I can always tell when someone is a good church goer, sweet Colene. So much like my precious Della and her faithful husband Robert. We shall send you a card, along with a photo of Della and Robert with our ten grandchildren."

"Ten?" Colene couldn't control her laughter. "Two more kids and my best friend will have a perfect dozen! I bet Santa Claus has to make several trips down their chimney, just to deliver all those presents!"

"From meeting the very jolly man myself, my guess is that the black sack he carries has the same extraordinary abilities he possesses." Nathan laughed when he heard her give a surprised 'huh'? "Like I said my dear, little Abby was delivered by two very special friends, on a sleigh driven by nine-fast-reindeer." Nathan and Doren both laughed at the sound of what he just proclaimed to a straight A College student who had a top-paying job at the Riverside Airport. "Try not to figure it out, just let your faith take over by walking by faith, not by sight."

Suddenly there was a rustling noise high on the roof and the sound of 36 Reindeer paws prancing in place. "It appears you are right Colene about the Lord sending us transportation to Appalachia Village. I just count 9 Reindeer landing on our roof. Wouldn't you agree Doren?"

"Yes dear. With 4 paws each divided into the 36 we can hear moving in place up on our roof, it does make exactly 9 Reindeer!" Doren said loud enough for the listener to hear her. "I'm just glad we packed lightly."

"Abby did mention light speed was a possibility! Sorry to cut you off my dear, but we've got to go! Take care and Merry Christmas!" Nathan hung up before he got bombarded with questions and jumped when he heard a voice behind them. Swirling around, both Daniels saw a short fellow dressed in red and green, wearing a pointed cap topped with colorful tassels. There was no mistaking just what Nathan and Doren were looking at.

"You are one of Santa's Elves?" Nathan finally asked.

"It is my ears, is it not, Nathan Daniels! "Barnabas stated, rather than question his rider. "The ears always give us away, even before the pointed shoes we wear! But, it is the Holy Creator's way of making us appear different than our human counterparts!" He gave his polite smile after noticing their one piece of luggage each. "I see you are prepared and ready for takeoff!"

"Takeoff?" Doren asked with a swallow, treading the answer she was about to receive. "Santa parked his Reindeer in the backyard when our granddaughter paid us her visit. I was just"

"Just hoping you would not have to go up the chimney madam?" Barnabas gave a chuckle. "Santa parked back there due to everyone being awake in the neighborhood when he brought sweet Abby here. Now that the problem does not present itself due to everyone being in bed at this hour, we can travel the normal way."

"Normal for you perhaps, but I cannot see myself performing like a chimney sweep. Mister?" Doren was hoping this strange being had a little compassion for her fear of high places.

"Barnabas is the name madam, just plain Barnabas." Reading her thoughts, he knew she didn't know what he was or how he felt about humans. "Doren, rest assured I am aware of your fear of being elevated upward but you are perfectly safe with an angel of God."

"Elves are actually angels?" Nathan gave a relief laugh. "Well, I be darn! I never would have guessed."

"It's pretty easy to put together Nat." Barnabas had been studying both adults until he finally recalled them as children. "Nat, I recall you had six brothers and you where the youngest. You grew up on a farm, just like Robert with almost the same situation."

"Nathan, you never told me you grew up on a farm." Doren thought back and remembered her husband always changed the subject when she asked him about his younger days. "Weren't you happy as a child darling?"

"Except for my marring you and having Della, growing up with my loving family was one of my fondest memories." Nathan had tears in his eyes. "I let my pride and ambition blot out any memory of my family's poor existence but now looking back, all that ever mattered was how much we all loved and cared for each other."

"You really did care Nat." Barnabas took each suitcase and set them in the fireplace as Doren and Nathan watched on. "Santa received your letter when you were just six and you wrote: you didn't want a present because you wanted your sick brother to get the book Tom Sawyer because his old worn-out copy had to burned due to the bad germs on it."

"That's right Barnabas, I had forgotten." Tears ran down Nathan's face. "I still have that copy of Tom Sawyer, tucked safely away in my bedroom drawer."

"That's what your father sent you after your brother past away twenty-years-ago." Doren had walked over to comfort her beloved husband. "I could tell it had to be something sentimental but you weren't sharing anything with me back then."

"And Doren, what family secret did you keep from Nathan when you met the very successful lawyer?" Doren gave her husband a shy grin when he turned to looked down at her.

"I sort of told you that my father was a successful doctor and my mother was a top fashion model, when I was trying to impress you Nathan. After all, you had just stated you were in line for the next state court judge, then you had hopes of getting dominated for the supreme court down the road." She noticed his smile and felt more relaxed. "I know I should not have lied about my parents or my attending the community college instead of Wells Lady's College, but I could tell that you were falling in love with me and I was madly in love with you darling."

"You were absolutely right about my falling in love with you Doren. I still am, so I can confess that I did check into your brilliant story to learn my beloved had lied to me about herself and her parents." Seeing her bush, he pulled her into his arms. "My darling wife, my love for you made it impossible for me to walk away, especially since my silence about my own family was equal to your imaginary parents."

"This reminiscing on your romantic past is quite interesting but we must leave if you are to make it to the Mountain View Inn in Appalachia by midnight!" Barnabas had taken the Daniels by surprise. "Oh, pardon my failure to inform you that a reservation has been made in your name at the quant little inn since it will still be late when you arrive and your family are all nestled in their bed while visions of sugar plums dance in their heads!" the head elf laughed at his own statement as he waved his hand over the luggage and it disappeared up the chimney. "Now, which one of you wishes to go up the chimney first?" He noticed their hesitation. "I could put up the cladder, if you prefer."

"The cladder?" Nathan glanced down at his wife who was shrugging her shoulders. "Pray tell, how does a cladder work?"

"I was under the assumption you both had read your little girl Twas the Night Before Christmas many nights and you do not recall the phrase, 'There a rose such a cladder?'" Barnabas shook his head at their blank faces.

"We recall the phrase from the story book Barnabas but we assumed the writer meant 'There a rose such a rattling sound! You know, clatter-noise?'"

"Listen closely, as our time is hastily slipping away, a cladder is what humans call ladders." Barnabas heard a bell and nodded. "I am aware of the time Father Christmas, as soon as these travelers choose an exit." His eyes fell on the couple. "There are houses with no fireplaces! No fireplaces mean, NO CHIMNEYS! The Reindeer always land on the roofs and sometimes Santa makes his magic Cladder appear if he has to go down to ground level to enter a chimneyless house!" The elf grew loud. "CHOOSE NOW OR REMAIN HERE!"

"I will go up the chimney Doren and help you out when you come next!" Nathan walked inside the big fireplace. "Try to stay brave darling and keep thinking about Della and her big family!" with those last words, Barnabas waved his hand and Nathan flew up the chimney and out on the roof.

"Look Doren, if it will make it easier on you, I will flash up to the roof beside you! Are you coming with us? Your daughter is waiting for her big surprise." Barnabas held out his hand smiling as she walked inside the fireplace and up the chimney they rose.

Seated high on their three-story house's roof, the couple suddenly felt like children when Barnabas gave a whistle and away the Reindeer flew up with a flash, leaving the town of Claremont behind.

CHAPTER 25

The Asbury Farm: Christmas Morning

Robert opened his eyes just as dawn was breaking in the east and hearing the stillness filtering in from outside, he quickly recognized the sign and climbed from the covers to peer out. A warm smile crinkled his face at his first glimpse of a newly fallen snow on the mountain and he felt better for making each child their very own sled for their gifts this Christmas.

Not hearing his wife slipping from the covers, he closed his eyes when he felt her soft hand touch his arm. Looking out, Della noticed they had been blest with a white Christmas this year instead of a left-over snowfall. "Oh Robert, isn't it beautiful, when one can witness the silence of softly falling snow just before the daylight!"

"There's something about this Christmas Della that holds a miraculous optimum, a degree of something most favorable, that will lead to some sort of end." Robert wasn't sure why he declared such a statement, and on Christmas morning at that. He felt as though it was some invisible religious spirit that had inspired the words. "Della, what could my declaration mean or am I just waking from some sort of dream?"

"My dearest Robert, I was moved by your poetic words and felt a ray of hope that something good might happen on this Christmas morning that will bring peace to a bad situation, thus end the bad and start anew!" Della heard the obvious sounds of Children awaking and moving about inside their rooms. "The children are getting up darling and soon our peaceful moments will be erupted by screams of delight when our ten beautiful children raced downstairs to see if Santa Claus really did come last night."

"I just hope our little Abby isn't too heartbroken over her unanswered request from the one she believes in and obviously loves deeply." Robert slipped into his overalls and flannel shirt, over his winter thermals, then waited for Della to fasten up her warmups.

"We shall soon know darling." Della touched Robert face before giving him a loving kiss. "Knowing our precious angel, Abby will be all smiles when she comes down, even without a gift from the jolly man she admires." They walked out to noticed most of their gang was waiting for them in the upstairs hallway. "Hello my darlings, is everyone up and anxious to check under the tree?"

"Mama, there are nine of us here, waiting to go down, but we did not want to go down until our baby sister has joined us." Peter had taken a vote to wait on Abby, the one that gave them all the real Christmas spirit. "Clara checked in on her and found she was fast asleep."

"I tried waking her by calling her name, but the sweet thing just rolled over, never waking up." Clara spoke with a sister's concern. "Mama. Maybe Abby waited up for her friend and she got tuckered out, and that's why she is still asleep."

"Well, whatever it is, this is not like our little girl." Robert glanced down at Della, recalling his strange words and his wife's personal definition to what it meant. "Stay here and I will go to Abby and wake her up so she can join the family."

Della waited out in the hallway with the older children and knew by their quiet behavior, they were all concern over their little sister. Della glanced down the steps, her thoughts swirling in her head. "Since Abby hasn't got up yet and she is always the very first to get out of bed on Christmas morning, just maybe Nickolas did except her request then magically swept her away to wherever she needed to go and they didn't get back until he finished his deliveries." Della jumped when Abby's bedroom door opened and Robert walked out carrying his little girl, who was all smiles.

"Abby is just fine love ones, she is just tuckered out from her long visit with Santa Claus last night." The loving father gave his little girl a wink.

"Santa Claus?" Jacob pushed his way to the front. "Were you really with Ole St. Nick, kiddo? THE SANTA CLAUS THAT GOES HO-HO-HO?"

"That depends on if he is on Kringle Village side of the magic mirror or the Wonderland of Zion side!" Abby giggled. "Hey, what is everyone waiting for? Aren't you the least bit curious to find the presents you asked Santa for under our tree? Why, I bet mama or daddy haven't even went down to light up the tree or mantel yet! And just who do you suppose lit up this stair rail or have you even noticed the colorful lights all aglow?"

"Why, yes, it is lit up Abby." Robert smiled over at his wife, assuming she had plugged the lights in at the upstairs plug.

"Don't look at me Robert, I never touched the lights cord!" Della felt a new sense of magic sweep through her and waited for one of the children to confess to plugging in the stair rail lights, but she only received confused faces.

"Can't you all just believe without seeing who lit up all of our Christmas lights?" Abby proclaimed as she started down the steps, her family close behind. As predicted, the large family den was lit up in Christmas lights and unwrapped presents were placed around and under the large cedar. "See folks, my very favorite friend Nickolas can work miracles through his magic touch!"

"Abby is right!" Mary dropped to her knees to check out her set of twelve Nancy Drew mysteries. "Look mama, I ask Santa for a set of Nancy Drew mysteries and he brought me twelve books!"

Clara pulled out a long box with her name written on it. She was all smiles when she opened the lid and lifted out a beautiful blue dress with matching shoes. "Oh mama, this is even prettier than I had imagined! And matching shoes! It will be perfect for my senior prom!"

"And our Clara will be the prettiest debutant there, I guarantee!" Robert gave his oldest daughter a gentle hug. "Sarah, did you and the twins get your gloves and balls?"

"I sure did daddy!" Sarah held up her right hand, covered with the perfect fitted catcher's mitt and tossed her soft ball up with her left hand. "With a little practice, I'll be a shoe-in for first pitcher on our school team this spring!"

"And Robby and I can practice our swings with this really cool professional bat!" Bobby let his hand rub over the smooth Hickory wood.

"We can toss the baseball until my throw is right-on and like little sis, my hopes of being head pitcher for our team next season will improve greatly!" Robby had ambitions of playing every game in the new year and now he and his twin had the chance to practice at home.

Jacob had been searching for his red bike and grew more depressed when someone else called out about finding what they asked for. Peter and James were next, as they shared their finds with the family, a net, volley ball, and a complete badminton game. Jacob dropped his head, believing that Santa had not taken his letter serious. Abby had been observing her youngest brother and called out his name. Thinking she was going to scold him for his disbelief, he didn't even look her way.

"Jacob, have you tried checking behind the Christmas tree for that red bike?" Abby had seen the shiny red bike glistening from the lights. "That was probably the only space big enough for your gift brother."

Perking up from Abby's positive words, Jacob moved to the back of the tree and let out a yip. "My bike! Santa wasn't mad at me after all!" the overjoyed young man rolled the shiny-new red bike from behind the tree, a broad smile spread across his cute face. "Abby, which way to the North Pole?"

Abby giggled and pointed up "Nickolas Kristopher Kringle lives at the top of this world Jacob! The closest spot to heaven!"

Putting his palms to his lips, Jacob planted a big smack on them and held them straight up "Thank you, Santa Claus!" Hearing a train whistle beneath him, Jacob laughed. "Frank got his really cool train set!"

Abby continued giggling as she looked over at her parents, busy watching with happiness their children's joy. "Mama, I see a box with your name on it under the tree and a smaller box for you daddy." She watched her parents drop to their knees with their own child-like wonder, to find their gift from Santa.

"I could not have chosen a better dress for church services." Tears laced Della eyes when she noticed the shoes and shoulder bag to match. "I bet Mrs. Claus picked these out."

"Mama Martha is very talented mama." Everyone in the family stopped with Abby's remark. "Daddy Nickolas's wife is named Martha Kringle and she makes yummy hot chocolate with tons of marshmallows, whipped and fluffy! I enjoyed a mug with her, Nickolas and Simon before Daddy Nickolas had to be transformed into his Santa Clauss."

"Abby sweetheart, how long were you with the Kringle's?" Robert recalled checking in on his five-year-old before turning in for the night. "What time does Nickolas leave to deliver presents to all those children?" he glanced down at the present in his hand. "And all the adults who wrote him this year?"

"My very dear friend daddy Nickolas always prepares to leave the North Pole at exactly 8:00 p.m. and with the magic mirror

147

placing him in the Wonderland of Zion Santa Claus magically takes off north-south-east-and west!" Abby gave a big smile when they all stared at her confused. She just shrugged her shoulders and declared "He is magical, what more can I say!"

"You can tell us how you spent enough time with him to have hot chocolate and which way did he take you, north, south, east, or west?" Della also was aware their little girl was home in bed at 12:00a.m., so how could she have spent time with them? "Abby, your daddy saw you sleeping at 12 midnight and you stated that your friend left exactly at 8:00 p.m."

"That is absolutely right mama! Simon woke me up after everyone in the house fell asleep and said we were expected at the North Pole." Abby could tell they were having a hard time believing her story. "I was just like you, so I question my friend Simon about being too late, that Santa had to be gone already, so he explained to me that Jesus had placed the time backward so I could be arriving a 6:00 p.m. Nickolas took me on a tour of Kringle Village and the toy factory!" Abby giggled. "You should have seen all of Santa's joyful elves still busy happily making toys! We had hot chocolate when we returned from our fun tour and it sure did taste yummy and warm after being out in the coldest place on earth!"

Robert gave a soft laugh. "Well baby girl, after having all that excitement, no wonder you were warn out." He absentmindedly opened his gift and laughed out when he lifted the prize yoyo from its box." It took a few years waiting, but I finally got my one special gift from Santa!"

"Great going daddy! Let's see you do some of those tricks you've been bragging about!" Jacob enjoyed seeing his father so happy as he wrapped the string around his finger for the only trick he remembered then performed what was called the triple swirl." Robert smiled out at the happy faces on his family as he took a performer's bow. "Thank you, for your kind applause!"

"Robert darling, I am impressed." Della reached up to reward him with a kiss, then her attention fell on Abby's empty hands. "Abby, you haven't looked to see what Santa brought you sweetie."

Before Abby could respond, Jacob laid his bike over and stepped over. "What present mama? I was under the impression the little squirt didn't want any gift from her friend, just some kind of mission she needed his help on." He gave his little sister a loving smile. "Abby just filled us all in about her exciting visit with the Kringle's, didn't you sprout? I just bet our cute sister isn't expecting any more gifts after her magic time at the North Pole, right Abby?"

"I did tell Santa not to bring me anything for under the tree, but my very special friend insisted that not only Santa would have me something under the tree, but that he and mama Martha had a very special present, just for me." Abby paused momentarily, recalling Nickolas's words. "Nickolas promised that his and mama Martha's gift would be given to me by them, so I don't know when I will be getting that present, since neither one of them can leave the North Pole, except for Santa's one magic night."

"Baby girl, if your friend Nickolas told you he and Martha would be giving you that gift in person, then I believe somehow they will." Della took Abby's hand and led her to the tree. "After all the miracles that have come to our family, as well as the folks in town, living below the mountain, I can believe in almost anything being possible."

Abby squeezed her mama's hand and dropped on her knees to retrieve the two presents waiting underneath the large Christmas cedar, aglow in sparkling lights. "Mama, sometimes the things that seem the most impossible can bring a Christmas miracle." As Abby reached for the pretty doll she had dreamed of having, she was hoping that her grandparents had found their way there. "Look mama, It's Chatty Kathy! Is she as pretty as yours was?"

"I would say, they could pass for twins!" Della laughed, taking the doll from her daughter's outstretched arms and checked it out. "Why, this doll looks exactly like the one I had, probably long gone, packed up and shipped off to Goodwill!" she watched Abby open the other box and let out a happy squeal. "What has gotten you so excited?"

"My very own glass tea set mama!" Abby took out one of the teacups and held it up, revealing a beautiful Winter Rose. "Now I can have a tea party with my doll and all my sisters and you mama!"

"Just let us know little sis, we will bring the cookies." Clara enjoyed watching her baby sister so excited over her very first real toys.

"Hey Clara, are those tea cookies you girls are planning on taking to sprouts fancy tea party going to be as fake as her make believe tea?" Jacob tried to picture the women of the family seated around Abby's very small round toy table in her bedroom and he couldn't resist his chuckles. "I wouldn't want you ladies to get choked eating real cookies and drinking invisible tea!"

"I'll have you know brother Jacob, I will be pouring 'real' tea from my beautiful teapot." Abby glanced up at Jacob's stocking, hanging full next to her own and instantly noticed one long-black-stick protruding out the top. She giggled. "Jacob, you had better behave before Santa exchanges everything he placed inside your big stocking!"

Jacob, along with everyone else in the family, looked over at the mantle and noticed for the first time all the stuffed stockings and the large lump of coal standing out from all the others. "Brother, you must never forget, Santa Claus sees all and hears all. He knows if you've been bad or good, so"

"be good for goodness sake! Dang it, I keep forgetting!" Jacob blushed and slumped back to pick up his prize bike, feeling relieved that the jolly-old fat man didn't zap it away. "I'm sorry sprout, just read that card, waiting near the trunk of our tree."

"I forgive you Jacob even if you are a stinker!" Abby giggled and reached for her card, instantly noticing the writing wasn't from her friend Nickolas. She opened it and began reading to herself, when she noticed it mentioned her grandparent's names.

"Merry Christmas Sprout! I guess you wonder why your mischievous brother started calling you the same nickname I gave you." Abby smiled when she knew the card was from Barnabas, Nickolas's head elf. "Jacob kept calling you squirt and I could not picture such an adorable young girl being compared to an ejected liquid spurting out!" Abby tried to snaffle her giggles, knowing her brother was referring to the noun squirt, meaning very small and not the verb, squirt. "I replace the proper word in his head so he now calls you the same thing as I.

Now Sprout, do not share what I tell you in this letter because it will not be a surprise if your mama and daddy know its condense. Since Father Christmas cannot depart the North Pole except for the brief hours on Christmas Eve, then he had me to deliver your grandparents to you. They arrived just before midnight, the Lord's turn back time, and stayed at a little inn in the town below your mountain. We have arranged a way they can surprise your mama so I need you to get your favorite story book and have it ready to start reading at 8:00 sharp. When you get to the part where papa states: Ma-ma in her kerchief, please pause so your grandfather Nathan can take over the story while he and grandmother Doren stepped inside the den from where they will be hiding and waiting for Nat's cue to read." Abby's lips melted into a huge grin. "This is our secret Sprout, unlike the stick of coal I placed inside Jacob's stocking earlier." Once again, Abby covered her giggles.

Father Christmas has asked me to share something with you later, but for now, we must complete your dear mama's Christmas miracle. After your parents share their own Christmas presents made just for you children and what has made them completed by a blessing from heaven, I will share Nickolas's message to his very special friend and daughter. By the way, if you wonder why I can leave the North Pole when Nickolas cannot, it is because he is a heavenly immortal, I am one of God's angels, capable of descending throughout the entire earth.

The time draws nigh to the big surprise Sprout! Your grandparents await just inside the adjacent room. I will appear when the time is right. I do have one message from Father Christmas about Morgan Matthews big surprise. The rude boy was up to another trick, never knowing he was being observed by the one he was planning to play his prank on. Morgan had stolen his father's vodka and was about to empty some into the milk his little sister had left for Santa. Just as he lifted the bottle over the milk, Santa called out his name right behind him and it startled old Morgan so much that he dropped the bottle and it crashed to the floor, spilling every drop. Wide eyes with disbelief as to who he saw behind him, the usually big-mouth bully was speechless. After getting a fatherly lesson from the wise man he thought did not exist, Morgan broke down in tears and asked Santa to forgive his stubborn behavior. After Nickolas got Morgan's promise to be sweeter to his little sister and all the children at school, he gave Morgan his asked for gifts, the model Corvette and the Top Gun DVD. Then in Santa Claus tradition, Nickolas stepped inside the fireplace, gave a smile, touched his nose, and giving a nod, up the chimney he rose! Mission completed! Listen for the bells of eight! Your newfound friend, Barnabas.

CHAPTER 26

Della had whispered to Robert about leaving their gifts for the children until they had breakfast and after he agreed, she got everyone's attention. "Children, this has truly been a wonderful start for our family Christmas and your daddy and I wish to prolong the joyful act of giving by waiting until after we have had our breakfast to give you our gifts this year." Della waited for the anxious chatting between brothers and sisters as they wondered what they would be getting this Christmas from their loving parents. "Now, if I can get Clara and Mary to give me a hand in the kitchen while you boys can get some warmer clothes on to help your daddy milk Bessie and feed the animals their Christmas grain."

Abby noticed the old clock was about to chime 8:00, so she took her mama's hand. "Mama, could I please read our favorite book first." She noticed everyone watching her. "After all, it is daddy Nickolas's favorite book too and I thought since he made our Christmas so special, it would be the right thing to do."

"Sweetheart, couldn't it wait until after we have breakfast?" Della asked, noticing her little girl's sad face.

"Mama, it isn't a long book and even though it happened last night, I think we owe it to Santa Claus for making everyone's Christmas magical again." Abby heard the clock strike 8:00. "Please mama, let me read it now."

"Alright kids, have a seat and let your baby sister read this special story for us." Robert pulled Della down next to him. "Go ahead Abby, you can read us the story now."

"Thanks daddy, you won't regret it." Abby opened the book, but knowing it by heart, looked out at her family. "Twas the night before Christmas when all through the house, not a creature was stirring, not even a mouse, the stockings" the precious girl said each word clearly and knew she was drawing close to her grandpa Nathan's part. "The children were all nestled, all snug in their bed while visions of sugar plums danced in their heads." She pretended to cough and watched her mama when her grandpa and grandma stepped out, wearing a nightcap and a kerchief on their heads.

"Ma-ma in her kerchief and I in my cap had just settled down for a long winter's nap." Nathan and Doren fault the tears that filled their eyes as they watched their daughter rise slowly from her sofa, staring with uncertainty at just what she was seeing. Della clutched her chest as she called out softly, her children looking on at the strangers who had appeared and wondered why their mother was so shaken up.

"Mama? Daddy? Is it really you?"

"Della, my precious daughter, we are so sorry for hurting the only thing that made us both happy." Nathan could not control his own tears as he watched his beautiful daughter weeping in front of them. They watched Robert looped his protecting arm around the woman he loved, unsure himself of what had happened to changed the two people that drove them out and away from their life.

"I don't understand what made you change after all these years." Della finally found the words she needed to asked. "You made it clear to me and Robert, that we were not wanted or welcomed in your lives anymore."

"Yes, I'm afraid we did Della and we had to suffer the consequences of those horrible actions for many years." Doren reached out to the daughter she had missed ever since she walked away. "I would take it all back if I could darling but life does not offer us another chance to start over but with the renewal of our faith in the One that can, we came here with the hope of receiving your forgiveness so we can start over, this time by you and Robert excepting us."

"Della, your precious mother stated we were to blame for your leaving, but the truth is, I was the stubborn arrogant one that insisted you chose my way of taking your life forward." Nathan had humbled himself, after years of staring in the mirror to see himself for what he really was. "Maybe you think we don't deserve another chance and I could not blame you for that decision if that is your choice. But sweet child, all I'm asking if you choose to throw us out of your life, just let it be me, not your dear mother. I know she just did what she knew I wanted her to do but the instant it was done, we both blamed each other and drew apart, bitter toward each other. It was you that had brought life inside our home Della. It was you that made Christmas special for your mama and daddy. It was your little Abby that melted the darkness that had taken over our hearts and that precious child made Christmas come to life again by some beautiful miracle."

Della and Robert looked down at their little five-year-old angelic girl and suddenly realized what the Lord had asked her to do, to bring Christmas back, back into the hearts of someone in the family.

"Abby, this is where you were last night, saving my mama and daddy from their deep depression." Della noticed the tears falling from her daughter's big eyes. "Oh Abby, my beautiful baby. You had a dream about the home I grew up in. The Lord gave you the vision of Nickolas so he could help get you there and prepare what must have been a dark-dreary house when you arrived."

"That's right mama. Grandpa Nathan and Grandma Doren had lost all hope in seeing their little girl again and they both let Christmas die inside their hearts. Nickolas used his magic and made your home look exactly like it did when you were five." Abby smiled over at her grandmother. "Grandma Doren came down first and thought she was dreaming when she saw me with my back turned, the same way she remembered seeing you when you got your Chatty Kathy doll from Santa. After she found out I was really her granddaughter, your daddy was awakened and came down while I was playing the piano and singing his favorite song, Silent Night." Abby gave Nathan a big smile. "Isn't that right Grandpa Nathan?"

"That is exactly right Abby. You were seated at the piano just like our little five-year-old Della and your grandma was turning the pages for you, same as she had done for Della." Nathan chuckled recalling learning he hadn't gone mad. "When I found out that my angelic granddaughter was the smitten image of her dear mama, I felt a new kind of change inside me and I knew at that moment, the Lord had forgiven my unforgiveable actions toward my only child and renewed my faith. Why, Doren and I were feeling almost like children ourselves when we learned that Abby's very special friends were Santa Claus and Simon, her invisible guardian angel."

"Mama, you and daddy have made my Christmas complete, just as the Holy Spirit had spoken before daylight through my dearest Robert this morning." Della reached up to kiss Robert. "Remember those poetic words you didn't understand?"

"The Lord certainly has worked wonders Nathan, Doren." Robert smiled. "This has been a Christmas none of us will ever forget."

The grandparents and parents stopped speaking when they heard Peter clear his throat. "Is anyone going to introduce the rest of the grandchildren to our grandparents?"

"I certainly count ten, just as Abby told us you had Della." Nathan winked playfully at Robert. "I guess I mistook the sparks between you two back then."

"Your daughter has always had my love and devotion sir." Robert smiled before asking the kids to line up in order of their age. "Starting with our oldest, this is Peter, graduated last year and helps me at odd jobs in town and farming. Clara is in the 12th grade, and is graduating with honors due to her outstanding grades. James is in the 11th, Mary, the 10th and Frank the 9th, The twins, Robbie and Bobbie are both in the 8th grade, Jacob, 7th, and Sarah, the 6th grades, and our youngest you know. Abby is in Kindergarten "

"Well children, it might take some time to learn all your names but believe me when I say, you all already hold a special place in your grandparent's hearts." Doren wiped her tears away. "The fact that you belong to our daughter and our understanding loving son-in-law."

"Doren and I were hoping you would permit us to sale our home in California and purchase a small place somewhere close to our family." Nathan felt better about the prospect of being closer to their daughter and her family so they could be a part of their lives. "What do you say? Please, just be honest about how you feel."

"Daddy, you must know I never stopped needing my mama and daddy and having you come here to tell me you still love me means the world to me." Della felt for her husband's hand. "Robert is my husband and his feelings mean the most to me. So, even though the thoughts of you both being near us fills me with comfort, I must abide by Robert's decision."

"I can understand your devotion lies with the man you have always loved sweetheart, so Robert, it looks like our staying or going rest on your shoulders." Nathan gave the gentle man an understanding nod. "I won't hold what you say against you son. I know way too clearly how I treated you so just say what needs to be said and Doren and I will honor your wishes."

"You have asked to buy a place somewhere near us, is that correct?" Robert looked his father-in-law straight into his eyes and waited for him to acknowledge his words. "You said this would be my decision to make so I have made it. I will not permit you and Doren to buy a place anywhere near me and my family." Everyone turned to stare at the usually loving and thoughtful man and were all speechless until Robert continued. "The reason for my statement is this, why would I want my beautiful mother Doren and Father Nathan to live at any distance from us when they can live right here in our big family farmhouse."

There was a burst of relief laughter from the children as Della took around her caring husband. "Robert, you must be thinking about your parent's empty room, aren't you?"

Robert finally laughed and grabbed around Nathan before hugging Doren. "My parents have moved up to heaven and that extra large room has been setting vacant far too long! "

"Robert, what can I say?" Nathan had been taken back at first with his refusal only to learn this wonderful man his daughter had married was wanting them to move in with them.

"You can say yes, Nathan. Your daughter needs you near her! Your grandchildren need to know their other two grandparents and I need an extra hand on the farm." Robert teased. "Nathan, Doren, you are family and we need to be together, to share that love you both have found missing."

"With all our heart, we want to move in and be a big part of your family." Nathan couldn't control his tearful smile. "I insist on helping you son, even though I know you were joking. I did notice the tin roof needs a new coat of paint and that fine old barn, that looks like my daddy's, needs some tender attention."

"I realize things need fixing up Nathan, but money is short on the mountain." Robert noticed his father-in-law pull out his wallet.

"Correction son, money was short, the grandparents are selling their large estate, and now that we are a part of your family we need to fix up this beautiful old place, so we can preserve it for generations to come."

"Now I must correct you Nathan, you and Doren are a part of your own family, since my family has made you both a part of it." Robert smiled and gave the once untouchable man a big hug. "We will also except any help you wish to offer because I too wish to maintain this two-hundred-year-old Asbury Farm for our children, the grandchildren of your happiest years."

"Daddy, Robert is right. You will find life on this mountain is blessed with happiness and tight family bonds that will never outgrow the love we all feel for one another." Della noticed her boys holding their growling stomachs and laughed softly. "Being a devoted wife and mother to a house filled with growing children and one terrific husband, I have learned when my little flock need to eat." Her eyes found her six sons who gave their mother an embarrassed smile. "Mama and girls, shall we march to the kitchen and start preparing a big Christmas breakfast?"

"What can us men folk and boys do sweetheart while we are waiting?" Nathan noticed Robert pulling on a heavy coat as the boys started for the stairs to prepare for the outdoors. "I guess it's farm duties then."

"None of that is needed Asbury's and Daniels', so you can gather back in the den for last minute instructions before I fly off with Nickolas's guest!" Barnabas stepped from the kitchen door eating a sausage biscuit. As everyone stared at the unusually dressed stranger, except for Abby and the Daniels, who met him the previous night, the head elf gave the five-year-old a high-five. "Nice job taking directions Sprout!" hearing Jacob gasp at this fellow with pointed ears and dressed in unusual green pants and coat, trimmed with a red collar, a festive sash tied around his thin waist and a wide red cuff on the bottom of his pants, Barnabas knew Abby's cut-up brother was wondering why this person of magic was calling his little sister the same nickname that suddenly filled his head earlier. The elf gave the confuse young boy a playful wink before smiling down at the cute five-year-old. "Starting that old story exactly at 8:00 sharp gave everyone time to get over the shock of Nat and Doren's popping in dressed for their part. Brilliant!" he finished the biscuit as Della looked on, wondering where that food had come from. Reading the mother of ten's mind, Barnabas smiled.

"Della, you grew into such a beautiful lady and it was truly a blessing that your last child, sweet adorable Abby, looks exactly like you did at five." The handsome elf gave Abby's head a pat. "The sausage biscuit, you have been wondering about is only a small part of the large breakfast waiting in the kitchen for your hungry family. There is no need for you to worry where it came from so just consider it a gift from Santa. While it is being kept warm for you, there are a few things we must tie up before we depart for the North Pole."

Jacob suddenly realized what was standing in their den. "I get it now, you are one of Santa's elves, aren't you?"

"Look pal, if my pointed ears and turned up shoes had not alerted you as to what I was, pray tell why are you just now discovering that I, Barnabas, am a very high-ranking elf from the North Pole?" The head elf could only shake his head.

Blushing from the laughter around him and the obvious, pointed out by the elf named Barnabas, Jacob gave him a shaky grin, not wishing to have something else in his stocking replaced with coal, he respectfully said "You did mention a gift from Santa then announced you would be returning to the North Pole. Come to think of it, earlier you said you would be flying off." Jacob suddenly wondered if a sleigh was up on their roof attached with flying reindeer. "Are there?"

"Reindeer on your roof? Sorry to disappoint you kid, but only the big cheese lands on the roof, except for my stop last night. I parked the sleigh in the front yard, magically placed your grandparents in the small room next to this one and waited in the kitchen for the proper time to appear."

"Barnabas, are you taking our little girl up to visit Nickolas so he can give her the gift he promised?" Robert felt strange over letting their precious child go with this elf.

"Oh, you won't have to worry about your daughter traveling to the North Pole with me Robert." Barnabas gave the worried father a reassuring smile. "Elves are God's angels, that is why we are immortal and can remain with our immortal Father Christmas and his adoring wife Martha. Besides, you and Della will be going along with us, a request from the Kringle's." The elf snapped his finger, remembering Martha's instructions for him. "Speaking of Mother Christmas, she has sent Della a very special gift, meant for the whole family to enjoy. It lays invisible under the tree but I have the card she sent on me." Barnabas presented a red and green envelope from thin air. "I was to deliver the card but Santa delivered his wife's gift to you last night."

Della opened the very festive Christmas card and gave her little girl a bright smile while the other children asked her what it said. "It appears, Martha Kringle enjoyed watching your baby sister drink down every drop of her secret double-chocolate hot chocolate with extra fluffy-creamy "

"Marshmallows!" Abby called out proudly and a big box appeared under the Christmas tree. "Hurry mama, open mama Martha's gift!"

After Robert lifted the heavy box up and opened it, the family all cheered at the sight of cans of hot chocolate mix and tons of marshmallows. A note was attached on the top. "Christmas Greetings Della. I have everything here you need to keep making my delicious recipe for Hot Chocolate throughout the cold months on your mountain. All you need is some of old Bessie's great milk, Abby told me about! Then sit back in your easy chair and enjoy a little taste of Kringle Village. Love. Martha Kringle."

"Now that's done, it is time for Robert and Della to give their children the presents they have for them." Barnabas knowing what they were getting thought what a neat thing to have at the Pole, on fun day. "If either of you kids wish to exchange your parent's gift for one of my own created gifts, do not hesitate to ask!" Barnabas gave Robert a playful wink. "Your gift for carpentry is outstanding and even among our many talented elves in the toy factory, not a single one could outshine your remarkable gifts."

"Why, thank you Barnabas, that is a very moving approval for my humble abilities." Robert gratefully shared his handsome smile for the elf. "I must admit, I cannot whip one up as quickly as your talented group of toymakers and since I rather doubt any of my children will part from their own personalized gift, I would be happy to build one for you come next Christmas Barnabas."

A wide smile spread across the elf's cheerful face. "I would be most grateful to receive such a fine work of art."

"Daddy, could we see what has Barnabas so excited?" Peter had always spoken for his siblings and could tell all of them were as anxious as he was to see their gifts even Santa's elf wanted. "Now I know why you locked me out of your work shed and made me do my sawing under the grape arbor." Peter had guessed his daddy was making the kids something again for Christmas. Last Christmas their father had made them a large see-saw and a long wooden stand holding ten adult size swings, one for each child. No amount of use could wear out the carpenter's great skills.

"Peter, go to the large closet next to the old piano and let the family look inside. Your favorite color will tell you which belongs to who." Robert watched as the excited Asbury children found their sleds and joyfully chatting, pulled out their own sled. "Now, you are all ready for snow kids."

"Gee daddy, I almost hate the thoughts of sliding my brand-new sled down that dirty old snow bank." Mary was admiring the perfect pink sled when her father and mother called their attention at the doublewide window in the den, it's drapes still drawn close.

"Children, your daddy and I wanted to save this part until you opened the closet to find this year's special gift from us." Della smiled up at her devoted husband. "Although we won't be here to witness your first run down Antler Ridge due to escorting your baby sister to the North Pole, we both know God's special surprise will delight each one of our beautiful children." Della smiled up at her mate. "Daddy, will you do the honors and show the kids their own winter wonderland."

Robert happily acknowledged his wife's request and opened back the curtains to reveal a snow-covered ground as a gentle snow drifted down quietly, one snowflake upon another.

"Ah, the sounds of home!" Barnabas could actually hear each individual snowflake sing praises as it softly landed on the other carolers and it reminded him of the North Pole, where the sound of snow carolers never ran out. "The bells now ring out 10:00 and soon we must return to Kringle Village for Father and Mother Christmas awaits their dinner guest. The breakfast has been made ready, the farm animals have been fed, Bessie has been milked and the Holy Creator has provided the Christmas snow for you children's pleasure. The time for getting acquainted has come, grandparents to grandchildren!" Barnabas took Abby's hand. "God's Holy angels watch over your sledding to keep you from harm and to help the grandparents relax and enjoy watching the fun." He turned to Robert and Della, waved his hand over them and they found themselves in a set of Kringle Village wear as did their small daughter. "Now, we are set to fly off to the North Pole! Destination: Kringle Village! Merry Christmas Asbury Household!"

With a blink of his eye and a nod of his head, the small group were seated in a shiny red sled. With a click of his tongue and a flick of his finger, away the reindeer flew, not a moment to linger!

CHAPTER 27

When Barnabas arrived with the Kringle's special guest, the entire village was waiting, circling the village square, now dressed in their finest Christmas attire and singing the carols of Christmas. The live snowmen had stopped their dancing to get their first glimpse of the precious child they had been expecting. When Abby stepped from the big barn, jeers rang out from the happy elves and the snowmen started performing for the little girl they loved. Taking her parent's hands, Abby led the way around the busy town square, smiling at all the familiar faces as they blew colorful magic bubbles over their head before drifting down as giant suckers. Abby let go of her parents so she could catch a big red sucker with a yummy looking snowflake in the middle.

"Mama, you and daddy catch a lollipop, they taste super good! Mine taste like frosted Cinnamon and creamy vanilla marshmallow! Mumm, yummy!"

With so many lollipops drifting passed them, Robert and Della finally could not resist catching one and hoped they wouldn't ruin their appetite. Once again, Barnabas walked beside them, looking out at his entertaining friends.

"My dear Miss Della, have no fear eating that dream sickle, for anything made in Kringle Village has no measure or calories, so once eaten, the imaginary lollipop will amount to eating nothing."

"Then, are you saying, our dinner with the Kringle's will be imaginary food, once eaten we will still be hungry?" Della gazed down at the empty stick before it simply vanished. She forced a smile down at her watchful daughter. "Well Abby, I must say, we are definitely not in Kentucky anymore."

"Miss Della, you will get use to being in our enchanting village, where magic abounds and the wonders of childhood come to life." Barnabas gave his lopsided smile. "Take your cute kid there, overjoyed to be back where reality is dancing snowmen, colorful bubbles that become tasty lollipops, where elves live happily creating toys that come to life in this land of Childhood dreams. The place where every snowflake that falls, sing praises to their Creator until they land, to be a part of the frosty wonderland chorus on the snow-covered ground." The head elf grew respectful as he continued. "It is the place that our Lord put our leader, Father Christmas and his beautiful bride Martha, of 2,000-years. Like heaven, this place is Eternal and up until your angelic child was allowed entrance into it's realm, no human has ever set foot upon this magical dominion."

"Then, except my apology for being skeptical over this remarkable place. "Della could tell by Barnabas's great smile that he wasn't the lease bit upset. "I can see why our little Abby fell in love with your magical home. I guess I need to become like a little child if I am truly to believe in everything you have told me and can witness with my own eyes."

"I know how my wife feels Barnabas, for I too have felt somewhat out of place here." Robert looped his arm around Della's shoulders. "I guess our childhood has become a fond memory now that we have children of our own and must act like adults. Perhaps, you could help us believe again, like we did when we were Abby's age."

"That would be for Father Christmas to perform." Barnabas motioned them forward, toward the tallest house in the village. "Nickolas Kristopher Kringle is the one who can turn doubt into believing! Sorrow into joy! Frowns into laughter! Despair into hope!" when the elf reached the Kringle's front door, he gave Abby a wink. "And I must not leave out Father Christmas's special gift. Being human, like yourself, Nickolas would never have fake food served to his guest, especially when he would not eat make-believe food himself." Barnabas laughed along with the Asbury's. "You will find Martha is an expert cook and I guarantee you will not be disappointed." He opened the door and waved them inside. "We will find the Kringle's waiting in their warm den." Barnabas led them to the room as Abby ran ahead, knowing her way to her very special friends.

Seeing Nickolas and Martha seated by the fireplace, Abby ran over happily calling their names. "Daddy Nickolas! Mama Martha! We are finally here!" she ran over in Nickolas's outstretched arms.

"Our precious little Abby, it is truly a joy to see you at last!" Nickolas gave her a fatherly kiss. "I must admit, I found it hard to allow my excited elves to welcome your arrival after they begged me, since I wished to be the first to welcome you and your parents. You did not leave them in the village square with my elves did you child?"

"Oh no Nickolas, they were just too slow walking in here." Abby giggled when her friends laughed. "I know it hasn't been very long since we said goodbye in California Nickolas, but it seemed like forever to me."

"And to me as well, sweet girl." Nickolas smiled up at Abby's parents when they finally were escorted in by Barnabas. "I trust my head elf was describing our fair land to the adult in you both." He made them feel relaxed when he smiled and offered them a chair in front of the warm fireplace. "Warm yourself from the North Pole cold. I had no doubt Abby would fit right in to Kringle Village, the land of childlike dreams and wonder. Being adults when we arrived never wavered our magical beliefs since we had been playing the Giver of Gifts for many years while living and felt the enchanted powers that radiated from ever child we gave gifts to. It might take sometime before you grow into the wonderland belief that radiates from heaven and spills an oracle of divine occurrences between miracles and magic, occurring simultaneous at the same time."

Della and Robert had been staring in wonder at the young couple seated in matching plush green velvet reclining chairs and finally understood their little girl's comparisons between her very favorite friend Nickolas to that of the jolly-white hair Santa that brought joy to every good little girl and boy.

"I can tell Della and Robert have been left speechless Nickolas darling, taking in two very different people than the ones they had been expecting to see." Martha stood to collect the loving child who had hopped from Nickolas's lap to give her a big hug. "Abby, do you suppose your mama and daddy might feel better if they knew why Nickolas and I remain so youthful at what apparently must be a very old age?"

"I certainly do mama Martha." Abby gave the radiant woman a big smile before turning toward her embarrassed parents. "Mama, daddy, you must know Nickolas and Martha are living in Eternity now, the same way all good souls will look when they go to join the Lord in heaven." Abby walked over beside her father. "Daddy, it is the way grandpa Henry and grandma Grace look right now in heaven. No heavenly soul will exceed over 33-years-old, the same age as Jesus was when he came back to heaven."

"My precious Abby, heaven holds many happy things, Christ Jesus being at the top, with the Father. The Spirit of God works below within us." Robert's attention fell on the beautiful couple. "I'm not sure how it could happen, that this magic place resembles heaven, but none the less, the portals of Paradise have opened up and kissed this part of earth, much like it did Eden, at the dawn of time."

"This truth that has been revealed to you, my brother, has come from the very portals to which you speak of." Nickolas joined Abby next to her parents and he smiled down at his little friend when he felt her take his hand. "Those many years ago when Martha and I made the hearts of needy children happy by giving them simple little toys in secret, we grew concern as to who would take over making the toys after we were gone. We could visualize each small child we had grown to love, step out of the front door only to find the little plant they had left out for their gift set empty and bare. The sadness and tears on each little face took hold on our hearts, so each of us wrote our own gift wish, for something we wanted more than anything else. Martha suggested that we placed them under her big plant and wait for morning before comparing the notes." Nickolas's eyes met Martha's "The following morning, both notes were gone. They had simply disappeared."

"You didn't suspect each other? Thinking either he or she might have got up early to slip them out from under the plant and see what their mate wanted, then try to get it for them?" Della could not see anyone in their small town, stooping to stealing something that they obviously did not know anything about?

"Neither of us found them missing until I returned with the wonderful news about our Messiah being born and that I had seen him with my own eyes." Nickolas noticed Abby's parents grew pale over the powerful revelation he had just freely given.

"You where in Bethlehem then, just like Abby dreamed you were!" Robert finally spoke up. "Tell us Nickolas, how did it feel to be one of the first to see the face of God?"

"Dear friend, it is a night I shall never forget even though it has been over 2,000 years." Nickolas felt the usual tears that came when he spoke about the holy night Jesus was born. "I was one of the shepherds, tending the sheep on the hillside outside of the city. First, we noticed the magnificent star, shining its long rays down upon the stable in Bethlehem. Then the Angel appeared, frightening every shepherd among us until he spoke, then the sky lit up with a heavenly chorus of angels, praising God with song." Nickolas knew

Robert and Della were hanging on each word that he spoke concerning the birth of Jesus. "We lined up to see Jesus and when I stepped up, I heard Him say my name. It was obvious from my brother shepherd's actions they had not heard the Lord speaking. His words were intended for my ears only and that is when Jesus told me that he had Martha and my notes, then he held out his little hand and I saw our folded notes. As I knelled at the infant Jesus's manger, Abby could see the thing I could not. For a brief moment I was transformed into Santa Claus. Then he asked me to bring Martha there to see Him and that is when he said he would reveal His answer concerning the notes." Nickolas helped Della up. "My dear ones, there are many other glorious things Martha and I witnessed when our Savior lived, but time does no permit our sharing them this day. The table is set and if my special guest is as hungry as I am, then I say it is time to share a Christmas dinner."

"I don't know about everyone else Daddy Nickolas, but I am starving!" Abby rubbed her empty stomach. "We missed breakfast because of all the excitement of finding presents from you under our good smelling tree! Then Grandpa and Grandma showed up and everyone felt warm and fuzzy, sort of like my bedroom slippers."

The four adults laughed as Martha led the way to the large dining room where a big Christmas feast was laid out. The happy group enjoyed their meal and true to Barnabas's words, the Kringle's enjoy good food as much as the Asbury family. Friendly elves kept them served with warm coffee and a cream-covered chocolate drink for Abby, topped with a peppermint stick. The dessert was a triple-layer cake, with each layer being a different flavor that blended well with each other. The bottom layer was rich chocolate, the middle layer was strawberry, and the top layer was coconut. The thick frosting danced around with swirls of chocolate and coconut, and luscious strawberries crowned the top.

Abby stared down at the huge piece placed in front of her, and with bright eyes smiling declared "This looks too pretty to eat, but like mama always says, eat everything on you plate Abby. So, I will gladly eat this yummy cake!" she dug in, icing painting her nose with swirling colors.

Nickolas chuckled as he reached over to clean Abby's face. "Abby, I am aware that Barnabas filled you in about Morgan Matthews refreshing realization of learning Santa Claus is real and not the myth he announced to his little sister as well as the entire school." Father Christmas enjoyed this sweet child's giggles. "I thought you might like to hear about your little school mate Cindy and how she responded to your request gifts to her."

"Thank you, Nickolas! I'm bubbling over with happiness for Cindy! I did ask you to give her the present you wanted to give me, didn't I? What did my friend get that would have been mine?"

"Your precious little friend fell asleep on Christmas Eve, feeling very sad and left out as usual. That is, until she was awaken by prancing and pawing on her roof, directly over her head." Nickolas gave Abby a wink when she sat up smiling.

"Santa woke Cindy up on purpose, didn't you, jolly ole St. Nickolas?" Abby excitedly scooped another bite of Martha's yummy cake into her open mouth, chewing it quickly. "Then what happened?"

"When little Cindy slipped down her stairs, now lit with Christmas lights, she instantly noticed their shabby tree had become a big-full Christmas tree, covered in lights and overflowing with presents for her and her parents. Her big brown eyes looked around the room for me until I became visible for her inside her stone fireplace. Cindy's scared face melted into an angelic smile as she thanked me." Nickolas recalled what happened next. "Cindy's parents had heard the reindeer and discovered what their little girl had come down to see. With tearful eyes, they thanked me as well. Under their revived tree they would find new clothes for the parents and Cindy, a large box of apples, soap and towels. Cindy would find the special gift we spoke of, her very first doll, the Christmas doll named Holly." Nickolas watched Abby to see her reaction for giving her friend the doll she had dreamed about and only saw a sweet giving heart smiling back. "Before I left, I told them they now own one very large milk cow so Cindy can have all the milk she needs. Then I waved my hand over them and left them standing in their new Kringle Village woolen coats, hats, boots, scarves and gloves, looking at their milk cow standing in their new barn."

Abby jumped up to give her Daddy Nickolas a very loving thank you, Santa, hug. "Santa gave Cindy every thing she needed! You remembered everything!"

"That is because the loving child that asked Santa to help her, made it possible for me to know what to take this poor child and her family."

CHAPTER 28

Kringle's Den

"Alright Abby, it's time to exchange our gifts to each other." Nickolas placed a large, wrapped package in front of the sweet little girl he and Martha had grown to love. "It is something you can always remember us by Abby, unlike all the other Children who grow out of believing.

Abby puckered up, large tears filling her big blue eyes. "Please Daddy Nickolas, tell me this is not goodbye. I will never forget you Nickolas." Her sad eyes turned to Martha. "I can never forget you Mama Martha! I don't want to leave if I cannot come back!" The tears turned to weeping. "I love you both! A person can never forget someone they love." Her little hand wiped at her tears. "You love me too, don't you Daddy Nickolas?" she bit her quivering lip. "Mama Martha, don't you love me?"

"Oh Abby, we love you more than we have any child we have ever known, and that is a lot." Now Martha was fighting tears. "We live in two different worlds sweet girl and the Lord allowed us this one Christmas to have you with us. It won't be easy for us to say goodbye either but darling, you have got a wonderful big family to love you." Her eyes fell on Abby's parents, now sharing the sad tears with their precious little girl. "Abby, you have made this Christmas the happiest one we have ever had. Nickolas and I finally knew how it felt to have our own little girl, if just for a short time."

"Abby, Martha is right. Not only did you save Christmas for me, you helped filled that empty place inside my heart that never knew the love of having our own special child." Nickolas walked over and lifted Abby up in his arms. "Abby, if I could see you again it would make my heart sing and there is no shortage of love here in Kringle Village for you." He tearfully kissed her forehead. "But it is not up to me or Martha. If it were, you would be a frequent guest at the North Pole, but we must follow the Lord's wishes Abby."

"Surely Jesus understands how much we love each other Daddy Nickolas." Abby sniffed. "If I were older I might understand you thinking I would forget you like every adult who loses their belief in Santa Claus, but not me! I will 'never' forget you, no matter how old I get! A daughter does not forget their parents! I am your daughter, same as I am to my mama and daddy! They know how much I love them and they would never keep me from loving you, the same way!"

"Excuse me Nickolas, but Abby is right about having enough love for two sets of parents." Robert had seen the raw emotions on this special couple and he could almost feel their deep love for his little girl. "Nickolas, Martha, the fact is I too believe as my precious daughter does, that our faithful-loving Lord will not strip away this deep affection the three of you have for one another. From what I hear, it was an act of Jesus that brought you all together, so I cannot believe the God that made you feel so much for each other would deliberately keep you a part now that his mission has been fulfilled."

"My good friend Robert, we cannot dispute the Almighty's will, even matters of the heart. But, if there were a slim chance that Martha and I were blessed to have Abby remain a daughter of our heart, then I assure you, we would welcome her presence as often as it were possible." Nickolas could tell by Abby's sweet smile that she understood her leaving was as hard on them as it was on her. "Abby, you do know how much you are loved by me and Martha, do you not?"

"I know daddy Nickolas, because I can see it in your eyes and feel it in my heart." Abby rapped her tiny arms around his neck and whispered in his ear. "I will love you and Martha forever!"

Della had been observing her little girl's reactions and she said a silent prayer that the Lord would find a way to keep the love burning inside their beautiful hearts for one another alive. She heard the unusual clock standing in the entrance hallway chime out: North Pole time: Christmas. Kentucky time: 2:00p.m. Della knew they had nine more children waiting at home with her parents, who had just arrived before she took off with Robert and Abby to the North Pole. "Abby, sweetheart, wouldn't you like to see Martha and Nickolas open the present you made for them?"

"That sounds wonderful mama." Abby commented softly. "I think we need something meaningful to distract from our leaving." She noticed her wrapped present under their tree and gave Nickolas a sweet kiss on the cheek before sliding down to go get the present.

She waited for her dear friends to be seated then she gave them her best smile. "Like mama said, I made this gift, well most of it. Daddy sawed out the figures and animals, the inside of the stable, the rafters and the manger. I drew them off before he cut them out and I painted them after. The real falling snow was a gift from Simon. It won first place in our school and it even got high marks from my brother Jacob." Abby laughed along with the adults. "I wrote a card with it. With all the neat things you have here at Kringle Village, I hope it meets with the master toymaker's approval." Abby placed the box in Nickolas's hand and watched him open it up, Martha watching on closely.

"Abby, I must confess I knew you had made a snow globe for a school contest and I did barely it. The Lord told me what was in it and how you knew of me." Nickolas knew he must be honest with this sweet child that meant so much to him and his wife. "Jesus told me about the dream you had and how you saw me knelling at the manger." Nickolas reached for Abby's small hand. "Abby, when the Lord brings someone like you into His everlasting realm, it must be made clear to the recipient why He is allowing a living mortal into the portals of Heaven and why their coming concerns the one they come in to see. So, this is why I know these things that were made known unto me by the Lord." Nickolas gave her a big smile. "Martha and I stood far from you, invisible with the Lord, when you won 1st place "

Abby's reassuring smile helped Nickolas and Martha relax as he lifted off the lid to pull out the beautiful snow globe. "Oh Abby, you have gotten every detail right, down to the number of sheep that followed us from the hills." Nickolas held it over for Martha to check out, giving it a gentle shake. The snow started falling softly as Mrs. Kringle watched on with delight.

"Your Simon has done a heavenly mini-miracle inside your compassionate snow globe, sweet child." Spotting the note in the box, Martha reached in and handed it to her husband as she took the snow globe for safe keeping. "Read it allowed dear so we all can here our precious heart daughter's words."

"Daddy Nickolas, Mama Martha, now you can look inside this magical snow globe and remember those special moments with baby Jesus by seeing it happening on the other side, the moment I saw a shepherd become Santa Claus for the very first time. The amount of love I poured into this magical globe cannot be measured anymore than the amount of love you both felt when you looked into the face of our Savior on that very first Holy Night of Christmas. As a child, I just want to thank you both for making children happy all around the world and say, Abby Asbury loves you with all my heart! Just ask Jesus, He knows I never tell lies. A Blessed Noel to my very special parents. Abby."

"Oh Abby" Nickolas pulled the angelic child into his arms and hugged her as Martha gently rubbed her blonde hair. "Mama Martha and your daddy Nickolas will forever keep you in our heart. The most loving gift will find the center place on our mantle so it will be the first thing we see when we gather in to rest."

Martha got up to opened the door for Barnabas so he could lift up their large gift for Abby. Smiling cheerfully, the head elf settled it gently on the floor. "You might wish to open such a big delicate gift on the floor sweet child."

"Nickolas laid it out earlier for me Barnabas but sad words interrupted his giving it to me." Abby smiled, eyes wide with surprised delight at such a big package. "Wow, this big box is just for me?"

"That it is my charming daughter, made just for one Abby Asbury, to keep and cherish throughout her long-happy life." Nickolas helped her off his lap and got down on the floor with her, waving Martha and Abby's parents over. "Gather around parents and see what our precious girl has got."

With her father's help opening the sealed lid, Abby noticed the round-glass top and knew instantly she had a very large snow globe of her own. Being too heavy for such a small child to lift up, Nickolas gave her a hand pulling out the amazing heavenly snow globe. With childlike excitement, Abby noticed the Kringle's looking from their large picture window overlooking the village square. The large den looked exactly as it did where she sat. There was an actual fire blazing in the large fireplace and the little girl could swear she smelt the embers burning and heard the crackling of the flames. Just outside the window, Abby could see the funny snowmen playfully dancing then stopped, looked inside and waved, causing the little girl to giggle. She watched the elves coming from the big barns leading the reindeer and when they reached the corner, they would sweep out their hand toward the window and kept pacing around. The toy factory was alive with happy busy elves and the sounds and smells of the North Pole fill the air. Her globe had real snow falling and she could actually hear each snowflake singing praises as it fell.

"Can you hear the snowflakes singing mama?" Abby asked, her little face still focused on the place she had grown to love. "This is such a magical world! It's like living real life daydreams filled with unbelievable fantasy!" Abby's attention was drawn to the giant mirror that transformed Nickolas into Santa Claus. "Look mama, daddy." She pointed to the mirror with no reflections. "See that giant mirror? That is the magic mirror that Nickolas, Simon and I stepped through before I flew off in a sleigh to help grandpa and grandma Daniels." Abby's sad eyes glanced up at Nickolas, who had been enjoying her happy excitement and he realized what was on her sweet mind.

"Abby, you are wondering if you will see me inside that snow globe stepping through the magic mirror, are you not?"

"I know if you do daddy Nickolas, this time I won't be with you." A big tear ran down her cheeks. "Will I?"

"Abby, everything you have been seeing inside your very special memory snow globe was the things you did and saw when you came to visit us, right?" Nickolas gave her a reassuring smile. The reason you cannot see yourself inside the globe is because it is you that is actually inside there reliving everything in person. Look again outside the window then wave back at the snowmen when they wave at you and tell me what you see."

Abby waited for the snowmen to stop and wave at her, so she waved back and instantly saw her hand waving, in front of herself "I saw my hand! I was waving right inside the snow globe!"

"We all saw Abby's hand inside the globe!" Robert had gotten down to look closely and the instant Abby raised her hand, it went up inside the globe. "How the heck can my little girl be two places at the same time."

"In the outside world it would be impossible, but in heaven anything is possible if you just believe." Nickolas pointed to his and Martha's figures standing by the mantle, both looking directly at Abby. Martha reached out her hand toward her and Abby slowly reached out her hand and gasped when Martha took it and led her across the room and stopped at the mirror, then Abby and her

171

parents stared at the reflections inside the magic mirror. Standing next to Martha smiling out at those watching stood Abby.

Della whispered "Abby wave and see if your reflection waves back." The confused mother had noticed her daughter's big smile the moment the reflection showed up.

"It is me mama, but I will wave if you want me to." Abby gave herself a big wave and the mirror image waved with her. "Well, it's me alright!" she giggled. "That means, come Christmas Eve, Nickolas, Simon and I will be stepping through the magic mirror!" Abby gave a big smile up at Nickolas. "I can see now what you meant by these image's being my very best memory of how I spent Christmas Eve when I was five-years-old, at the North Pole with the real Santa Claus and his caring wife!" Abby reached up to touch his young face. "Daddy Nickolas, will these images only appear on Christmas eve and Christmas day, like today and just be still images that stand frozen through time the rest of the year?"

"Abby, the image's you see today reflects the things we did yesterday so this very special globe, that was not made by human hands, retains this one particular memory in time so it must be viewed at the Holy of Holy's miracle birth." Nickolas could read her questioning eyes. "My precious child, although I can make many remarkable gifts now that I am blessed with Christmas magic, I could never create such an amazing-real-life snow globe that permits you to actually become a part of what is going on inside the globe." Nickolas gazed down with so much love, Abby couldn't help but smile. "Darling child, you have been given a most treasured gift by our Lord Jesus Himself. It is His loving way of giving a gift that gives over and over again, to celebrate His birth that first Christmas morning."

"Your friend Nickolas is correct Abby." All four adults and young Abby turned at the sudden sound of a soft gentle voice behind them. There was no mistaking the one standing lend and tall, dressed in a white robe that glowed even brighter from the light that radiated around the Son of God. Jesus spread out his arms, palms down, revealing the loving sacrifice He had made for all mankind on that cross. The gapping holes in his hands marked the place where the large Roman spike nails pierced through, so knowing the incredible love their Savior had for them, both the Asbury's and the Kringle's dropped to their knees, out of respect for the King of Kings.

Being a child and seeing the one who had been with her throughout her witnessing, Abby stepped over to where he stood, smiled up into his glorious eyes, then walked into his outstretched arms. Both Jesus and Abby closed their eyes as the love radiated from one to the other. His arms enfolded around her as Jesus gently lifted the small child into his arms. "Abby, I created your snow globe as a special gift to be given by Nickolas and Martha, who I know love you as their own. While they lived on earth, their hearts longed for a child of their own, but none ever game for them. We knew how much they wanted children and as each prayed separately, cried out to us, if they could not have a lot of children then please just permit them to have one baby. Either girl or boy, that never mattered, their hearts just ached for a baby to love. Both Holy Father and Holy spirit agreed with me, we felt their pain but it was always meant for this loving couple to one day find another way of having children and unlike the birth parents of a few children, Nickolas and Martha would be magical parents of many children, as much as the sand grains in the oceans and seas."

"Jesus, if I was only one of these little sand grains lying on the ocean floor, why did Mama Martha and Daddy Nickolas love me like I was their daughter?" Abby asked sadly. "Jesus, I know it wasn't make believe. I could see how sad they were when Nickolas mentioned having to tell me goodbye and that we lived in two separate worlds!" Abby couldn't control the quiver in her voice when big tear drops started falling. "Jesus, I love daddy Nickolas and mama Martha, just like I love my dear mama and daddy. When I'm on the Appalachia Mountain, I am with my loving mama and daddy! When I'm at Kringle Village, I am the loving daughter of Daddy Nickolas and Mama Martha. I just love them all Jesus! Please, don't take me away from Nickolas and Martha. I heard them say, they had known many children over their years at the North Pole and when they started making toys in Bethlehem, but for the first time they knew how it felt to have their own little girl," Abby choked up as she finished "If only for a little while."

"Abby, most prayer request come to us asking for something they want or need desperately and they don't get the answer they are seeking from us." Jesus gently rubbed his fingers through her soft hair. "You are asking for a difficult thing, yet even with your young age, you wisely have shown me how strong your faith is by asking me to permit yourself as a daughter to both the Asbury's, who rightfully had you, and the Kringle's, whose non-stop prayers for a child of their own while they yet lived among the earthly living, had great faith also, that never wavered from that need inside their caring hearts. I have full authority as your Savior to decide the fate of this parent-daughter relationship continuing."

The Lord's attention fell on the four kneeling. "Please, rise to your feet and come forward." Jesus waited for the Asbury's and Kringle's to move up close. "As my witnesses, you have heard the child's plea, to remain a faithful daughter to both Robert and Della, as well as Nickolas and Martha. What do you say about the matter, Robert? You are Abby's birth father and have shown me you are both a devoted husband and a loving and caring father to all your children. You are aware I know all, so be truthful in your words and speak those things that concern your heart."

"As Abby's daddy, she will always be my precious baby girl and I know I can speak for myself and my beloved Della over this unusual situation between our little girl and these two-amazing people." Robert felt Della squeeze his hand and knowing her well, could tell her heart was in the same place. The exchanged between the loving couple did not go unnoticed by their Lord. "Lord, we witnessed the deep love shared between our little girl and the Kringle's and believe me when I say, no one knows more about our precious Abby's heart than her beautiful mother and I and we both can say, without one doubt, the mother and father relationship the Kringle's feel for Abby is just as real as our own."

"Della, do you agree with your husband?" Jesus asked softly.

"Lord, I agree with all my heart, especially when I witnessed their deep affection for one another." Della fault her own tears. "At first, it felt strange that two complete strangers could love my little girl the same way I do, her own mother. But after listening to their words and seeing their emotional tears, it was as if somehow our souls were connected all because of Abby. Lord Jesus, there are fake tears, even selfish tears, but the tears we witnessed came straight from their hearts. Sad, forever tears, with no hope of seeing one another again. If you are asking our permission to share Abby's love with Martha and Nickolas, I can only say, love is something that needs no permission to give. Love comes from you Lord, so if its pure, like our Abby and the Kringle's, then it can only be right and needs to last for all Eternity."

"Well said, Della, Robert." Jesus turned to the Kringle's. "You have felt a close bond to Abby every since you met her, we have known this might happen once you actually had her in your presence. This great love you feel for this one single child is far different than the love you have shared with all the children you have served since you began handing out your toys to them. Can you explain why this little girl felt like a daughter instead of just another precious little lamb of mine?"

"Jesus, the moment Abby stepped inside the den she immediately entered my heart and I knew the love I felt for her was something special." Martha looked into Abby's big blue eyes and could see pure love looking back. "Lord, I cannot explain why I felt the motherly bond with Abby, but none-the-less it existed and my heart ached, knowing our time together would be brief. I remember hoping the same bond did not find its way inside that sweet child's heart so at the time of our parting she would not be heartbroken." Martha's tears reflected those in Abby's eyes. "Jesus, this dear child was not spared the dreadful pain of our certain separation and effected the three of us in a way that has never been felt before, even when Nickolas and my hopes were crushed after learning we would never have a child of our own."

"Jesus, my brother, my Savior, Martha has described everything that I felt when I heard Abby's sweet voice call out to us." Nickolas had wrapped his arm around his devoted wife who had chosen an Eternity with him, helping make glad the hearts of children instead of enjoying the wonders of heaven. "My heart kept singing, this small child could have been ours and to hear her call me daddy, lifts up my soul with a completeness of something which was always missing in our joyful-busy life. Like Martha, I too dreaded the moment we had to say goodbye to our little girl. Martha nor I discussed our deep feelings for Abby but there was really no need, for this wonderful woman I married so many anniversaries ago can feel what I feel, as though our minds now think as one."

"I can see why each one of you hold a deep affection for Abby. She is both loving and caring. Although her years are young, it is plain to see the great wisdom in one so small." Jesus turned to look at the little girl he held in his loving arms. "I am sure you have wondered why the Lord Most High would choose such a small child to be His smallest witness, but I believe Abby can tell you and how she learned to speak far better than many adults around her, who listen in wonder. It is alright to tell the people you love Abby. I will replace all your memory of your time in heaven and why you had to return the first time. Once heard, they will love you all the more."

"Alright Jesus, I will share with my parents why I am filled with so much Christ-like knowledge." Abby waited for Jesus to lower her to the floor, then she stepped over and smiled down at each loving face. "Perhaps you have heard it told that in heaven little souls are made and infants to very young children remember what heaven looked like before they left, to be given to their mama and daddy. My little soul was created over 2,000-years-ago and I was placed inside a beautiful mother womb the instant my daddy sewed my seed. My mother became very sick soon after and got a high fever, and never knowing I was there, she lost me and I was taken back up to heaven. When I arrived back, I searched for Jesus but I could not find Him. Then I remembered what Jesus had told me before I went down to be with my parents. He told me we would be conceived at the same time then be born on the exact night." Abby noticed all four parents were crying. "I think the Holy Family had this miraculous plan in motion and hadn't seen my mama getting caught out in the cold rain while daddy was away watching sheep. The couple down on earth had really wanted a baby but they never knew one had been sent, if only for a little while." Abby watched Martha clutch her chest, the reality of what Abby had told them. "After Jesus was born, Simon spirited me back down to earth to witness for myself the tiny Holy child and that is when I saw my daddy for the first-time. Then Simon took me to see my mother before we went back to Heaven. I watched her looking down at a ragdoll she had just made that looked exactly like me and I listened sadly to her sorrowful words as she said 'I made you to look like I picture my own little girl so I will name you Abbrey. It was sad to leave my mama and daddy, but I was never born so I had to go back." Abby noticed all 4 parents were crying and she tried hard not to. "In heaven, the Lord allows lost babies to grow into childhood like I did, and stopped at five. Being in heaven for over 2,000-years never felt that long, for I was with Jesus and He was teaching the children many beautiful things." Abby turned to give Jesus a big smile. "One day Jesus took me for a long walk in the garden of pink roses. We listened to the roses sing as we walked, then Jesus told me I would be sent back down to earth to become the 10th child of a very loving mother and father. I asked Jesus if that loving mother would lose me like my first mother did, and be unhappy like she was? That's when our beautiful Savior told me I would be born to Della and Robert Asbury and grow up in a large happy loving family with two wonderful parents." Abby got down to kiss them then turned to Martha and Nickolas. "Jesus also told me about you both and how you had shared toys with good children all over the earth. He said your Giver of Gifts name, known by children everywhere, was Santa Claus. He told me when I grow up to the age you are in heaven, past secrets will come to light and you will find love in that beautiful heart of yours for that man and his beautiful wife. And, Jesus was right, I did love you the moment I saw you. I guess my dream about being at Bethlehem to witness baby Jesus and see you daddy Nickolas, was just a beautiful memory that came back to life, same as my snow globe."

"I can tell by your tears Nickolas, Martha, you now know why this immediate father and mother connection you felt that ingulfed your complete being, was so powerful." Jesus had moved over next to Abby and lifted up one parent at a time. "Abby feels like your daughter because she is the little daughter you conceived over 2,000-years-ago then lost her over your sudden illness, with no knowledge of her existence." Jesus looked on at their overwhelming emotional realization over what happened without their knowledge.

"Jesus, why did not the physician tell us Martha had a miscarriage?" Nickolas could not take his eyes off the little girl they almost had and wanted so desperately. "Was she just too soon to show? Was Abby too small to see?"

"And, what brought on the sudden fever Lord that caused me to lose my baby girl?" Martha could not control her tears. "Was it your plan that we not have a child so we could become this Giver of Gifts to all children?"

"I could never take back the beautiful soul once given Martha." Jesus remained gentle and compassionate. "We had heard your pleas for a baby many a time. Both you and Nickolas. "We did have you picked to be our Eternal Giver of Gifts from the beginning. After watching the incredible love, you both possessed for making children happy, the Father and I knew we had found our choice a perfect fit to be Kris Kringle, Santa Claus. Then your pleas for a child increased so we felt compelled to give you one and start Our search for a new Santa Claus. The fever was not sent on you by your heaven Creator, it was an unfortunate illness that spread throughout Bethlehem and you contacted it through the rain."

"So, if we had our beautiful Abby, then we would not have been chosen as the Giver of Gifts?" Nickolas pondered what they would have given up to have the angelic little girl for their own. Then his attention fell on the Asbury's. "And, if we did have Abby, then Della and Robert would have never been blessed to have this incredible child who touches everyone she meets with pure love. Della's parents would still be living in their darkness with no hope for a renewed Christmas Spirit." His eyes fell on the snow globe Abby had made him and tears filled his eyes. "And, I would not have this special gift from the little girl that stole all our hearts. Things did have a way of working out for everyone. All the children who have believed in us Lord and have felt the joys of a childlike Christmas and know the real meaning of why we celebrate it every year on your birthday. For Della and Robert, who have shared both their love to us as well as their gift to willingly share their precious child with us. For me and Martha, to continued our joy of making glad the hearts of children while being able to know our beautiful little girl and share her love with her other parents. For our Abby, the one who helped put Christmas back inside my heart and fill that empty place inside my soul where she once lived briefly but has return in our lives completely." Nickolas's eyes met the Lord's. "And we owe it all to you, our blessed Lord. As always, you know what we needed, that one thing that has always been missing in our life, and you made the hearts of Abby's birth parents except us for who we are and feeling the love, we hold for this child filled with the kiss of heaven. Simply said, thank you, Lord Jesus!"

"Because of that bond between both parents, this child can be free to visit those she loves within the veil of heaven's portals." Jesus knelt down at Abby. "The snow globe you have is filled with heaven's miracles Abby, so whenever you shake it, if the figures come to life, you will know a visit is at hand. Listen out for sleigh bells and be watchful. Barnabas will appear and escort you and Simon to the North Pole. You will remain at your home on the farm while school is in session and at other family celebrations, but your visits to Kringle Village will continue as long as you live. A child does not outgrow their parents nor will your belief in Santa Claus be forgotten after you cross through the portal of toy land." Jesus stood up. "Have your hot chocolate that Martha wishes to serve before leaving for your mountain. Robert, have Nickolas show you his first attempt at carving a toy donkey then asked him what made it special to me." Jesus put out his palm and the carved donkey magically appeared. He handed it to Nickolas. "Merry Christmas Nickolas, your handsome misfit did very well carrying me through that crowd, on my way to Jerusalem." Jesus gave Abby a hug. "Abby, we are very proud of you! Never forget, I am always with you. Look on the other side of your globe and relive my Holy birth. My gift to you."

"The first Christmas! Thank you, Jesus, for everything!" Abby looped her little arms around his strong neck. "I love you Jesus and I will never forget you are by my side." With one last smile, the King of Kings was gone. Abby took her mama's hand. "Mama Martha is going to make her famous hot chocolate mama, I bet she would let you watch how she does it, then you will know firsthand!"

"Martha, I almost forgot to thank you for that very lovely gift you sent me to share with the family." Della patted Abby's head. "Thanks sweetheart for reminding me and I would love to watch you Martha, if that is alright with you?" Della quickly checked her watch. "Then I am afraid we must ask Barnabas to take us back to the farm. I imagine the other kids are wondering when we're getting home so I can make them some of your great recipe."

"I would love to teach you my tricks on the perfect mug of double fudge hot chocolate with whipped marshmallows!" Martha led the way while speaking. "I will make enough to send back to your family, then you can enjoy another mug with them there."

"Daddy, mama has gone with Martha to make the hot chocolate, so why don't you ask daddy Nickolas about the donkey Jesus gave him back." Abby followed her two daddies to the mantle were Nickolas had placed his very special carving next to Abby gift to them. Abby giggled at the funny little donkey. "Jesus called him a misfit. I think he is cute Nickolas. I see why Jesus chose him, he is special, like you are."

"Thank you, that is very sweet Abby." Nicolas gave an embarrassed grin to Robert. "I believe the Lord has a sense of humor

Robert. He knows perfectly well the great talent he gave you with carpentry and how your gifts are sought after among your town's people." Nickolas held the sad little donkey up. "This was my very first attempt at carving a toy. It was not fit for anything except my deep pocket. I kept it hidden there as a reminder of how I first got started."

Robert took the misfit, as Jesus called it, and studied its form. "I can tell you chose a block of wood too short and narrow to carve out four equal legs. The short mane tells me you ran out of wood just below the donkey's jaw and as for the bobtail, I cannot say why it is so short. There should have been enough wood there to make it longer."

"And there was a longer tail, for a brief time until I accidentally broke it off at the last shaving." Nickolas made a face. "I had offered baby Jesus a perfect angel carving but it became Mary's and Jesus wanted the sad donkey hidden inside my pocket." Nickolas smiled as he remembered seeing his donkey years later outside of Jerusalem. "You may recall Jesus going up to Jerusalem riding on a colt, the fold of a donkey, When I noticed that one of its legs was shorter than the other three and its mane and tail were also short, I knew the Savior had transformed my little misfit into his glorious ride through the crowds, cheering Him with praises."

The story told and Martha's special hot chocolate finished, the Asbury's were saying their goodbyes. Robert and Nickolas bonded in a hug, fresh tears had begun to fall, with the uncertain feeling of ever seeing each other again. Robert spoke, choking up.

"My friend, I pray this is not goodbye forever. I now know how our little Abby felt when she thought she wouldn't see the ones she loved so dearly again."

"My brother, the four of us share something precious and she is a blessing from God, to all of us." Nickolas had sent for Barnabas and watched him stepped through the opening quietly, giving them time to say their goodbyes. "We serve a loving Lord and He knows our hearts more than anyone. Perhaps we won't meet often, dear ones, but deep down inside me, I feel there is miracles that happened only at Christmas time, when the portals of heaven are opened through the magic mirror and the Kringle's can venture out to places beyond the North Pole." Nickolas had felt the Spirit of Christmas spark inside him as he looked into the eyes of the family he loved.

"I found out this Christmas I could split five times and now that our daughter will be apart of the Christmas season, I will invite my Martha, who has wondered long enough how it must feel to fly above the clouds on Christmas Eve with Santa Claus." He gave a great smile when Martha laughed. "I know the other four of myself will rejoice to know the fifth part will be delivering gifts to only one family each year!" Nickolas waved his hands and their warm coats, hats and gloves adorned them. "Listen for the reindeer on your roof next Christmas eve. Sweet peace!" Nickolas waved his hand and they found themselves back on the sleigh and up in the air.

There was a distinct sound of sleigh bells ringing above them as they looked upward. Abby smiled and gave a big wave. "Goodbye Santa! See you soon!"

Robert and Della waved as well, although they saw no one above them, just ringing bells. They called out in unison "Merry Christmas Kringle's!"

"HO-HO-HO! A MERRY CHRISTMAS TO ALL, AND TO ALL A GOOD YEAR, MY BEAUTIFUL FAMILY!" the spirit of Santa was gone and Abby sat back on the soft seat between her parents. Her attention went to the large thermos her mother was holding and Abby suddenly couldn't control her giggles.

"Abby, sweetheart, what has turned your giggle box upside-down?" Della shrugged her shoulders when Robert glanced down at his giggling daughter.

"I was just picturing Jacob's white nose after he dunked his mouth down in Martha's hot chocolate covered in fluffy mouth-watering marshmallows!" her giggles overflowed into her parents as they laughed along with her.

"I would bet all nine of your brothers and sisters wind up with sticky-white marshmallow noses!" Robert gave his daughter a wink. "Just like our Abby did when drank hers down."

"It's the only way to enjoy mama Martha's hot chocolate daddy, like you and mama did!" Abby gave them a big grin when she heard Barnabas chuckle.

"Abby, I didn't think anyone noticed our mishap after that first sip," Della blushed when the head elf turned around to give her a smile. "Well, it was standing so tall and fluffy above the mug, one could only hope of getting a marshmallow nose just the first sip."

"Mama, Mama Martha's hot chocolate is just too good to resist diving into! She makes the very best!"

"I agree 100% Abby!" Della gave her daughter a big smile.

"Mama, you make the very best chocolate cake ever!" Abby giggled when her daddy agreed. "And daddy, you and daddy Nickolas have something in common. You both build beautiful things, with or without a marshmallow mustache!"

Barnabas chuckled louder. "I might take to calling you three, the Asbury family with the marshmallow nose." He glanced back and noticed Abby had grown quiet and her little lips started puckering up. "Hey Kiddo, why the sad face? You have just been given cheery news by the Lord, permitting you to visit the big cheese on special occasions."

"I know Barnabas, and I really appreciate Jesus's beautiful gift to us." Abby looked down at her hands holding tight to the snow globe. "We haven't been gone hardly anytime and I already miss Nickolas and Martha. It wouldn't be so hard to wait if I knew how they were doing or could hear their voice. Unlike the rest of the world, that can communicate through modern technology, cell phones and landlines, the North Pole does not require worldwide connection to the outside. In other words, I cannot call mama Martha or Daddy Nickolas to chat!"

"Not with these devices you spoke of Sprout, but you can contact the Kringle's anytime from your snow globe." Barnabas gave her a positive nod, then trained his ears on a familiar sound before adding. "Listen Sprout, can you hear the sleigh bells?"

Abby strained her ears until the distinct sound of sleigh bells chimed out nearby. Her first response was to look back up, and noticed Barnabas shaking his head.

"The bells are not coming from the sky kiddo. The reindeer have taken us far from the North Pole and in a few minutes, the Appalachia Mountain will be rising in front of us. Try looking down, in your cute little lap."

"The, snow globe?" Abby lifted it up and laughed when she noticed the village square come to life after she gave it a shake. Then she stopped laughing and stared up at the head elf. "Wait a second Barnabas! Nickolas told me this was a memory snow globe and it could only come to life on Christmas Eve and Christmas Day. He told me I could relive our time together when I was five!"

"That is exactly what the big cheese told you Sprout, but that was before Jesus opened up the portals to the North Pole for you and the Kringle's to be together." Barnabas said proudly, knowing he had brought out Abby's sudden smile. "Just give it another shake, ring your sleigh bells and call out to the Kringle's! Simple."

"Simple?" Abby asked with big eyes. "Simple enough to shake my beautiful snow globe Barnabas! Simple enough for me to call out to Mama Martha and Daddy Nickolas, but where are my sleigh bells? It cannot work without sleigh bells, can it?"

"It cannot! So, you need to bend down and fetch the new set of Sleigh bells at her tiny-little feet!" Barnabas smiled. "Better give it a try before we reach your farmland."

Abby shook the globe, rang the bells, then called out their names, and instantly saw them appear.

"Hello sweet daughter! I see you found your sleigh bells I sent with Barnabas." Nickolas gave her a smile. "Did you miss us already Abby?"

"Well, I was bothered about never talking to you, the North Pole without a telephone and all. Then Barnabas told me I could get in touch through my beautiful gift now that Jesus has allowed us to be a family." Abby giggled, just glad to see them happy. "I feel much better now so I had better go since Barnabas said our home was coming into view. This is not goodbye mama and daddy, so I will say, I'll be seeing you soon! I love you both very much!"

"We love you too baby girl. Be a good girl for your mama's and daddy's and continue saying your prayers. Martha and I will be seeing you soon." Nickolas and Martha blew their little girl a kiss and the globe went dark.

"This has been my second-best Christmas ever!" Abby proclaimed.

"Your second?" Robert glance over at Della, thinking in her short five-years which Christmas could possibly match this one. "Abby darling, what could be better than this Christmas? You got your Christmas wish to witness with Santa Claus, you saved Christmas for both Nickolas and your grandparents, which made you mama 's Christmas special reuniting with her parents. You won first place for your magic snow globe and you got to visit Nickolas and Martha at the North Pole and become family with them."

"That is why this Christmas is my second favorite daddy." Abby looked up with sincere eyes. "My very first favorite Christmas is the one where Jesus was born and became our King and Savior. If Jesus hadn't been born to save us, then we would not have Christmas and Nickolas would not have been chosen as the Giver of Gifts, to blest the hearts of children everywhere, forever." Abby hugged her father when she noticed his tears and gentle smile. "I bet that first Christmas is your very favorite Christmas too, isn't it daddy?"

"It would be right and good if all God's children could see through the eyes of a child and find the birthday of our Lord and King was every Christian's very favorite Christmas." Robert smiled toward heaven. "Thank you Lord for giving us Christmas by coming to earth as our Messiah and thank you Jesus for giving us Easter, so we can all rejoice with you in heaven one day. And, thank you Lord for given two-sets of lucky parents this beautiful child who has renewed the true Christmas Spirit in many a heart."

"REMEMBER, MY LOVE ONES, IF YOU BELIEVE LIKE A LITTLE CHILD, YOU WILL BE MINE FOREVER!" came the soft voice from heaven. "Abby, well done, my little faithful witness."